DOPE, LOVE, & KARMA

HE PLAYED WITH MY HEART

DEDRA B.

Love, Dope, and Karma

Copyright © 2018 by Dedra B.

Published by Mz. Lady P Presents

www.mzladypresents.com

ACKNOWLEDGMENTS

First and fore most I would like to thank God for giving me the patience and talent to push through this book! My mommy, I know you're in heaven smiling, I love and miss you soooo much!!! My daddy, I love you old man!

Chris, I love you forever!

My love Chubby thanks for being you baby, I love you to pieces!!! We in this forever!

Camille you are my auntie, momma, and best friend all wrapped in one! You've been here since day one and I'm lucky to have such an amazing, smart, and beautiful person in my life. I love you!

My sister gurl Patrice thanks for always listening to these crazy storylines and real life problems, I love you!!

My sister Chelsea I love you and my Niecy Pooh! I will be here for y'all no matter what!

Von, my sister!! I love you thanks for always having my back!!!

S/O to the best mother figure a girl could ask for Vivian Smart you have been nothing more than a blessing to me, I love you, and thanks for all you do!!!

My entire family blood and extended I love you all!!!

To my main thangs Trenae, CoCo, and B Capri, the bond we have formed can never be broken! We started out as a group of authors talking. I can now proudly claim you all as my friends and sisters. Thanks for being y'all, I love y'all!

My MLPP team, remember sky is the limit, we can go as far as we want! Let's continue to motivate one another and dominate the charts all 2018! Last but not least my super dope publisher Mz.Lady P, thank you for allowing and welcoming to be a part of this dope publishing family, I appreciate all that you do!!!

ONE

KYANA

Back in the day, where it all it began...

Damn, looking this good should be a crime. I ran my hands over my perfectly shaped seventeen-year-old body. My ass and thighs were the largest things on my body outside of the huge gold hoop earrings that hung from my ears. I had a ring on every finger, and a gold chain with my name engraved on the charm that hung from my neck. I rocked a pair of stonewash overall shorts with one strap unhooked, a white sports bra, and a pair of fresh K-Swiss sneakers.

I applied my clear lip gloss and blew myself a kiss before power walking down the hallway only to witness my mother sitting at the kitchen table of our two-bedroom apartment sniffing lines. In a matter of seconds, she was slumped over and high as fuck as usual. I walked over and put one arm around my neck as she looked up at me and smiled with powder residue on her nose. I walked her over to the dusty couch that sat in our living room and laid her down to sleep it off. I often wished for siblings to share this responsibility, but I knew my mom was done. I never knew my father, but my mother always told me he was a handsome hoe from around the way, so I'm sure I have siblings somewhere out there. I don't care to know who he is. My mother is all I have, and I love her no matter what she does.

I used to be known around the neighborhood as "Powder nose Shelly's daughter" until I made a name for myself as a hustler. I learned how to get money on my own at an early age to get whatever I wanted. Whether it was holding crack for the dealers or doing hair around the hood, I was easily bringing in about three hundred dollars a week, after my mother took her fifty-dollar drug fee. I made sure I kept the latest kicks, and my hair stayed laid. I'm that little bitch that even the grown bitches hate to see coming because they knew there was no competing with me. Every nigga in the hood wanted me, but I only had my eye on one guy— Kayo Castillo.

"A'Nekaaaaaa!" I yelled up to the second floor of the court way building my best friend lived in.

Two seconds later, she came flying down the stairs wearing a pair of neon pink leggings, a lime green sports bra, and a pair of lime green high-top Reeboks. Her hair was in a fan ponytail with what looked like a hundred blow pop suckers sticking through it. Unlike my high yellow ass, Neka has the prettiest mocha skin tone that I have ever laid eyes on, not to mention a banging ass body to match it. Even though she's labeled as the neighborhood hoe, I absolutely love my best friend. I was used to beating bitches' heads in because Neka was fucking their men. I didn't care if people thought I was a hoe too, even though I'm still a virgin.

Neka stayed with a man that kept her pockets full, and she always made sure I was straight and vice versa. Her mother is a full-blown heroin addict, so she spent most of her time at my house or out with her dips. Neka didn't ask to be this way. She was forced to fuck at an early age. Thanks to her mother, every nigga in the hood knew what her young pussy felt like.

"Bitch, it's too hot to be walking all the way to the candy store. My fat ass tired from running down here," Neka said as sweat beaded up on her forehead.

"It's only two blocks away, damn. You don't get tired when you chase them niggas," I replied, laughing.

"Sholl in the hell don't. Speaking of niggas, I know you only want to take this long ass walk so that we can walk past Kayo and Santana's fine, Puerto Rican asses. But, I got a thing for Rio's sexy black ass, I just know he got a big dick!" she said before blowing a huge bubble with her gum and popping it.

"How can you tell?"

"That print, you have to look at the dick print, girl."

"Oh ok."

"You better leave Kayo alone. Them Ricans be packing, so he's gone tear the lining out yo little virgin ass."

"And I'm gone let him! I promise he's gone be mine one day."

"Well, I just wanna fuck his friend, Rio. I ain't trying to make him mine. I might fuck Santana again too," she replied, laughing.

"AGAIN!? You're something else. I pray you grow out of your hoeish ways."

"If the money's right, we fucking tonight," she replied, causing us to bust out laughing.

Kayo was this fine, and I do mean fine, ass mixed nigga from Puerto Rico. I heard someone put a hit out on him and his older brother, Santana, so his mother sent them to the states to live with their father until she straightened things out, but they never went back. A million different stories are floating around about them. My favorite one is about his mother being the head of some Puerto Rican Cartel. I don't how true it is, but that's how powerful I want to be one day.

Moving them to the states really didn't make a difference because word on the streets is they're making all the money in the streets. I can see him going straight to the top, but he needs a girl like me to help him get there. Even though he's two years older than me, I know for a fact I could get him. But every time I see him, he has a different bitch with him, so it's kind of hard to get his attention.

I touched my headband to make sure it was still in place as my real hair hung down to the middle of my back. I looked up the street and saw a small crowd of guys standing in front of the candy store that Kayo's father owned. I knew he was in the midst of them. I pulled my phone off my hip and acted like I was checking it as we walked past. Just as I suspected, he was standing there alongside Santana, Rio, and a few other guys.

I felt a hand grab my arm and just knew it was my man, so I turned around with a huge smile spread across my face. I looked up and almost threw up in my mouth because I stood face to face with one of the ugliest niggas I have ever seen in my life. I mean, this nigga was butt ass ugly. He looked like an uglier version of the rapper Flavor Flav. I know his momma was mad as hell she had to claim him.

"Where you going, baby? I'm right here," he said, smiling and showing a mouth full of yellow teeth.

"Man, she doesn't want your ugly ass, estupido!" Santana said with a slight chuckle.

"I'm not looking for your ass, and let go of my arm, please."

"Fuck you, bitch! You ain't shit just like yo hype ass momma. That's why I fucked her for a bag of blow," he said, using the street slang for my mother's drug of choice before releasing his grip and slightly pushing me.

"I ain't shit, and your mouth looks like shit. You look like you suck dicks for a living, I'll spit on yo real ugly ass!" I replied, causing everyone to bust out laughing including Kayo while steam came from the ugly nigga's ears.

I was laughing right along with everyone else because I was over the hype jokes. It used to bother me, and I would cry, but hell, everyone knew my mother had a habit, so I learned to laugh right along with everyone else. It wasn't until it felt like someone took a bat to my mouth I realized this ugly muthafucka had just punched me.

I heard Neka yell, "You bitch ass nigga!" as she charged him.

I fell back, but someone grabbed me. I looked up and into Rio's face. Neka was right, he is really handsome. He sat me down on a nearby crate because I was dazed. He ran over to help Kayo and the other guys stomp the shit out of the ugly dude, pushing Neka out the way. I was still in shock. I can't believe this nigga punched me in the mouth. I sucked my bottom lip to stop the bleeding, and I could feel it swelling. Someone finally broke up the fight, as everyone asked was I okay. Kayo was the last person to walk up.

"You cool?"

"Yeah, I'm fine. Thanks," I replied, covering my mouth so that he couldn't see the swelling.

"No thanks needed. I will never watch another man hurt mine," he replied, flashing the sexiest smile I had ever seen.

"Yours, huh?" I asked as he grabbed my hand and helped me up off the crate that I was sitting on.

Just as he was about to answer me, police cars came flying toward us. Everyone took off running, but it was too late for Kayo to run, so he quickly emptied his pockets and placed his stuff in my pocket. He looked me in my eyes as he put his hands in the air as if it was a practiced routine. I had no idea what he placed in my pocket, and I didn't care. The police walked right past me and grabbed him, throwing him against the car right next to his best friend, Rio. The officers told Neka and me to walk off. I nodded at Kayo and did as I was told.

When we made it back to our block, we sat on my porch and talked about everything that had taken place earlier and how they beat the shit out of dude. I already knew Neka and Rio had hit it off because she wasn't the type to take no for an answer. I wouldn't be surprised if she were spending the night with him. I never removed anything from my pockets as I sat and waited on Kayo to appear. The streetlights popped on, indicating it was starting to get late. I walked Neka halfway home and started walking back toward my house. I felt someone tap my shoulder and almost had a heart attack until realized it was Kayo and Rio. I still had my hand over my heart as I let out a sigh of relief.

"You thought it was that nigga from earlier coming to get his lick back, didn't you?" Rio said, causing all of us to laugh. Rio is one of those funny but real niggas.

"Fuck you, Rio," I replied.

"Where's my baby at?" he asked, and I thought it was so cute.

"She just went in. I can call her back out if you want me to," I replied.

"Nah, I'll see her tomorrow," he said, walking ahead of us to holler at the niggas on the corner.

"Here you go," I said, turning my attention to Kayo. I reached into my pocket, pulling out an eight ball of crack and a wad of twenty-dollar bills.

"Thanks, you a real bitch, no disrespect. That was some real shit you did today, and I appreciate it," he said, peeling off ten twenties and holding them out for me grab.

"None taken, I'll do anything for mine," I replied, reciting his exact words from earlier, also meaning every word.

I stood up and walked toward my front door without taking the money he was offering. I wasn't looking for a reward, and I didn't want him to think I was anything like the gold digging females he was used to. I liked everything about this boy from his high yellow complexion that matched mine perfectly, to the toothpick that hung out of the side of his mouth. I didn't even know he knew my name until he called out, stopping me dead in my tracks as I turned around.

"Same time tomorrow?" he asked. I nodded my head in agreeance and closed the door.

TWO
KAYO

"I've been watching you
    for so very long
      trying to get my nerve built up to be so strong
      I really want to meet you
      but I'm kind of scared
      cause you're the kind of lady
      with so much class
      get my thoughts together
      for the very next day
      but when I see you lady
      I forget what to say
      your eyes and hair
      such a beautiful tone
      the way you dress and walk
      it really turns me on."

I SANG along with the lead singer of the R&B group, Jodeci, in my best singing voice. Even though the song was old, he described exactly how I was feeling about Kyana to a tee. I always saw her walking past, but I never approached her because she was younger than me, however, after the shit she did yesterday, I have to have her now. She held me down, and she didn't even know me, so I can only imagine how hard she's gone go for me when I mold her little ass. I couldn't get past how mature she was for her age. You would only know how young she was if she told you. Everything about her turned me on, especially the way she walked away without taking my money. Any other bitch would've taken it in a heartbeat, which is why I planned on showing her a good time today.

"Surgido fuera de la vagina?" Santana asked, standing in the doorway of my bedroom.

"How can I be sprung off the pussy and this our first date, tonto!" I replied, laughing.

"That young pussy is gone have your head gone. I fucked a few young ones, and it ain't shit to play with."

"Yo dick gone fall off," I replied, laughing and shaking my head.

My brother is my best friend outside of Rio. I swear I will lay down my life for his if need be. I can talk to him about anything and vice versa, even though he's a couple of years older than me. We come from a very dangerous family. Our mother, Amelia Castillo, is the leader of the CC (Castillo Cartel) and is a very dangerous woman. My grandfather passed the cartel to her once he knew she was done with my father. My grandfather was a racist piece of shit, may he rest in peace. My brother and I are next in line to run it, but I have no intentions of going back to Puerto Rico. I want to build my own empire here.

My mother has only been to the states twice throughout her entire life. Once was to handle business and the second time was to let my father know face to face that if anything happened to her boys, there would be trouble for the entire city. My father came back to the states years ago because my grandfather wanted him dead after he found out it was a black man that made his only child run away from home. My father was in the service and based in Puerto Rico when he met my mother, she loved him, but she knew his life would be taken, so she cut him off. My brother and I got mixed up in some shit, so we ended up coming to the states with my father. He's a cool little man and well known around the neighborhood because he owns one of the best candy stores on the west side. He saw what I did to Kyana and told me not to mess up that girl's life, but those were not my intentions with her because I know she's special.

I made sure I got a fresh haircut and a brand new head to toe outfit. I bought a red Chicago Bulls jersey, a pair of black Levi shorts, and the new red and black Jordan 11's that came out this morning. Rio and I told the girls to be ready around three o'clock, but I don't think I can wait that long to see her. I had a few bitches that thought we were an item, but I'm gone dead all of that shit depending on how this date turns out. I know two years is a big gap in age, but I have to see what's to her. I'm willing to take that chance. I'd be a damn fool to let another nigga get her.

I grabbed my cell phone to call Rio.

"Hello."

"What's up, nigga?"

"What time you gone be ready?"

"Damn, it's only one o'clock, nigga. But fuck all that, did you see how thick Neka's little ass is?"

"Yeah, she's definitely holding, but you better be careful. I heard she's a lil hoe."

"Well, she's about to be my little hoe, I fucks with her," Rio replied, causing me to laugh.

"I'm about to leave out so be ready. I'll blow when I'm outside," I replied, hanging up the phone.

I walked outside, and it had to be at least ninety degrees. I instantly took my shirt off and let my gold rope chain hang. I made sure my 1998 Lexus SC300 was washed and waxed. I shook up with some of the guys as they looked at my shoes and wished they had them. I hopped in my car and let "Computer Love" blast through my speakers as I hit a few blocks to kill time. I pulled up in front of Rio's crib, but I didn't have to blow because this nigga was already outside in the middle of a dice game. I pulled over and caught a park before hopping out and placing a few side bets. I made an easy five hundred dollars to put in Kyana's pocket before telling Rio let's ride.

I turned down Kyana's block, and it was packed. Everybody was outside. The guys on the block turned the fire hydrant on for the kids, and they were having a ball. I double parked in front of her house and waited for her to come out. Neka walked up wearing practically nothing as Rio got out to hug her. Neka was one thick ass little girl, but far from my type, I would have to be drunk to hit her.

After I waited for about ten minutes, I saw my baby walking out wearing a Chicago Bulls t-shirt, tucked in a pair of black daisy dukes, as the girls called short shorts, with the same shoe I was wearing. I couldn't help but smile as I watched her throw her wide hips as she walked towards me smiling. I jumped out to open the door for her while Rio and Neka climbed in the back.

"You trying to match my fly, huh?"

"I guess so," she replied, blowing a bubble with her gum.

I turned the music all the way up and headed to the movies to see the new horror movie, *The Faculty* that everybody was talking about. I thought I was doing good by catching an early show, but it was still packed. I lucked up on a park a few rows away from the door. I walked around, opened her door, and we walked toward the entrance hand in hand. Everything was good until I heard the voice of a bitch that I couldn't seem to get rid of. All four of us stopped walking and turned around as I cursed under my breath.

"Kayoooo!" the female yelled, sprinting over with her friends in tow.

"What man?" I replied clearly annoyed.

"Can I get forty dollars for the show?" she asked, causing Neka to look at Kyana and laugh.

I already knew this shit was about to go left when shorty turned her attention from me to Kyana.

"Kayo, who the fuck is this?" she asked while pointing at Kyana, who didn't seem fazed at all.

"Why, damn?"

"Because I asked so tell me before I beat her ass up."

I saw Kyana screw her face up and tilt her head to the side. I know I should've killed the situation, but I wanted to see how Kyana was going to react. I wasn't going to let her get her ass whooped, but I wanted to see how far she was going to go. I watched Neka as her body language changed and she balled her fist up. I like how she goes so hard for Kyana.

"Baby, you couldn't beat my ass if I gave you a head start. If you were smart, you would walk off and act like you didn't just say that dumb shit out of your mouth," Kyana calmly replied, shifting her weight to one side with one hand behind her back.

"You look like a lil ass girl, so I'm gone give you a pass. Kayo, be at my house when you're done with your little sister."

"Yeah, this lil ass girl got the juice, and he won't be at your house because he's gone be knee deep in this lil ass pussy. You can catch him tomorrow, bitch," Kyana replied, shocking the shit out of me.

"Yeah, ok. We'll see."

"Yeah, we will. Baby, I'll go pay for our tickets with "my" money while you dismiss this broke duck," Kyana sarcastically said, walking off.

"Here, baby!" I yelled out. She stopped and turned around, taking the wad of cash from the dice game out of my hand, winking at ole girl.

Embarrassment was written all over baby girl's face. She just rolled her eyes and walked off.

I prayed all the way into the show that she was serious about me being knee deep in that lil pussy; it just looks like her shit good. Once we got inside, I caught up to her and let her order whatever she wanted before we headed to the show. I made sure we split up from Rio and Neka and sat all the way in the back because I hated when people try to squeeze pass me. We watched the previews, and my favorite part came when they turn the lights off. I put my arm around her as she laid her head on my shoulder. Ten minutes into the movies, I felt her hand rub against my dick. I thought it was a mistake, so I thought nothing of it until she grabbed it and slightly massaged it through my shorts. I tried to keep my hands to myself and be a gentleman, but fuck it. I pulled her shirt out of her shorts. We were the only people in our row, so I knew no one could see us unless they turned around. I lifted her shirt and bra with one swift move and pushed her back. I started licking around her small but perfect nipples. I could smell the baby powder that she dumped in her shirt as I explored her with my tongue. She let out low moans as she squirmed in her seat. She lifted my head up, brought me face to face with her, and kissed me like I have never been kissed before. I went to stick my hand in her pants, but she stopped me.

"What's wrong?" I asked in a low tone.

"Nothing, I'm sorry."

"Sorry for what, baby?"

"Leading you on. Kayo, I'm a virgin, and this is not how I pictured losing virginity."

"It's cool, baby. Let's just watch the movie," I replied, leaning back in my seat.

ONCE THE MOVIE WAS OVER, we grabbed something to eat and dropped Neka and Rio off. I could tell Kyana was in her feelings because she wasn't doing much talking. She just stared off out the window. I put my hand on her thigh, and she slightly jumped, which confirmed that was indeed in deep thought. I grabbed her hand, and it was damn near soaking wet from sweat.

"Baby, you know you don't have to do anything you don't want to do. I will never force you."

"I know, Kayo. I just see how the guys do Neka, and I don't want to be that girl. I mean, I'm pretty sure if I fuck you on our first date, you're going to think I'm a hoe and tell all of your friends. I'll have a label by the morning," she said, looking up at me.

"Kyana, I'm not that type of nigga. No one will know our business unless you tell them, and the only label you will ever have while dealing with me is "my girl." And please don't ever compare yourself to Neka. You all are two different breeds of females," I replied, meaning every word.

"I hear you," she said, looking back out of the window.

"I tell you what. We can chill and watch TV. I won't make any foul moves. I just want to be around you. I'll take you home when you're ready," I said. She shook her head up and down and smiled.

We pulled up to my house, and my block was still live. These nosey ass people never sleep. It's a Saturday night, so I know Santana is out somewhere being a hoe, and I'll have the house to myself. We walked up to the porch, and all the niggas looked at Kyana. I knew she was fine as hell. I knew I was gone have to make shit official with her very soon because these niggas out here are vultures. I walked her to my room and told her to make herself comfortable, so she climbed on my queen-sized bed.

I turned on one of my favorite movies, *New Jack City*, and climbed into the bed behind her. I pulled her back on my chest and ran my fingers through her hair. Everything about this moment felt so right. I know I might be moving too fast, but I could see myself fucking with shorty for the rest of my life. I can't believe I've been overlooking her all this time. I felt myself nodding off, but the touch of her hand running down my arm and woke me up. Her touch alone had my dick on the rise. I moved back so that she couldn't feel it, but she poked her ass out and slowly grinded against me. She eventually flipped over and faced me, tracing my lips with her finger. I didn't move my hands at all because I didn't want to scare her. She leaned in, parted my lips with her tongue, and I followed her lead. She sat straight up in the bed and pulled her shirt over her head. I stood up, locked the door, and cut the light off. Before I could get back in the bed, she was helping me out of my shirt.

I pressed play on my stereo, and the same Jodeci song was still on repeat from earlier. I sat down and pulled her between my legs. I could tell this was nervous because she immediately covered herself with her hands, but I pulled them down to let her know that it's ok. I leaned in and took one breast at a time into my mouth, making sure I showed them equal attention. I flicked my tongue over her harden nipples, and she moaned and placed my hand between her legs. I managed to unbutton her shorts, and she wasted no time stepping out of them. I never took my shorts off. If she wanted it, she would have to get it.

I laid her down on the bed, spread her legs apart, and went in head first. I placed her small pearl between my lips and kissed it like I was kissing her lips. She placed her heads on my head and grinded her hips. I picked up the pace, locked onto her clit, and sucked it. I knew she was about to wet my entire face up, but that's exactly what I wanted. Two seconds later, she was shaking uncontrollably.

"You cool, baby?" I asked, laying there motionless.

"Why you do me like that?"

"You didn't like it?"

"I loved it!" she replied, sitting up and unbuckling my shorts.

"You sure this is what you want?"

"Yes, this is all I want for the rest of my life."

THREE

KYANA

"Ooouuuuu you fucked him, didn't you?" Neka asked as soon my foot touched the first step.

She must've been sitting on my porch all morning waiting on me. I took a seat next to her but quickly stood back up because I was sore. I knew it was going to hurt but not like this, but what's crazy is I can't wait to do it again.

"Come on with the details, bitch. Is his dick big?"

"Bitch, don't worry about it. Just know I'm sore as fuck. It hurt like hell in the beginning, but then it felt so fuckin' good. It felt like he was controlling body."

"Aww shit, did he eat it?"

"Yes, he did that first."

"Aw ok, Kayo knows what he's doing, huh?"

"Yes girl, that's my baby."

"I bet, but you better get ready because your momma's been looking for your ass all night, and she is pissed off."

"Girl, can't nothing and nobody blow my mood. I'll holler at you later. I'm about to take a bath and a nap."

"Ok."

I placed my key in the door, but before I could turn it, my mother snatched it open.

"Where have you been all night? I was worried sick."

"Was you worried sick or sick because I didn't leave you money for your fix?"

"Let me tell you something, Kyana. I'm your mother before anything, so like I said I was worried sick about YOU. I don't mind you staying out because I rather you do in my face than behind my back, but please tell me where you end up. Now how was it?"

"How was what?"

"Losing your virginity, you're not walking like that for nothing. We're going to make you an appointment to get on some birth control too."

"Mommy, it hurt like hell, and I promised to not to stay out without letting you know again," I said, handing her one of the hundred-dollar bills Kayo gave me.

Once that money touched her hand, she was out the door. I slowly walked to my room to undress and take a bath. I sat in the tub and soaked for a while, and my body was so relaxed. I finally climbed out after cleansing myself. I stood in front the mirror and looked at my naked body. My innocence was gone, and I'm officially a woman — Kayo's woman. I smiled and took it all in as I fell back on my bed, and before I knew it, I dozed off.

I HAD BEEN spending time with Kayo nonstop, and we were insepa-rable. If I wasn't at his house, I was on the phone with him. I knew Neka was starting to get jealous because I didn't have time to kick it anymore, but between Kayo and doing hair, I was tired as hell. I laid across my bed and took a quick nap after my last head. It wasn't until I heard a loud commotion outside of the window that I jumped out of bed. I grabbed a t-shirt and a pair of biking shorts and ran to the front porch. There was always some type of drama on our block, and my nosey ass was always front and center.

When I made it to the porch, I noticed a crowd of girls in front of Neka's house. I stepped down off the porch and asked one of my neighbors what was going. She said they came to jump Neka, and that was all I needed to hear. I sprinted back up my stairs and ran to my room. I rubbed a decent amount of Vaseline on my face before sliding my blade on the side of my shorts. On my way back out, I grabbed my steel bat from behind the door. I ran out the back door and came up through the vacant lot next to Neka's house. The crowd had moved to the middle of the street, Neka was fighting two females, while the others swung from the crowd. I ran up and hit one bitch in the back dropping her. Opening up the crowd, I made my way to the middle where Neka was.

"You bitches better back the fuck up!" I said, tapping the bat on the ground.

They all backed up. I was giving Neka enough time to get her second wind because ain't no way these bitches walking off this block after jumping my friend. I gave Neka that look, and when she gave me a nod, I knew it was time to act a fool. I handed her the bat, grabbed the closest bitch to me, and started swinging.

"Get this bitch off of me, she is cutting meeee!" the girl yelled as my razor ripped through her skin.

It wasn't until I felt someone grab me around the waist that I stopped swinging. I looked behind me to see who grabbed me, and it was my mother.

"Let me go, they jumping Neka!" I screamed.

"Kyana, give me the damn blade. Neka is fine; those guys have her. Go in the house. These heffas called the police," my mother said, pushing me toward our house.

I looked around for my friend, and when I saw her on her porch along with Rio and Santana, I was relieved. I walked into the house and grabbed the cordless phone, and dialed Kayo's number, I didn't see him with the guys, so I wonder where he was. He picked up on the first ring.

"What's up, baby?"

"Nothing much, what are you doing?"

"I just pulled up on your block. Come outside."

"Ok," I replied.

I jumped up and ran to the bathroom to brush my hair up into a high ponytail. I slipped on a bra and a tank because my shirt was all ripped up. I walked back into the living room, and my mother was sitting on the couch watching TV.

"Now, where are you going, Kyana? You don't need to go back out there."

"I promise I'm not gone fight, . I'm just going to talk to Kayo."

I just smiled and walked toward the front door. I stood on the porch for a minute before he came walking up the street. My mother came and stood in the doorway,

"You better watch that one there with a real close eye," she said, referring to Neka as she playfully pushed Kayo toward my house.

My mother had this fucked up perception about Neka, but I know she would never cross me. I love my friend to death, but I will kill her dead over Kayo Castillo.

"Hey, baby!" I said excitedly as my mother closed the door.

"What up," he dryly replied.

"Umm ok, what's wrong with you?"

"Why were you fighting? That shit had nothing to do with you, I don't like that shit," Kayo said with a serious face.

"I couldn't let them jump her, Kayo."

"So, you're super save- a-hoe, huh?"

"Really nigga? If it were Santana or Rio, you would be on the same shit so gone with that shit." I stepped back.

"You wanna fight me now?" he said, flashing a sexy smile.

I didn't give a fuck about that smile or shit else. He has me so fucked up right now.

"Look, baby. I don't want to argue, but if you gone be with me, that shit stops right now, Neka better learn how to keep her mouth and her legs closed because I would hate to have to shake the hood for fucking with mine."

"Yours, huh?"

"Yeah, mine for now and for forever."

FOUR

KYANA

"Kyana get ready to push, baby!" I heard my mother say as I reflected back to two years ago on where it all started and what put me in this painful situation.

Who would've thought an innocent date the movies would lead to me being in labor for thirty-nine hours? I looked around the room for Kayo, but he was nowhere in sight.

"Where the hell is Kayoooo?!" I yelled as a contraction hit me with full force.

Two seconds later, he came through the door with Neka. I managed to force a smile when I saw her. I was glad she made it just in time to see to her godchildren make their grand entrance into the world. I pray to God my body snaps back like Neka's did being that she had just given birth six weeks earlier to a beautiful baby boy, and her stomach was flat as hell. I stood right next to Rio when she delivered the baby. I had never seen a man cry until that day. He absolutely adores her. They let me do the honors of naming my godson, and I promised to always treat "Sincere Young" like my own. I still didn't understand why she didn't give him any parts of Rio's name, but I guess that's something they agreed upon. Ever since she found out she was pregnant, she'd changed toward him. Even now, she doesn't really want him to touch her, and she always has an attitude. I believe she's suffering from postpartum depression, and I just pray I don't experience it.

I can't even believe I carried not one but two babies inside of me for almost eight months. I was too big to go full term so here I am lying in this uncomfortable ass bed with everyone observing my vagina like it's a piece of fine art. I would've never thought in a million years that Kayo and I would be bringing children into the world. I mean, I always joked about it, but it's really happening. I can't lie, though; I wouldn't have it any other way. This man has been nothing but good to me. However, right now, I want to kill him for putting these fucking babies inside of me. I promised him that once we were able to live comfortably, I would give him a baby, but damn, I didn't sign up for none of this shit.

"Kayo, why did you do this to me?" I asked with warm tears running down my face. This pain is unbearable.

"Baby, it's ok. I just need you to breathe," he replied, rubbing my sweaty forehead.

"Move, Kayo. You suck at this," I heard Neka say. She came and took his place as my coach.

"I'm here, best friend. Remember when we were seventeen and talked about this day? You said, and I quote, *"When me and Kayo have our first baby, I'm gone take it like a gangster."* Well, I need you to calm down and be that G," she said, popping a piece of ice into my mouth and rubbing my hair.

"Neka, I didn't know it was gone feel like this. It hurts so bad, and it feels like I'm gone shit on myself," I said, trying to hold it in.

"That means it's time to push, baby. They're ready to come out," Neka said. Kayo grabbed one foot while my mother grabbed the other, and Neka held my hand.

"Ok, Ms. Jones I need you to push!" my doctor said, and I did as I was told.

I looked down at Kayo and laughed to myself because he looked like he was going to pass out. My mother just looked at me and smiled. I'm so grateful that she got herself clean and healthy. Kayo and I checked her in rehab, and she never looked back. I smiled back, but I don't know how much longer I can do this. I'm exhausted, and I didn't have time to get an epidural. I don't know what the fuck I was thinking fucking Kayo without protection.

"Here come's baby number one! Give me one more big push," she said. I screamed and pushed with everything in me.

The sound of crying was like music to my ears, but I wasn't done. My nurse made me push two more times until the second baby was out. I started to panic because unlike the first baby this one wasn't crying. I tried to sit up, but I couldn't move.

"What's wrong with my baby, why isn't she crying? Momma, why isn't my baby crying."

My mother patted my leg and told me to relax and that she's just stubborn. Kayo walked up to me and kissed me on my forehead. When I heard both of my babies crying, I started crying. Neka just stood back smiling and winking at me. The nurses walked over with two beautiful, light-skinned little girls with a head full of hair that changed my life, London and Paree Castillo, born May 17, 1999.

FIVE

KAYO

Present Day

"Y'ALL, this is it. Wait until Kyana sees this shit," I said, pulling up in front the house that I purchased a few weeks ago.

"Damnnnn, nigga, this a mansion. This how you going? I knew that young pussy was gone have you sprung, this nigga is buying houses!" Santana said, shaking my hand while he looked around.

"Hell yeah, the girls are growing up so fast, and they need a home to come up in. I promised Kyana she would have a brand new house before the year was out. I have to give my baby what she wants. This is where I'm bringing her after her surprise birthday party tonight."

I really wish I could have my mother and Kyana in the same room, but I knew she would never come to the states for something so simple. I sent her pictures of her grandchildren so that she could see how much they resemble her. She always says she will see them one day, so I left it at that. I knew better than to keep pressing the issue with her. My dad wanted nothing to do with me once he found out I was heavy in the drug game, so Kyana and my team is my family.

"That's dope. Shit, I'm gone cry if she doesn't. But dig this. I brought Neka's ass a crib, and she's still acting funny. I swear the best thing that came out of this shit is my son," Rio replied, looking depressed.

"Now you knew better than to wife a hoe!" Santana said with no filter.

"Fuck you, Santana," Rio replied, hitting the blunt one last time before putting it out.

I wasn't used to seeing this side of Rio. The nigga wasn't anything short of a killer. He took no shit from no one, except Neka. She was really doing a number on my homie, but that's what happens when you turn a fuck into your future.

"Yeah, I love that lil dude like he my own. Let's go," I said, hopping out of my '02 Range Rover. I had to trade in my coupe for a family truck.

I was still wowed by the huge water fountain that sat in the center of the winding driveway. The entire house was lit up, and it was gorgeous. Trees surrounded it, and the neighbor's house had to be at least a half block down. The house sits on three acres, averaging out to about seven thousand square feet. I made sure there was a pool in the backyard for the kids and a Jacuzzi for us. Space would no longer be an issue. With five bedrooms and five bathrooms, everyone should be comfortable. The grass was neatly cut, and the bushes were trimmed nicely.

It's time for me to make everything official. This woman has given me everything I've asked her for, so it's only right I do right by her. She makes sure any money we bring in from the streets is squeaky clean by running it through the restaurant she opened, along with the car wash and laundromat that she forced me to open. I always knew she had a head on her shoulders, but the moves she's been making over the last couple of years have shown me that she deserves the world and some. I was already running the drug game when I met her, but she definitely helped me take it to the next level. We were bringing in at least two hundred thousand a week, and she made sure we had paperwork to back up every cent. I made sure I put every-thing in her name. I trust her with my life because she's the most loyal and honest person I have ever met. Kyana was all about family. She made sure Rio made nothing short of us, and I love her for that.

We walked up to the door and walked in. It smelled brand new. You could still smell the fresh paint that covered the tall walls. I already had the bedrooms fully furnished because I knew once she stepped foot in here tonight, she wasn't going to leave. I even set up a room with a Kobe Bryant theme for Sincere because that's his favorite basketball player. I knew Kyana wouldn't mind because she was in love with the kid.

Our master bedroom looks bigger than most one-bedroom apart-ments. I made sure we had two separate walk-in closets, alongside a his and her shower with an oval Jacuzzi tub that sat in between. The entire upper level belonged to us. I didn't bother decorating anything because I knew she was going to redo everything and add her own touch to it. I started throwing the linen I bought from Walmart on the bed before my phone started vibrating. I felt the pockets on my jogging suit, trying to locate my phone. I pulled it out and smiled as Kyana's name flashed across my screen before hitting the speaker button and placing it on the nightstand.

"What's up, birthday girl?"

"Nothing, what are you doing? I miss you."

"Finishing up your birthday shopping, I got you some dope shit."

"Baby, you know you don't have to do that. I have enough of everything. Besides, I don't think I can fit anything else in my closet," she replied, laughing.

Little did she know, she had a brand new spacious closet to fill.

"Okay well, I'll take it all back."

"No, no, no! I'll make some room. I want my shit!" she replied as we both started laughing.

"Ok, your mother is coming over to watch the girls tonight. I need you to be dressed and on the porch by eight o'clock, Kyana. I have reservations, so please be ready, baby. I'm sending a car for you."

"Ok, love you!" she replied. I could tell she was smiling from ear to ear.

"Love you too, baby."

I pressed the end button on the phone, but it immediately vibrated and alerted me of a text. I never saved numbers in my phone, so I have no idea who the fuck this is.

773-988-3254: Kayo

Me: What's up, who dis?

773-988-3254: Tanya, damn.

Me: Aw, what's up stranger? I haven't heard from you in a minute.

773-988-3254: Kayo, I'm pregnant.

Me: So, what the fuck you telling me for, I know I'm not the only nigga you been with.

773-988-3254: Yes, you are. I know you don't want that stuck up ass BM of yours to find out, so I suggest you help me get rid of it before I pay her a visit.

Me: You right, baby. I'm tripping. I'll be over tomorrow.

773-988-3254: Thank you.

SIX

KYANA

My whole life has changed (My whole life has changed)
    Since you came in (since you came in)
    I knew back then (I knew back then)
    You were that special one (you were that one)
    I'm so in love (so in love)
    So deep in love (so deep in love)
    You make my life complete (you complete me)
    You are so sweet (are so sweet)
    No one competes (no one competes)
    Glad you came into my life (my life)
    You blind me with your love (love)
    with you, I have no sight (no sight)

I LET Ginuwine sing to me as I stepped into my tub filled with cherry blossom bubble bath and let the hot water soothe my body. I swear running behind two toddlers will make every bone on your body ache. I'm glad Kayo arranged for my mother to come over because I need a break. I can't believe I'm turning twenty-two years old. It's true what they say time waits for nothing. I can't complain though, my life is great! I have my family, my businesses, and the perfect man. I couldn't ask for anything more, or I would be being greedy.

I dried my body off and danced to the music before walking over to my vanity and dolling myself up. I was going for a natural look, so I applied the minimum makeup and topped it off with a gold-shimmered lipstick. I decided to leave my rollers in until I slipped the all black haltered mini dress on. I'm extremely blessed. I already had a nice ass body, but after giving birth, everything grew for the better. I went from an A cup to a full C, my ass sat so high up on my back that you could sit a cup on it, and my stomach snapped back in place perfectly— minus the few stretch marks I had on my sides. I knew I was highly favored because I just knew after having twins my body was going to be destroyed.

I took the rollers out of my head and let my curls fall down my back freely as I looked myself over in the mirror. I noticed my mother and girls watching me. They were giggling, and she looked like she wanted to cry. She walked over to me and helped me put my chain on. I bent down on my stilettos so she could see.

"You look beautiful, baby. Don't your mommy look pretty, girls?"

"Yesssss!" they said in unison.

"Thanks. I love you all."

"I love you too, more than you will ever know, Kyana. Thanks for never giving up on me."

"Aww, mommy, I will never give up on you. You're gone make me ruin my makeup."

If someone would've told me years ago that my mother would be clean, I would've looked at them like they were crazy. I guess her almost losing her life from an overdose and a praying daughter opened her eyes.

"I don't want to do that, birthday girl. You better get going. Your car will be here any minute now. Go on," she said, fanning me out the room.

I carefully walked down the stairs and headed outside. The summer breeze felt like silk blowing across my bare skin. I looked down at my watch, and when I looked back up an all white limousine pulled up. A white older gentleman walked around the car and opened the back passenger door for me to get in. I waved goodbye to my kids as they watched me from the porch, I just knew Kayo was inside waiting on me with a huge smile, but to my surprise, the car was empty. I was about to text him when the partition came down, and the driver handed me a piece of folded paper. I immediately opened it and began reading.

Hey baby,

I know you're probably wondering where I am, but that's for me to know and you to find out. So just sit back, ride, and know this is going to be the best birthday you've ever had, I promise.

See you soon!

I SMILED and reflected back on the past five years of my life with this man, and I love him more each and every day. He has helped mold me into the woman I am today. I've always been a hustler, but together we've created an empire. I already knew the ins and outs about the drug game from the guys in the hood, but Kayo gave me hands-on experience— enough to where I could look at a brick and tell if it was short or stepped on. Everyone knows we are not to be fucked with in the streets because like I said before, I will do anything for mine, and that includes killing. I never intended getting caught up in this lifestyle, but once you're in, it's almost impossible to get out. I made a vow never to hide anything from my girls, so I knew I would have to explain this shit to them one day. I just hope they understand I do this for them.

The sound of loud music pulled me out of my thoughts as I looked out the window to see what looked like a million people. *It must be a celebrity appearance at this club tonight.* I sat back in my seat and beat myself up for telling Kayo that I didn't want a party. I know we would've brought the city out. Neka and I always threw each other parties even if it was just the two of us there. I really don't know what's gotten into her, but my feelings are truly hurt because she's usually the first to call me, but here it is nine o'clock at night, and I haven't heard from her. I damn sure wasn't calling her ass first on my birthday. As of today, I will not try to keep anyone around who doesn't want to be here.

The driver went around the block before pulling in front of the same club but came to a complete stop. Before exiting the car, I looked around while I waited for him to open my door. I stepped out, and all eyes were on me, so I smiled, trying not to look too confused. I looked toward the door and saw Kayo walking toward me in a custom fitted suit, looking like a million bucks with Rio, Santana, and Neka in tow. I couldn't help but smile when I saw them. Kayo was holding the biggest bouquet of white roses that I had ever seen in one hand and a wireless microphone in the other. I couldn't help but wonder what this man had up his sleeve.

"Babbbbyyyy! I know you didn't. How did y'all get this pass me?" I yelled. Kayo put the mic in the air, and the music stopped.

"Come on now, baby, it's your birthday. You should've known how I was coming."

"And Neka, you knew and didn't tell me? We keeping secrets now?" I asked, playfully punching her in the arm.

"That's why I've been dodging you. I would've ruined it," she replied with that smile I love to see.

"Ok, ok, ok, I need everyone's attention. I have some shit to say. The faster I get this out, the faster we can party all muthafuckin' night long," Kayo said, grabbing my hand and pulling me to the middle of the red carpet that we were standing on.

I looked over at Neka, and she looked just as confused as I did. I don't know if I'm tripping, but it looks like Rio is getting a little teary-eyed. I stood there looking up at Kayo as he whispered something in Santana's ear. It was then I felt butterflies forming in my stomach. Kayo took a black box from Rio and dropped down to one knee, confirming what I thought was about to happen. I looked over and smiled at my best friend, but she stood there crying harder than I was. Words cannot describe how I was feeling right now. I have to be the luckiest woman in the world.

"Kyana, I've loved you since the day I laid eyes on you. I've wanted to protect you since that day that nigga hit you in the mouth on the block. I knew you were the one for me that day you held me down without asking any questions, and I knew you were going to be my wife when you blessed me with two beautiful daughters. I want you now and forever. Kyana, will you..."

"YESSSSSSS!" I replied before he could finish his question, jumping up and down as he placed the biggest rock I have ever laid eyes on my finger.

"Yeahhhhhh, let's party, baby!" he yelled, and the crowd went wild.

———

IT WAS ALMOST four o'clock in the morning, and I was all partied out, so I told Kayo I was ready to go home. I don't know if it was the Vodka I was drinking or the blunts that I smoked, but I was feeling really good. I leaned over and started massaging Kayo's dick right in front of Rio and Neka. I didn't give a fuck. It's my birthday, and I can do what I want.

"Damn, don't nobody want to see that!" Neka yelled over the music.

"Close your eyes then, bitch." I shot back. I wasn't in the mood for her attitude tonight, and I guess she sensed it because she stood up and walked off.

"Let's go, baby," I said.

I stood up and grabbed Kayo's hand before he told Rio we were leaving.

We passed Santana and three chicks on the way out; he is truly a lady's man. I'm glad I chose the good brother.

Kayo put me in the front seat of his truck and climbed in. My liquor was starting to wear off as the morning breeze came from every direction. I realized we had been driving for almost an hour. I wasn't that damn drunk, and I knew our house wasn't this far away from that club.

"Where are you going?" I finally asked.

"Home," he said. I sat straight up in my seat when he pulled up to a house that looked like it belonged to a celebrity.

"Kayo, don't play with me. Whose house is this?"

"It's yours, baby. Happy Birthday."

"Ohhhhhh My Goooooodddd!" I screamed while kicking my feet before jumping out and running up the stairs with him in tow. He grabbed my hands before we went in.

My night couldn't get any better, an engagement and a house all in the same night!

"I love you, Kyana."

"I love you, Kayo. Please don't change."

"I'll never do anything to hurt you."

SEVEN

KYANA

Six months later

I stood still so that my mother could place my tiara on top of my head with my huge barrel curls that hung over my right shoulder. I can't believe this day is finally here. I'm nervous and happy. I have been planning this wedding in my head since the first day I laid eyes on Kayo. The love I have for this man is unexplainable. I'm ready to become one with the man I love and party with the two hundred people that are here to witness our union.

I sat down in the makeup chair as my makeup artist touched up my face. I tried to be still, but I couldn't help but notice my best friend and maid of honor staring at me crying. I knew my best friend was happy for me, but damn, she was crying more than me like something else was bothering her. I didn't have time for a pity party on my wedding day so whatever it is will have to wait until the morning. I did, however, get up and wrap my arms around her to show her I care.

I made sure everyone in my wedding was dressed to perfection, but my mermaid dress was the dress of all dresses. It is custom made to hug every curve on my body and fitted from the chest to the knees and flared out to an extremely long train. I had to have at least two thousand shiny rhinestones placed to perfection throughout my dress. This dress ran Kayo a cool fifty thousand dollars, with an additional ten a piece for the girl's dresses, which were a semi-exact replica of my gown.

I hired the best wedding planner money could buy because I didn't want any flaws in my extravagant wedding. I went over the top because I don't believe in budgets, money is made to be spent. I rented the entire JW Marriot Chicago Hotel out for my special day. I put every single guest in a room for the night because I knew the open bar reception was going to put everyone down. I paid a cool seventy thousand to make this hotel ours for a night, which was a great deal for this beautiful venue. The venue sits on 44,000 square feet. It has hand-made royal chandeliers and enough floor space to bring any vision to life. Kayo had not one say so in this wedding; I even designed the suits they were wearing.

I looked at the door as my wedding planner peeked her head in as she talked over a walkie-talkie.

"Ten minutes to show time, beautiful," she softly said as I stood to my feet.

"You ready, baby?" my mother asked, standing in front of me and grabbing my hands.

"As ready as I can be, mommy."

"Well, I'm not ready to give you away. No matter what you will always be my baby and my strength, I love you more than life," my mother said as I tried not to cry.

"I will always be yours, mommy. I love you too, but I'm getting hot in this dress," I said. We both laughed and followed my planner to the door.

I stood behind the ivory satin curtain that separated me from the rest of my life. I felt the butterflies flying around in my stomach as singer Monica's song, "For You, I Will," came through the speakers. I broke the traditional rules of a man giving a woman away because the only person I had my entire life was my mother, so she's walking me down the aisle. Neka walked out with Rio first, followed by my girls. They wasted no time tossing white and red rose petals over their heads as everyone snapped pictures. Sincere was up next carrying an ivory satin pillow with a ring attached to it. He was so handsome in his little suit as he tried to concentrate on not dropping the pillow. I took a deep breath when the curtains were pulled back, and everyone in the room stood to their feet. I made it halfway down the aisle before the tears started falling from every set of eyes in the building. Kayo stood at the altar and wiped his eyes with a handkerchief as I made my way to him. I stood across from him with the biggest smile on my face. The pastor read a scripture and asked us to individually repeat after him.

"I, Kyana Jones, take Kayo Castillo, to be my lawfully wedded husband, to have and to hold from this day forward. For better, for worse. For richer, for poorer. In sickness and in health, 'til death do us part, and I pledge my faithfulness as a sign and seal of unbroken fidelity," I said as tears fell from my eyes.

"I, Kayo Castillo, take Kyana Jones, to be my lawfully wedded wife, to have and to hold from this day forward. For better, for worse. For richer, for poorer. In sickness and in health, 'til death do us part, and I pledge my faithfulness as a sign and seal of unbroken fidelity," Kayo repeated, looking me dead in the eyes.

"It's my privilege to introduce to you, Mr. and Mrs. Kayo Castillo."

EIGHT

KAYO

"Who pussy is this?" I asked while I had her bent over with her legs were spread apart.

"Yours, daddy!" she screamed as I rammed all ten inches inside of her.

"Who else you been giving my pussy to?" I asked now getting inside of her head.

"Nobody, Kayo. I swear you're the only person I want."

"Make me know it," I replied, smacking her ass so hard that I could see my handprint.

I had her ass up in the air and her face to the floor, pounding her pussy. She managed to grab the nightstand that held a picture of her and her grandmother. I leaned over and flipped it down because it looked like the lady was staring at me. She found her rhythm and started throwing her ass back, making me remember why I started fucking her in the first place.

I met Tanya last year at the gas station. She was drinking with a group of her friends and was bold enough to walk to my truck and pull the passenger side door open. Rio instantly pulled his .9mm out and aimed it at her as fear covered her face. I laughed when she backed away. It wasn't until she damn near ran back over to her friends I saw how thick she was in the Apple Bottom jeans that cover her ass. I told Rio to chill. I hopped out and jogged over to her and the group of chicks she was with. I could tell from her conversation she was actually a good girl that probably came from a strict household. I gave her my number and told her I was taking her out to make up for the incident. I knew I should've left her right there in that gas station when I found out she was only eighteen years old, but her body and my dick wouldn't allow me to let her get away. I ended up taking the girl's virginity, and the rest is history.

I did my little shit, but I always made sure bitches knew who Kyana was and made it clear she was not to be fucked with. I would never allow what I do in the streets to affect my home. I don't tolerate bitches overstepping their boundaries. That's the quickest way to get cut off. It didn't matter one way or another because Kyana knows how bitches operate, so she doesn't believe the shit she hears in the streets. I can have a bitch sitting next to me, and someone can see me, call Kyana and tell her, but if she doesn't see it for herself, she gone put their ass right in their place. I know she's not stupid, though, that's why I have to handle this situation right after I bust this nut. They weren't lying when they said pregnant pussy was the best pussy.

Once I let my kids shoot off into the Magnum that was covering my dick, I pulled my Nike shorts up and laid across her bed. I should've got back to her sooner, she texted me about this shit months ago, but I was busy with the wedding and shit. I watched her as she bounced her ass around her room before walking to the bathroom. I actually liked this girl, but she fucked up when she threatened to go to Kyana. She came back smelling like strawberries and climbed into the bed next to me. I just shook my head and handed her one of the blunts I already had rolled up. She wasted no time grabbing the lighter and flaming it up. I shared a lot of shit, but my blunts weren't one. I let her finish smoking and get relaxed before I reached into my pocket and pulled out a wad of cash. I watched her eyes grow wide and angry covered her face.

"So, it's that easy, huh?" she asked, sitting straight up on the bed.

"It's real easy. You can't have that baby."

"First of all, I'm six months, and an abortion is out of the question. I bet you didn't make that bitch get an abortion when she got pregnant. I've been nothing but good to you, Kayo. What does she have that I don't?"

"Everything and I'm not trying to lose her over a fuck."

"A fuck, huh? You are a weak man, and I hate I got involved with a piece of shit like you. I actually feel sorry for that bitch because she has to spend the rest of her life with you!"

Before I knew it, I hauled off and slapped fire from her for disrespecting Kyana. I knew for a fact she was trying to play me like I'm one of these weak ass niggas. She wasn't a hood bitch, so I know it was one of her hoodrat ass friends that put her up to the shit. I snatched her out of bed by her hair and dragged her down the hall to her living room. She had that same terrified look she had on her face the day I met her.

"SIT YO ASS DOWN, BITCH!" I yelled, and my voice echoed throughout her tiny apartment.

I stood there and looked at the bitch while she sat on the couch shaking her leg uncontrollably. This could all be so simple, but this bitch clearly got me fucked up talking about taking this shit to Kyana. She looked at me with pleading eyes, waiting on me to react.

"So when you going to get the abortion?" I said, walking toward her, making her jump to her feet.

"Really Kayo? You're not going to even give me the option to keep my baby?"

"Option? You just texted me and asked me to help you get rid of it, so who are you playing with? Listen, Tanya, I'm not one of these lil weak ass niggas you're used to playing with, and that's probably not even my baby," I replied, handing her the test, she looked at it and broke completely down.

"Kayo, this is your baby, and I texted you months ago. I was willing to get rid of it, but you took your sweet time getting back to me and now it's too late."

"Tanya, you are looking for a family, and I'm not it. I'm married. I haven't heard from you in months, and out of the blue, you text talking about you're carrying my seed. Sounds like some bullshit to me, baby," I replied with a chuckle.

"Fuck you! I'm not lying. You are the only person I have ever been with. I swear to God you have me so fucked up. I'm gone drag your ass all through the court system to make sure we we're good. You're a poor excuse for a man! I hate you! GET OUT!" she yelled, pointing to the door and crying hysterically.

I almost felt bad because I knew she was probably telling the truth about not being with anyone else, but I don't know who the fuck she thinks she's talking to. I backhanded her, causing her fall back and fall flat on her ass. She looked up at me with pure hate in her eyes.

"Just get the fuck out, bitch ass nigga. Keep your money because I'M KEEPING MY BABY!" she screamed, grabbing her face.

"Over yo dead body," I replied, aiming my pistol at her stomach, releasing two bullets killing her and my unborn baby.

NINE

KYANA

"SHHHHHH," I said to the girls, flopping on the couch and throwing my legs across Kayo.

I was trying to listen to the news while they reported another death. Chicago was becoming a war zone, but I can't complain because Kayo and I have contributed to a large portion of it.

"This is Cindy Combs, reporting live from the Humbolt Park area, where an eighteen-year-old woman was found unresponsive by a relative with multiple gunshot wombs to the abdomen. First responders were able to resuscitate the victim and transport her to Norwegian Hospital, where she was later pronounced dead. No suspects are in custody."

"Damn, I know her family is sick."

"Yeah, that is fucked up, but I'm not surprised. That's a normal day in Chicago. I'm about to ride up to the car wash to meet the contractors," Kayo replied gently removing my legs so he could stand up.

"Ok well, I'm gone drop the girls off to my mom and see if Neka wants to go shopping."

"Ok, here's some money for the two of you. Have fun," he replied, handing me five stacks of hundred-dollar bills with rubber bands holding them together.

"Thanks, baby," I replied, dropping the money in my purse that sat on the coffee table.

I jumped up and grabbed the girls to get them ready. I was really excited because I rarely had time for myself between running the businesses and keeping up with them. I pulled their hair up into one ponytail and put them in matching dresses. I dressed down similar to them, slipping on an all white fitted dress that fit my body like a glove. I let my hair hang down my back and threw a pair of Chanel shades over my eyes. I strapped my babies in the back of my brand new Jaguar S type.

It felt like I had been driving forever. I hated that my mother refused to let me move her out of the hood. It was so much shit happening that I almost hated letting my kids visit her house, but she was the only person, outside Kayo and myself, I trusted them with. I came up off the expressway at Homan and noticed a black car riding my bumper. I looked back at my girls who were sound asleep. I thanked God because I didn't want them to the side of me that was about to come out.

I reached down on the side of my seat and wrapped my hand around the .9mm pistol that I kept in my car while keeping an eye on the car trailing me. I made a left turn onto Homan and another left at the stop sign. They did the same confirming that they were definitely following me. I knew Kayo was in the area, but I couldn't get my phone out of my purse without stopping, and that wasn't an option, not with my babies in the car. I pulled up to a red light and went for my phone, but before I could grab it, I heard a loud knock on my window, followed by glass shattering and my girls screaming. I stepped on the gas while the guy ran back to his car. I was doing at least eighty miles per hour up the side streets trying to get my babies to my mother's house.

I turned up my old block and it was packed. My mother stood on the front porch of the house she raised me in as everyone looked in my direction. I jumped out, snatched the girls out as quickly as possible and passed them off to the closest person to me then grabbed my gun off the seat.

I knew I only had a few seconds to warn everybody, so I yelled, "PLEASE GO IN THE HOUSE, GET THE KIDS OFF THE SIDEWALK! MOMMA, TAKE THE GIRLS IN!"

"Kyana, what's wrong?" she yelled, and she started praying aloud.

"Momma, just go in and call Kayo NOW!" I yelled. She hurried in and closed the door.

I kneeled down on the side of a parked car and left my car double-parked a few cars up to throw them off. My timing was perfect because a few seconds later, the car pulled up and opened fire on my car. I could hear people screaming from every direction as shots rang out. I crept up behind the guy emptying my entire clip into his back while a guy that I had never seen before opened fire on the passenger. I'm not sure where the tall, handsome guy came from, but I owed him for riding with me.

A few minutes later, Kayo, along with Rio, Santana, and twenty other niggas pulled up and hopped out. The guys quickly moved both cars and bodies before the police even got a chance to show up. Kayo paced the ground and cursed in Spanish before walking over to me. I was looking around for the guy who helped me. I looked in every direction, but it's like he disappeared into thin air.

"Baby, you ok?" Kayo asked, holding my hands.

"I'm good, but we have to move my momma. She can't stay here," I said, running my hands over my hair.

"Ok, she can stay at our crib until we find her a house. Who else was shooting with you because I know your gun only holds fifteen rounds, and it's well over thirty holes in them niggas?"

"Baby, I don't know, it was a tall guy. He was here when I got here. He stood right on the side of me and got down. I looked for him to thank him, but he was gone."

"I have to find out who this nigga is. I owe him my life for saving yours. I don't want you in the streets for a while, Kyana."

"That's easier said than done Kayo, and you know that."

"This was too close of a call. I need you to stand down and stay out the way, baby. I can't lose you."

"Ok, Kayo."

TEN

NEKA

"Hey best friend, what's going on?"

"Nothing much."

"I feel like you've changed right before my eyes, I don't even know who you are anymore. You know I'm gone always keep shit real with you. I feel like you've changed."

"Kyana, it's not like that, I just need to get myself together. I can't do Rio anymore; it's been going on too long. I have lost myself trying to love him. This shit wasn't supposed to go this far in the first place. I said I would wait until Sincere was old enough to understand and that time is now."

"Neka, nobody forced you to stay with that man. You had plenty time to leave. Why would wait until a child is involved to decide you want out? That's ass backwards. I don't care how old Sincere is, the shit is still going to hurt that baby. That's his father. So, when exactly do you plan on walking away from your family?"

"I plan on moving out around Christmas. I'm in the process of looking for a place for me and my baby. There is nothing left. I hate the sight of Rio."

"Really bitch? You're going to break the man's heart on Christmas? You're cold-blooded."

"I don't care. I'm not about to keep wasting my time with that nigga. Fuck that. I have to do what's best for me. My pussy doesn't even get wet for the nigga anymore," I replied, becoming annoyed.

"How long have I been I knowing you, Neka? I know when you lose interest it's clearly because you're fucking someone new. So, tell me who the mystery guy is that's breaking up your happy home."

"He's no mystery, and I've been fucking with him. And happy home? That home hasn't been happy since you had the girls so you do the math. Rio is too clingy. I had to get me a suite for a few days to get some fucking air. All he wants to do is cuddle and shit. I need to breathe. This shit is my fault. I should've fucked him and kept it moving."

"That's crazy. I knew you were cheating on that man a long time ago. So wait... what you're saying is you're tired of this man treating you like a woman is supposed to be treated? I'll tell you this. You know I will stand behind you in whatever decision you make, but don't wait until he starts loving someone else to start loving him. You have a good one."

"I can treat myself like a woman. I don't need no nigga for that. And as far as him loving someone else, he'll be doing me a favor. I don't care who he ends up with. Hell, you want him?"

"Bitch, please, I would never go behind you. That's a huge no-no. Bitches get killed for shit like that, and besides I'm good, I like cuddling with Kayo," she replied, laughing.

"I bet, but anyway room service is knocking, and I have a spa appointment in a few minutes. I'll talk to you later."

"Ok, I love you."

"Love you too," I replied, ending the call as someone slightly knocked.

I unlocked the door to my room and watched the man that I loved walk in. He stood in the doorway of the bedroom while I pressed the end button on my phone. I licked my lips as he walked toward me.

He stood there giving me the sexiest look ever, and a huge smile spread across my face. He leaned down and kissed my perfectly full set of lips. I stood up and dropped the towel I had wrapped around my body, exposing my size 32-D breasts that drove him crazy. He ran his hands through my bone straight hair before grabbing a handful of my ass. I could easily put any video vixen's body to shame. I had a natural shape that most bitches paid top dollar for.

I could have any nigga I want, and I've proved that plenty of times. I slowed down a lot since having my son and being with Rio, but I was slowly getting back to the old Neka. Bitches hate me because their men love me, but they will never bring that shit to me because I'm known for beating bitches.

"You miss daddy?" he asked, pulling me on top of him and falling back on the bed.

"What's that a trick question? Let me show you," I replied, spinning around and putting my freshly shaved pussy in his face.

I pulled his dick out his sweatpants and slowly spelled my name with my tongue over the head. I felt his tongue slide across my swollen clit, causing me to spread my legs wider and give him full access. I rolled my hips and took his entire dick into my mouth. I mastered the art of sucking dick at an early age. My mom started selling me to the hood at the tender age of twelve to support her drug habit. I didn't mind though because I made sure they paid me and my momma for my services.

"Damn, Neka."

"Shut up and eat this pussy," I replied, and he did as he was told.

After getting his dick hard as I wanted it to be, I stood up and positioned myself over it. I teased him a little by bouncing on the tip. He immediately pulled me down, putting all ten inches inside of me. I moaned out in pain and pleasure. I have had my share of dicks, and his is definitely in my top five. He wrapped his arms around my waist locking me down while he drilled in and out of my pussy. In one swift move, he flipped me over on my knees with my ass up and proceeded to lay the pipe. I couldn't control myself while he punished my insides. I began to work my pussy muscles, which caused him to lose control and fall on my back. He flipped me over, pushed my legs up to my shoulders, and fucked the shit out of me.

"Baby... damn, what the fuck?" I yelled while digging my nails into his back.

"Say my muthafuckin' name," he said while going deeper.

"Babbbbbyyy... wait! I can't... Ohhhhh!"

"I SAID SAY MY FUCKIN' NAME!" he yelled, speeding up the pace and smacking my ass.

"KAYOOOOOOOO!"

ELEVEN
KYANA

HANG ALL THE MISTLETOE

I'm gonna get to know you better,
    This Christmas
    And as we trim the tree
    How much fun it's gonna be together,
    This Christmas
    The fireside is blazing bright
    We're caroling through the night
    And this Christmas will be
    A very special Christmas for me yeah

I STOOD BACK and took it all in, our lives were moving at a very fast pace, but I wouldn't have it any other way. When Kayo said that he wanted me to stand down, I didn't know he meant for years. The shootout happened five years ago, and he was still hesitant about me handling street business. I really had to watch how I move now that my girls are eight years old going on twenty.

I danced around my house in my Christmas pajamas, hanging the last stocking up in front of my fireplace. Being that Christmas is my favorite holiday, I had my house professionally decorated. I had a nine-foot Christmas tree sitting in the corner with at least three hundred gifts underneath, wrapped to perfection. I went all out for the girls and Sincere this year because I knew they were old enough to take care of their things now. I watched them stand around the tree in their pajamas trying to guess what each gift was, but they had no clue. I brought Sincere all of the latest Nerf guns along with a new PlayStation 3 and his favorite game NBA Live. I knew he was going to go crazy when he saw it. I got the girls all kind of shit, including the new Wii game system with all of the games, new bikes, and an entire bedroom makeover.

Kayo was just like me when it came to Christmas gifts. It was all about the kids and seeing them happy. So, for Christmas, I went all out and had a custom made $16,000 Bvlgari Diagono watch along with a brand new sixty-inch television for his man cave. I really didn't care what gifts I was receiving because seeing a smile on my family's face was enough for me. I thank God for putting us in a position to be able to buy any and everything we wanted. I will forever remain grateful and humble.

I walked into the kitchen where my mother was standing over the stove preparing her famous soul food. I knew I was going to have to hit the gym extra hard after this Christmas dinner. She made two of everything because we had a house full coming over. Santana arrived with some girl about an hour ago, and I made a mental note to curse him out. I told him about bringing strays where my family lays their head. Neka and Rio had just walked in, and I could tell Neka was on bullshit with him already from the look her face. Rio remained humble and forced a smile as he carried a bunch of gifts. I walked over to help him free his hands since Neka's dumb ass just stood there and watched the man struggle. I can't lie. I love my best friend, but Rio deserves someone better than her.

"Ho! Ho! Hooo! Merry Christmas!" I heard Kayo say as he came down the stairs dressed in a full Santa costume, causing the kids to laugh.

I couldn't help but laugh because he looked ridiculous in that shit, but he would do anything to see us smile, and I love him for that. The last of our guests were arriving just as he gathered all of the children around the tree to open their gifts. I sat on the couch with my camera ready to capture every moment. I watched as the children's faces lit up with excitement while they ripped through the wrapping paper. I always celebrated on Christmas Eve so that the kids could play all day on Christmas. Once they were done, I walked over, sat on Santa's lap, and pulled a box from behind my back.

"What's this, Mrs. Claus?"

"A little sum-sum for Santa," I replied, smiling.

He wasted no time opening his gift like a big kid. He looked up at me, grabbed my face, and just stared. I was nervous because I thought he didn't like it, but then he smiled and pulled me in for a kiss. I felt all eyes on us as we kissed as if we were the only two present.

"Thank you, baby. Let me change and go grab your gifts from my office," he said, kissing my forehead.

I couldn't help but notice the dirty looks my mother was shooting in Neka's direction. She never cared for Neka. She always said Neka was a "hot ass," and nothing but trouble. I always took up for Neka because it always seemed like everyone was so against her, but that's my dog. I will kill or be killed for my best friend. She may not be shit to most, but she's everything to me, even when she's acting like a brat.

"Mommy, why are you looking at her like that? Please don't be rude tonight," I whispered, watching Neka walk with Sincere toward his room.

"She's trouble. Oh Lord, please open my baby's eyes," she said, looking up like she was speaking directly to God.

"She's not as bad as you think she is. She has a good heart. Ma, just let it go, please. For meeeee," I said, grabbing her face and planting kisses everywhere.

"Oh, Kyana, stop. Go round everyone up for dinner, please."

"Yes, ma'am. Rio, we're about to eat!" I yelled, walking to Sincere's room since it was first down the hall. I walked into Sincere's room, but he was so wrapped up in that video game he didn't even notice my presence.

"Wrap it up, Sin. It's time to eat," I said, walking out.

"Ok G momma, it's almost over!" he yelled back, calling me by the nickname he's called me ever since he could talk.

'I walked toward the back where Kayo's office is and heard whispering. I walked up and looked through the cracked door, noticing him and Neka having what looked like a heated conversation. I wanted to push the door open, but something told me to be still, so I did just that. I put my ear closer to the door so that I could really hear.

"I don't fucking get it, Kayo. The girls have been waking up to you every single morning since they've been born. Why does my son... no, our son, get the short end of the stick? He doesn't deserve to be treated like a stepchild!" Neka said with tears running down her face.

"Neka, you knew how shit was going to be. I told you I would take care of my son, and I've done that and more. Sincere is good on every level. Kyana and Rio suspect nothing, and now here you go putting feelings into the shit about to fuck everything up. I don't know what your motive is, but there will never be an us. I love my wife."

"Did you love her a couple of weeks ago when you came to my hotel room and put your face all in my pussy, Kayo? Did you fucking love her then? I tell you what, you better tell them or I will!" Neka said, slightly raising her voice.

"Bitch, if you don't lower your voice, I will kill you. This is not the time or place for you to start with this bullshit. All of my friends and family are out there. I suggest you take them feelings, put them in your back pocket, and sit on them because I'm not for the bullshit today."

"Well, you might as well get ready because I'm not hiding my son anymore. I don't care anymore. He's gone call you daddy like his sisters do. I'm sick of this shit."

"Come here, man, you gotta chill. That shit gone fuck the business up, and we all gone be broke. You have to think outside the box; this shit is way bigger than us," Kayo said, wiping her tears as mine fell to the floor.

I turned and power walked to the stairs. I heard my mother yell my name, but I couldn't stop. I made it to my room and locked the door, my legs gave out on me before I could make it to my bed. I laid on my floor in the fetal position as my heart felt like it was going to explode. What did I do wrong? I gave him chapters of my life that I can't get back. And Neka? I don't believe this shit. My mother was right on every level.

I tried to lift myself up off the floor, but my body felt like it weighed five hundred pounds, so I crawled on my hands and knees to my bed. I finally stood up. My first mind was to go downstairs, tell Rio what's up, and put a bullet in both of their heads. I have to get the fuck out of this house because I know if I look them in their faces, I'm going to end up spending the rest of my life in prison.

I went to the bathroom and washed my face. My eyes were so swollen from crying that they almost looked shut. My face was completely red, and my head was banging, which let me know my pressure was sky high. *Calm down, Kyana. Breathe,* I coached myself as I grabbed my Pelle Pelle coat out the closet and threw it on. I ran down the stairs and threw my hood over my head while everyone sat at the table waiting on me. I never stopped, I just yelled with tears falling from my eyes, "I'll be back. I have to run to Walgreens!"

I heard Kayo yelling for me, but I kept it moving. I hopped in my car and took off. I took off with no destination in mind. I just got on the expressway and drove. I knew everything was closed because it was Christmas, but I was starving, so I ended up in White Castle parking lot. I decided to get out and go inside because the drive-thru was line was long. I was surprised to see this many people out on a major holiday. Maybe it's because we were having a decent winter. It's cold as hell but no snow.

I got out and ran inside, totally forgetting I had on these thin ass pajamas while the Chicago winter wind beat my ass. I stepped up to the register as a group of guys came in behind me. I ordered my food and felt my pockets before realizing I rushed out of the house with no money, no purse, no nothing. I told the cashier to cancel my order and then turned to leave.

"I got her order," I heard one of the guys say, making me look up.

I couldn't figure out where I knew the guy from, but he looked familiar, and he was fine as hell. He stood about six feet even, toffee skin complexion, and a perfect set of teeth with dimples to match. He had a fresh haircut with enough waves to make anyone seasick. I ran my hand over my wild hair as he spoke to me.

"What's up, Ms. Killer?" he asked, followed by a chuckle.

Then it dawned on me. He was the guy that stood next to me in the shootout a while back. I don't know how this man always pops up when I'm in kill mode, but I'm glad he's here so I can thank him.

"How are you doing, Mr. Saved My Ass? I've been looking for you. I never got a chance to thank you before you vanished into thin air," I said, forcing a smile.

"My name is Waun and a thank you is not necessary. I've also been looking for you Ms. Kyana," he said, carrying our food over to an empty table.

"How do you know my name?" I said still standing just in case he said the wrong shit.

"Everyone knows your name. You run the city. You can have a seat. I don't bite," he said as I slid into the seat.

"So, tell me, Waun, why have you been looking for me?"

"I want to work with you. I'm gone keep shit funky with you. I'm a killer, nothing more nothing less. Watching you handle yourself when you were clearly outnumbered, let me know you're a true boss. It was simply kill or be killed, and that's what I live by," he replied, looking directly into the eyes.

"Oh, I know you're a killer, I saw you in action, but how did you end up on that block that day? That's my area, and I've never seen or heard of you," I asked, watching his body language.

"I was coming from my baby mother's crib and saw how fast you were passing your kids off, so I knew something was about to go down. When I saw you duck down behind the car and draw your gun, I joined you off instinct," he said, biting his burger.

"Wait, who's your baby mother? I might know her. I lived on that block my whole life, so I'm pretty sure I know her," I said, awaiting a response.

"Tasha, but she had just moved over there around the time of the shootout. Enough about me. What brings you to White Castle on Christmas Eve? You should be with your family."

"Long story. I lost a couple of people I loved tonight, and this was the only place open, so here I am."

"Damn, I'm sorry. They died on Christmas Eve?"

"Nah, they're not deceased yet, but I think you're ready for your first job. Welcome."

"Say no more."

I SAT and talked to Waun for about an hour before we parted ways. I'm glad I bumped into him because I could definitely use a nigga like him on my team. I know for a fact shit is about to get real ugly around my parts, but I'm ready. I thought long and hard about my next move. I plan on professionally going about things. Even though I gave Waun the green light on Kayo and Neka, I instantly thought about Sincere and the girls and called it off. I don't care what's going on, I still love that kid, and I don't want to hurt him like that, but I have to hit them where it hurts.

I found a few twenties in my car and decided to stop by Walgreens to grab a home DNA test and some other shit to throw Kayo and everyone else off. I pulled into my driveway and noticed Rio's car was still here, so everyone was still inside. I took a breath and mentally prepared myself to stand face to face with the two people who intentionally broke my heart. I jumped out and ran inside, and everyone looked at me with a stale face.

"Why weren't you answering your phone, Kyana?" Kayo finally spoke.

"I'm sorry. I left it here on the charger. I went to five different Walgreens, and they were closed. Hell, I had to drive all the way to the hood."

"You had us worried to death. I hope you got what you needed."

"I did," I replied, holding the bag up in the air before running upstairs.

Neka came upstairs right behind me and closed my bedroom door before whispering, "Come on spill it, who is he? I know you are cheating on Kayo, I knew you weren't ready to get married."

"What are you talking about? I went to the store," I nonchalantly replied as I got my clothes out for the bath I was about to take.

"Righhhhhhtttt, I knew it was only a matter of time. I'll be waiting on the call when you tell me you're ready to leave Kayo," she said, walking toward the door as Rio called her name.

"I bet you will. Oh, leave Sincere here tonight. I'm taking them to take pictures in the morning," I replied, walking into my bathroom.

"Ok."

I decided to wear a red lace thong teddy with the fishnet stockings to match and a pair of red six-inch stilettos. I wanted my last night with my husband to be everything he ever dreamed of. Plus, I need him in a deep sleep tonight so that I can swab his mouth along with Sincere's. I just need proof. I poured the cherry bubble bath that he loved into the tub before stepping out of my clothes. I looked at myself in the mirror and realized this is the beginning of the rest of my life as a single woman. I turned Mary J. Blige's song, "Not Gon Cry" on and put it on repeat. I never thought it would end like this, but it explains why she cried so hard when I got proposed to and even harder when I got married. I replayed their conversation over in my head. I had to laugh because they have been fucking for years and this little boy that I have grown to love is actually my husband's biological son!

While all the time that I was loving you
You were busy loving yourself
I would stop breathing if you told me to
Now you're busy loving someone else
Eleven years out of my life
Besides, the kids I have nothing to show
Wasted my years a fool of a wife
I shoulda left your ass a long time ago
Well I'm not goin' cry,
I'm not goin' cry,
I'm not goin' shed no tears
No, I'm not goin' cry,
It's not the time
Cause you're not worth my tears
Well I'm not goin' cry,
I'm not goin' cry,
I'm not goin' shed no tears
No, I'm not goin' cry,
It's not the time,
Cause you're not worth my tears

"EIGHT FUCKING YEARS!" I screamed, breaking down again.

I pulled myself together and climbed into the tub. I thought about just letting my head go under the water or simply slitting my wrist, but I have my babies to live for. I scrubbed my body and stepped out. I decided to put on some makeup and let my hair hang. I slipped onto my lingerie, and I looked myself over. My body at twenty-seven still looks as good as it did ten years ago when I met his weak ass.

I walked out the bathroom and lit a few candles at the same time Kayo was walking in. He stood there and stared at me like he loved me. I knew that was a lie, but I played along. I walked over to him, wrapped my arms his neck, and he wrapped his arms around my waist. I walked him over to the bed, and he laid back as I kissed and licked his neck. I allowed his hands to roam all over my body so that he could remember what he had.

"You gone start some shit with all of those people downstairs."

"I don't care, do you love me?" I whispered in his ear.

"Yes, more than life, baby," he replied as I slid down to his now brick hard dick.

He grabbed me and pulled me over to the bed. All I could think about was him fucking Neka as tears fell from my eyes onto his chest. He never once asked what was wrong, as he held me. I couldn't help but think how this entire marriage was a joke, but I promise I will have the last laugh.

TWELVE
KAYO

"Nigga, ten or four!" I yelled, placing my bet on the dice.

It was cold as hell outside, so we decided to shoot dice inside of my car wash. I was up about eight hundred dollars when a fine ass white woman came strolling in looking like a boss. I stood up to greet her with a hand full of money in my hand. She had on a full-length mink with a pair of matching stiletto boots. Luckily, we were having a decent winter with no snow, or she would've been busted her ass. Everything about this woman spoke money down to the Louis bag that hung from her shoulder. I knew it cost a bag because I had just brought Kyana the exact same one.

"Hello Ms. Lady, how can I help you?"

"Hello, are you Kayo Castillo?" she asked, accepting my handshake.

"Maybe, how can I help you beautiful?"

"Business opportunity."

"Well yeah, I'm Kayo. Let's talk. You wanna follow me to my office?" I asked, licking my lips.

"You've been served," she replied, handing me two envelopes before strutting out the same way she came in.

Rio came and stood next to me as I watched the bitch walk out. I immediately walked to my office and closed the door behind me. I know this dumb bitch Neka did not put me on child support. I swear to God I regret ever fucking with that bitch, damn. I tossed the envelopes on my desk and leaned back in my chair while running my hands over my face. How the fuck am I going to explain this shit to Kyana without her finding out about Neka and me? Fuck! I finally picked one of the envelopes up and opened it. I sat straight up in my chair after reading the first line.

Decree of Divorce.

What the fuck is going on? This shit has to be a mistake. Kyana and I have been good. I know this has to be a mistake. I picked up the second envelope and opened it. I think my heart stopped beating when I read the results of a paternity test stating I was 99.9 percent the father of Sincere Young.

"FUCK!" I slammed my fist down on the desk so hard that it started bleeding. Tears formed in my eyes because I can't lose my family. I jumped up and stormed out of my office telling Rio to lock up when they leave.

I jumped in my car and did the dash home. When I pulled up, I saw a U-Haul truck parked in the driveway and some workers moving shit from the house. I jumped out without turning the car off and ran up the steps. When I walked in, Kyana was coming down the stairs with a few of her belongings, while giving orders to the movers.

"That's his shit leave it," she said to the mover.

I stepped in front of her and looked her in her eyes. All I saw was pain. Pain that was caused by me, I didn't know what to say because I wasn't prepared to lose the best thing that ever happened to me.

"Baby, please don't go. Let me fix this. Kyana, I fucked up. Baby, please."

"Kayo, what did I do to deserve this? I gave you all of me. I never even looked at another man, and you do me like this? And with Neka? Out all of the million bitches in the city, you chose Neka? All this time you two were having an affair right under my nose, and you didn't even care enough to protect yourself, STUPID! I can't believe you. I can't even stand to look at you!" she yelled before slapping the shit out of me.

I couldn't even react because everything that she was saying was right, I fucked up, and I know from the pain in her voice that there is no possible way I could fix it.

"Kyana, I never meant to hurt you. I need help. Please don't leave me, baby. Not like this. I need you and my girls. She's a hoe, and she doesn't mean shit to me, I love you!"

"No, you don't Kayo because if you loved me, we wouldn't be having this conversation and you wouldn't have a child with that bitch. You don't have to worry about me and my kids and you damn sure don't need us. You have Neka and Sincere, and FYI I mailed a copy of the results to Rio as well. I feel so sorry for that baby, and I pray to God he grows up to be nothing like his dog ass parents. Y'all have a good life, and I'll see you in court," she said stepping around me, walkng out the door and my life forever.

I walked into my office after they were done moving my family out of the house. I didn't even get a chance to see my girls. I put my Usher CD in, let it blast through the surround sounds, and grabbed my bottle of Hennessy. I sat down, placed my pistol on the desk, and turned the bottle up, drinking half the bottle in on gulp.

Every time I was in L.A. I was with my ex-girlfriend
Every time you called, I told you
Baby, I'm workin' (no)
I was out doin my dirt (oh)
Wasn't thinkin' 'bout you gettin' hurt
(I) was hand in hand in the Beverly Center like man
Not givin' a damn who sees me
So gone
So wrong
Thinkin' like I didn't have you sittin' at home
Thinkin' about me
Bein' a good girl that you are

But you probably believe you got a good man
I mean I never would do the things I'ma 'bout to tell you I've done
Brace yourself
It ain't good
But it would be even worse if you heard this from somebody else

I PICKED my gun up and put up to my head. I was about to pull the trigger when the door flew open. I instantly turned the gun from myself to the door, and Neka stood there staring at me. Everything in me told me to shoot her and then myself because neither one of us deserved to live, but I still had to think about Sincere. Through all of this bullshit, he didn't ask to be here.

"What the fuck do you want? It's your fucking fault my baby left me and is taking everything I have, you bitch!" I yelled slurring since the liquor was taking effect.

"Kayo, she was going to find out eventually, but it's ok, I have some money put up for us, and we can leave here," she replied. I tilted my head and wrapped my hand tighter around my gun.

"You don't get it, do you? I lost EVERYTHING— my family, my businesses, my money, my life! That little shit you have is nothing. I have to start from the bottom, bitch," I replied, slamming my gun down and crying like a baby.

Neka walked over, wrapped her arms around me, and held me. I wished it was Kyana. I pushed her off me and took another drink. Her voice was starting to annoy me, but she was definitely on to something.

"Rio has well over a couple of million dollars in a couple of accounts that I have access to and one more with another million set aside for Sincere when he turns 18. All we have to do is get him out the picture, and we're good. You won't even miss the money Kyana took from you. I told I got you, baby."

"I can't do no shit like that. Plus, shit is about get real. He knows about us. Kyana mailed him a copy of the paternity test."

"Well, that means we don't have time to play. Let's do this."

I pulled my phone out and dialed Rio's number on speaker without thinking twice. I had no other choice because starting from the bottom wasn't an option.

"Yo." He answered on the first ring.

"Change of plans; I need you to move that shipment we received earlier from the carwash and take it to the trap ASAP."

"No problem, I'm still at the carwash anyway about to pack it up and move it out now."

"Good looking, bro. I'll meet you at the trap."

"Yup," he replied, ending the call. Neka pulled her cell phone from her bra.

"911, what's your emergency?" the dispatcher spoke through the phone.

"I want to anonymously report a possible drug transaction."

"Ok, what's the location, ma'am?"

"Near the Family First carwash on Sacramento and Roosevelt, the guy is driving a silver BMW 750i. Please hurry before he gets away, I just want the drugs off the streets," Neka said, smiling and sounding like a concerned citizen before ending the call.

Fuck it. I don't have shit else to lose.

THIRTEEN

KYANA

I looked down as a weird ass number flashed across my screen. I hesitated to answer because I thought it was Kayo calling from another number again. I was confused when the operator said I have a call from "Mario Wilson", an inmate at Cook County Correctional Center. I quickly pressed one and accepted the call. I had no idea he was locked up.

"Yo Kyana, I need you to get me a lawyer and come see me today. My visiting hours start at three o'clock. I already put you on the list. You're not gone believe this shit."

"I'm on it, and I'll be there. See you in a lil bit," I said before the line went dead.

I wonder how long he's been in there. I had turned my phone off the day I moved out of my house because I didn't want to talk to anyone. I wonder if he got a chance to see the copy of the results I sent to him. I have so many questions. I could tell some serious shit was going on from the tone he was speaking in. I immediately called my lawyer and told her to meet me at the county in about an hour. Depending on the charges, this bitch would have him out in a few hours.

I was staying at a hotel until all of this court shit was over. I sent the girls with my mother until I could find us a new house. I explained to them what was going on without leaving anything out, except that Sincere is their real brother. I never wanted to turn them against their father, but I told them he would no longer be present because he had another family. Every time the bullshit crossed my mind, I broke down crying. They really have me fucked up, but this too shall pass.

I slipped on a jean outfit and a pair of wheat Timbs. I had to make sure my clothes weren't too tight because the correctional officers at the county were always on bullshit and would turn my ass around at the door. I walked down the hall to the elevator and stepped on. The doors were closing, but someone stuck their foot between the doors, and they slid back open. I knew exactly who it was when I saw my name in cursive across their hand. I instantly slipped my hand in my purse and wrapped it around my pistol because Kayo was losing his mind, leaving messages on my phone saying what he was going to do to me if I divorced him.

"So this is where we at, Kyana? You can't even hold a fucking conversation with me?"

"Kayo, we don't have shit to talk about, I wish you leave me the fuck alone. I would hate to have to get a restraining order on you, or better yet shoot you!"

"You think I give a fuck about a piece paper and don't threaten me because that shit will make me fuck you up in this elevator. I'm sorry, baby, just hear me out, damn," he said, walking up so close to my face that I could smell the liquor on his breath.

"You're drunk right now, so I suggest you get the fuck out of my face and go sleep that shit off," I said, pushing him to the side and stepping off the elevator.

"I made you! I made you, Kyana!" he yelled, slurring with every word and causing everyone to look in our direction.

"Yeah and you destroyed me too, Kayo. Don't forget that part!" I replied walking out of the hotel as valet pulled up in my car.

I will be glad when this divorce is final, and I don't have to see or hear from this man again. I would be lying if I said I didn't miss everything about Kayo, but I'll be damned if I take him back. What would I be teaching my girls? That it's ok to let a nigga do what he wants to do as long as he comes home, fuck that. I refuse to allow them to take any kind of bullshit from a man. I won't allow it.

I PARKED my car and walked up the steps a while the ghetto girls lined up to see their boyfriends and baby daddies. I thank God I didn't grow up to become a product of my environment because I would fit right in with these hood boos. I stood near the door and watched my bossy ass lawyer walk toward me. It didn't matter what kind weather it was. This bitch rocked her stilettos. I made a vow to myself I would step my shit up to her level one way or another. I really had no choice because soon I will be running the entire operation by myself. I planned on taking everything from Kayo, and I want to see if Neka can be half the woman I was to him and help him get it all back. I doubt it though with her nothing ass.

"How did you beat me here?"

"I was already here with another client when you called. I looked over Mr. Wilson's charges, and Kyana he was caught with a lot of shit. They want to give him some real time, but I will work my ass off to get some of that time knocked off," she replied, sounding like she came from the hood. You wouldn't know she was white unless you saw her.

"Damn, Rio. I don't understand. He would never get caught slipping like that. Something isn't adding up. Where was he when they took him into custody?" I asked, folding my arms across my chest as she opened a manila folder she was holding that I'm guessing contained his information.

"Sacramento and Roosevelt Road."

"Dirty muthafucka! I will pay you whatever to get him out of here, just make it happen. I'll be in touch," I said, hurrying to get in line to be searched.

Once I made it to the waiting area, I had to wait what seemed like another hour before these slow ass people brought the inmates out. I rolled my eyes and stood up when I saw Rio walking out wearing an orange shirt. He looked like shit, so I could tell he was in here stressing. His facial hair had grown wildly. He took a seat behind the thick glass that separated us before picking up the phone.

"Man Kyana, that bitch stole all of my money, so I couldn't bond out if I wanted to. I'm gone kill her if I get out, so they better keep me in this bitch. Kayo won't answer his phone, is he good? Is my son ok?" he asked, confirming that he didn't get a chance to see the papers I sent to him.

"Don't talk like that right now, not here. I got my lawyer on top of it, and she's the best in the city. But listen, she didn't do this shit by herself, Rio. Kayo helped her. I hate to tell you this shit while you're locked up, but fuck it. You deserve to know. I overheard him and Neka talking on Christmas and found out Sincere is Kayo's son. That's why I ran out the house that night. I needed proof, so I brought a home DNA test and swabbed him and Sin. The results came back 99.9% positive confirming that Kayo is Sincere's biological father," I said as tears fell from both of our eyes.

"Nah Kyana, that's my son. He looks just me man. Kayo? Nah, he wouldn't do no shit like this. Not to me," he said, shaking his head.

"I'm sorry, Rio, it fucked me up too, but it's ok. I need you to stay focused so that we can get you out of here. Don't worry about nothing. You know I got you and that lil money they stole I'll have it back and then some for you whenever you touch back down. They gone get what's coming to them in the process."

"Either they gone kill me, or I'm gone kill them but either way, it's some bodies dropping around this bitch." He said.

FOURTEEN

KAYO

"Damn Kyana... that shit feels so fucking good," I said, gripping the back of her head and forcing my dick deeper into her mouth.

"Fuck you!" Neka yelled, jumping to her feet and walking to the bathroom.

I had been slipping up and calling her Kyana since I let her and Sincere temporarily stay with me. I tried not to think about Kyana, but I can't seem to get her off my mind. The thought of her moving on and possibly being with another nigga is killing. I swear if I see her talking to any nigga, I'm gone kill them both. I know I sound crazy, but I mean that shit. I made Kyana into the boss she is, and I'll be damned if I sit back and watch another nigga reap the benefits. I'm gone give her this divorce, but I'm gone make her life a living hell until she has nobody to turn to but me.

I thought about how bogus I was for setting Rio up. I never thought shit would come down to this where I would have to turn on my own homie, but I can't start over. I worked too hard to have everything taken away from me. I have become accustomed to this lifestyle, and I will maintain it by any means necessary. I'm not worried about Rio retaliating because the amount of shit he was caught with, they could dig Johnnie Cochran up to represent him, and he still wouldn't walk.

Neka walked up and tried to kiss me on the lips. I was fixing my tie in the mirror preparing for this stupid ass divorce court, but I quickly turned my head, I don't know where she got the idea of thinking she could fill Kyana's shoes, but she could never. Don't get me wrong Neka is a straight rider and will ride til the wheels fall off, but I'm not trying to wife the bitch. The only thing she had going for her was the head on her shoulders. The bitch could suck a golf ball through a straw. The only reason I haven't killed her because I needed that lil money until I can get my money back flowing steadily. I was nowhere near ready to let Kyana go, but little does she know I'm not going anywhere.

"Kayo, Kayo!" Neka yelled like she wasn't standing right in front of me.

"What? Damn!" I asked clearly annoyed.

"Never mind. You must be thinking about Kyana again. I don't get you. She's about to take your ass to cleaners and yet you're still running up behind her like a fucking puppy, stupid."

Before I knew it, I had grabbed her face and applied maximum pressure, causing her to yell out in pain and tears to fill her eyes.

"Who the fuck do you think you're talking to? I'm not Rio, and you're damn sure not Kyana, so don't get shit fucked up. I will beat the fuck out of you if you ever-" I stopped in mid-sentence and released my grip when I noticed my son standing in the doorway.

"Pop, why are you making my momma cry?" Sincere asked with a twisted face.

"I'm not crying, baby. I had something in my eye, and he was blowing it," Neka jumped right in and cleared the air.

"You was gone beat me up, Sin?" I asked, scooping him up off the floor and tickling him while he laughed and begged me to stop.

Neka stood there smiling like I wasn't just about to fuck her up. She walked over, grabbed Sin, and told him to go get his bag ready so that he could get dropped off to the babysitter. I had Neka to drive me to the courthouse and told her to wait in the car because I didn't need her smart mouth ass adding fuel to the fire. I know whenever Kyana catches her ass it's gone be ugly.

I adjusted my fitted suit jacket, and followed my lawyer into the courtroom. Even in the midst of all of this bullshit, Kyana looked as good as the first day I laid eyes on her. She stood next to the same bitch that walked into the car wash and gave me the divorce papers. I saw Kyana look at me and roll her eyes. I just stood there and waited for the judge to start this bullshit ass divorce. I had mentally prepared myself to have everything snatched away from me.

I knew for a fact all of my possessions were going to be stripped away when a bitch walked out in that black robe. I know all women stick together when it comes to men cheating, so I just took a seat and waited for her to grill the fuck out of me. I didn't say a word as Kyana's lawyer made me look like public enemy number one. My lawyer tried his best to make sense of my actions, but there was no win. Kyana walked away with everything except the house and cars. The only good thing that came from this shit is they denied her claim for full custody of the girls and granted me unsupervised weekends twice a month and all school breaks. I was happy with that because that means I still get to see her.

Kyana shook her lawyer's hand, flipped her Chanel shades down over her eyes, and walked out without looking in my direction. I jumped up and followed her outside. I caught up with her and grabbed her arm. To my surprise, she stopped to hear what I had to say. I had no idea what was about to come out of my mouth, but I had to say something to her just in case this is my last time talking to her.

"I just want to tell you that I'm sorry for putting you through this bullshit. I hope we can remain friends and just know I'm always here if you need me," I said. She shook her head and smiled.

"You think I want you as a friend? I thought you were one of the realest niggas in the world when I first met you, but lately, I've been seeing the bitch in you. I know you and your bitch set Rio up, but don't worry I'm gone do your job and be a real friend to him. He won't be down for long, and you know shit gone get real when he comes home. Fuck out my face," she replied, waving me off.

I wanted to slap the fuck out her for disrespecting me. Ever since she found out about Neka, her mouth has become reckless. I tolerate a lot of shit, but disrespect is not one. Who the fuck does she think I am? I have never feared another human being. Rio is a killer; don't get me wrong, but he's far from stupid. Everybody knows ain't no such thing as friends in this game. It's every man for themselves. I had to do what I had to do, and I'm sure he would've done the same thing if he was in my shoes.

"Kyana, you need to choose your words wisely before you speak to me. I don't give a fuck about you thinking I set Rio up, but you will talk to me like you have a head on your shoulders before I knock it off."

"Show me, Kayo. You know ain't no bitch in me. I suggest you and your bitch come up with a business plan with all of the money y'all stole because I'm gone make sure y'all don't make no money on the streets. Now I have a few businesses to run," she replied, walking toward the door.

"Man, have my kids ready when me and my bitch pull up!" I spat, and she stopped dead in her tracks. I knew I struck a nerve, which was my intention.

"You bitch ass nigga, you will never see my kids. Better finish playing house with that hoe, and if you bring her anywhere near me, I'm killing you and her."

"Is that a threat?"

"No Kayo, that's a promise. I will not play with you!"

FIFTEEN

KYANA

"Go directly to the location he arranged for you all to meet. Be careful not to blow your cover because Kayo is far from dumb. He will size you up, and if he notices anything flaw about you, he will kill you. Make sure you give him the brick on top. It's the only one with pure cocaine. If you fuck this up, I'm gone kill you myself!"

"Relax. I'm no amateur, boss lady. I got this shit. I'm known for my dope along with my gun game. I am the connect which is why he's been going out of his way to meet with me," Waun said arrogantly, preparing to meet with Kayo.

I knew Kayo was hard up for a new connect, but I told him I was going to make sure he didn't make any money on the streets, and I meant that shit. It just so happens that he came looking for Waun, and Waun now works for me, so shit is working in my favor. Waun wasn't lying. His name was thick in the streets on the dope side. I did a little research on him myself, and his shit was A-1 pure cocaine.

I sat in the back of the laundromat we once owned together and wrapped ten bricks of pure drywall mixed with a little pure cocaine. I was going to get Rio's money back one way or another. I know Kayo like the back of my hand, and I knew he was going buy all of this shit because I made sure Waun made him an offer he couldn't refuse—ten bricks for $260,000. I have the nigga right where I want him. Once he buys this shit and tries to move it, his reputation will be ruined. What's a king with no power?

I placed the bricks in two black duffle bags and passed them off to a couple of my workers to load the car while I gave Waun one last practice run before he left. I can't wait until this shit blows up in Kayo's face. I have other plans for Neka's ass, and I planned on hitting her where it hurts. They will both regret the day they crossed a real bitch.

After Waun left, I sat behind my desk and looked over some paperwork before I heard a knock on my door. I guess I didn't answer fast enough because that knock soon turned into a bang. I jumped up with my pistol in my hand and walked over to the door.

"Who the fuck is it?"

"Mmmmiiiiiii-Miss Kyana, it's me Haaarold," one of the little stuttering kids that always hung around the neighborhood announced himself. I snatched the door and looked at the out of breath kid.

"What's wrong? Is someone after you?" I asked, peeking my head out of the door.

"Nnnnnooo, your cccccarwash is on ffiiire. It's on fire!"

I grabbed my purse and ran out of the door with the little boy right on my heels. Kayo made sure all of our businesses were located at least a block away, so I ran right past my car and straight to the carwash. By the time I made it, the fire department had got the fire under control and saved what was left of the carwash, which was practically nothing. I stood back and waited to speak to a detective. I reached into my purse, pulled a few twenties out, and handed them to my little messenger. His eyes lit up like a Christmas tree as he tried to thank me.

I pulled my phone from my bra and shot Kayo a nice little text.

Me: Lol, you love paying me, don't you? Did you

forget I have full coverage on this shit? You just blessed me with another big ass check, but you pulled yet another bitch nigga move. Baby, you know I'm not going out like that, so I'll be seeing you soon.

SIXTEEN
WAUN

My whole perception of Kyana was wrong. I just knew I was gone be able to slide right in and pick up where that nigga Kayo left off. I happen to be that nigga, and the ladies made it known. Every bitch in the city wanted to my Mrs., but that's a dead issue. I like my freedom and love my money, and I haven't come across one bitch that made me come close to changing my mind. I moved back to Chicago after a death in my family, and I don't plan on leaving anytime soon.

I know Kyana gave specific instructions not to make any stops before meeting Kayo, but fuck that. I'm my own man, and can't no bitch tell me what to do. I came up off the expressway and made my way to this thick lil bitch's crib that I met a few weeks ago at the club. I put the blunt I was smoking out in the ashtray and sprayed some Curve cologne on to reduce the weed smell.

I wasn't familiar with the neighborhood, so I made sure I was strapped extra tight, especially since it was a gang of niggas standing in front of the address she gave me. I caught a park and killed the engine before hopping out. I walked up to the gate and noticed the guys were a bunch of lil niggas no older than seventeen. There's always a tough guy that tries to make a name for himself in front guys.

"Aye, what you is, nigga?" he said, standing in front of the entrance to block me from going in.

I let a slight chuckle before running my hands over my face. I was high, and the shit is funny to me.

"Oh, you think shit a game, nigga. I said, what the fuck you is?" he asked, getting loud as his homies gathered around me.

"I'M A MUTHAFUCKIN' KILLA, NOW WHAT'S UP?" I yelled, pulling both of my pistols from my waist and pointed them in the tough boy's face. They all stood there froze as tears ran down the tough boy's face.

"I'm sorry, I was just playing," he said with pleading eyes, holding his hands up in a surrendering position.

"Well, I'm not," I said, cocking my guns trying not to laugh because piss started running down his legs. "Get the fuck on. Next time I'm killing you annnd them," I said, quoting Big Worm from the movie, *Friday*.

I shook my head and laughed to myself as they took off running. I finally made my way upstairs. This thirsty bitch opened the door before I could even knock. I walked in and looked around the small but neat apartment. I didn't even remember the way she looked in the face, but I remember that ass and how it sat up on her back. The shit instantly made my dick hard. I wasted no time. I was here for one thing and one thing only— some pussy. I pulled my dick out of my Polo jogging pants in one swift move, and she looked at me like I was crazy.

"I know you ain't call me over here to look at me do this, mufucka," I said.

She shifted her weight to one side and popped her lips.

"You don't even remember my name, huh?" she said, rolling her eyes.

"Does it matter, Keisha?" I said, praying that it was her own name tatted on her shoulder.

I'm guessing I got lucky because her entire demeanor changed in a matter of seconds, and she walked over and dropped to her knees. I leaned up against the wall as she gave the best head I had in years. I leaned my head back on the wall, gripped her head, and fucked her mouth, making her gag. I felt myself getting weak as my heart rate picked up. I knew I was about to nut, but I wasn't about to tell her ass, so a few seconds later, I let my kids go in her mouth. I held the back of her head while she tried to pull away.

I finally released my grip, and she spit my kids on the floor before yelling, "You a stupid muthafucka. Get out!"

"Shid, bye and thanks hoe," I replied, grabbing my guns and walking out.

I hopped in my car and headed toward the spot where Kayo wanted to meet. I was in my zone rapping along with the lyrics to Jay-z's song "Takeover" when an all white BMW cut in front of me. I could tell it was a female because most women can't drive and this dumb shit was proof. I managed to pull up on the side of the car and had to double look because I locked eyes with the finest bitch that I had ever seen. She looked over at me and flashed a perfect set of white teeth. There was no way in hell I was letting her fine ass get away. I motioned for her to pull over. When she pulled off leaving me at the light, I thought she was one of those stuck up bitches until she pulled over and waited on me to catch up. I jumped out my car as her Christian Louboutin red bottom stiletto touched the ground. I sized her up, and her body would give any video vixen a run for their money. Everything about this girl screamed money, and she reminded me of Kyana.

"What you doing in the hood, Ms. Lady?" I asked, trying to spark a conversation.

"Just riding. You can take a girl out the hood, but you can't take the hood out of a girl. It's my comfort zone," she replied like the boss she is.

"I hear that, what's your name beautiful?"

"Mena and yours?"

"Waun."

"I like that, nice and simple."

"Where's your man? I know you can't be single."

"Very, I haven't gotten lucky enough to find Mr. Right yet. I'm focused. I just graduated with my Bachelor's."

Today must be my lucky day. I haven't crossed paths with a bitch this badd ever! I know I gotta get my money up to fuck with a bitch of her caliber.

"Word? Congratulations, baby. Maybe I can take you out to celebrate one day."

"Thanks, and I don't see that being a problem. Take my number down," she replied. I pulled my phone out of my pocket before she could finish her sentence.

We hugged and said goodbye, and I watched her walk perfectly on her heels back to her car. I swear to God I needed her in my life. If she plays her cards right, I will give her the world. I walked back to my car on cloud nine.

"Mena just might be the woman I'll risk it all for."

SEVENTEEN

KAYO

"Nigga, did you get lost, and why is this shit so cheap?" Santana asked the nigga standing in front of me after he reached inside the bottom of a duffle bag and handed me a brick.

I made sure we met in one of my trap houses with about ten of my men present just in case this nigga tried anything funny. I wasn't really worried because I had heard nothing but good shit about his product, and I was in desperate need of new connect. I had been chasing this nigga down like he owed me money to cop some work from him, and he finally got back to me.

"Because I contemplated on bringing this bullshit. Yo ex-wife found out you were trying to work with me and tracked me down. Kyana made me an offer I couldn't resist, money talks, so I took the job. She mixed drywall and coke together, and here I am," he replied, completely catching me off guard.

"What the fuck did you just say?" I yelled while guns cocked and aimed at him from every direction.

He let out a chuckle, which let me know he was off as he handed me a small knife to cut the plastic that was covering the brick.

I know Kyana didn't have enough balls to play with me like this. I wasted no time poking a small hole in the plastic. I touched the powder with my index finger and rubbed it on my gums. I picked the shit up, threw it against the wall and pointed my gun at the nigga.

"Ok, I'll handle her, but what's yo motive, why are you snitching?"

"I want to work with you. I'm gone keep shit funky with you. Yeah, I move weight in my spare time, but I'm a killer, nothing more nothing less. From the looks of it, you need me on your team because ain't no way I should still be standing here talking to you, and all your niggas got guns drawn but ain't nobody let off a shot. Now either you gone kill me right now, or we gone do real business," he replied in a calm tone like eleven guns weren't pointed at him.

"How I know you not lying?"

"Because you haven't pulled the trigger."

"Ok Waun, let's talk about this bitch Kyana," I said.

I pulled my phone out and replied to message from the bitch herself, claiming I pulled a bitch move.

Me: I don't know what the fuck you talking about but Kyana, please find you somebody to play with because I'm not it. You'll see me soon? I'll be waiting on your tough ass."

I was really clueless about the shit she was talking about in that message. I haven't even started doing my dirt to her ass yet. I still can't believe the once love of my life has turned into my worst enemy, but if she wants to step into this world, that's on her. I will treat her like any other nigga that comes for me, and if that means making my kids motherless, then it will be done. The shit is gone be hard, but I have to teach her a lesson.

I dismissed everyone, except for Waun and Santana. I need to size the nigga up a little more and tell him exactly what I need him to do.

"I never caught your name, boss man," he said, taking the initiative to speak first.

"I never said my name, and I'm pretty sure if you talked to Kyana, she spoke highly of me before sending you to get killed. Now I'm going to ask you again... what's the real reason you dropped a dime on Kyana? Don't give me no bullshit because I have no problem blowing your brains out, and I won't think twice," I replied, taking my gun from my hip and resting it on my lap.

I wanted to see if the nigga's body language would change, but he had that same fearless ass smirk on his face, which confirmed two things— he was indeed crazy, and he wasn't afraid to die. Having a nigga like him around could be a gift and a curse, so I have to make sure he knows the type of nigga I am.

"Aight, Kayo, to be honest, I hate the bitch straight up. Her ego is a muthafucka, and I probably would've been killed her if it wasn't for the money I was making. She thinks she's unstoppable and can't be touched. I was hired a while back to kill you and some bitch you cheated on her with. Now I'm gone be honest. I accepted the job because I needed the money, but when I did my research and found out exactly who you were, and how much weight your name holds, I knew I was on the wrong team. Now like I said before you can kill me now, or we can do business."

I sat there in overall shock at the words that just left this nigga's mouth. I knew she hated me but to try and put a hit out on me was the biggest mistake she could've ever made. I'm on nothing but bullshit from this day forward, and I'm gone make sure Waun plays a big part in the shit since she wants to send him to me with this bullshit. I guess Kyana want to play big boy games. Well, game on bitch. I walked Waun out before speaking to Santana.

"That nigga looks crazy, but I like the way he moves."

"I don't trust him."

"Nigga, you don't know him!" I replied, laughing.

"You don't either. You're a Castillo nigga, so act like it with your friendly ass."

EIGHTEEN

KYANA

"Paree, sit yo ass down somewhere before I beat you!" I yelled to my bad seed. I swear she is Kayo's child, and I hate it.

"I didn't even do nothing, shoot," she shot back, rolling her little eyes.

"Bring yo ass here because you wanted to say shit!" I said, as she slowly walked toward me. I instantly popped her in her mouth and sent her on her way.

I swear my twins are like day and night. It scares me because Paree has all of Kayo's characteristics, but I'm gone break her up out of that shit one way or another. I always catch her doing devious shit to her sister and have to beat her ass. I know the divorce plays a huge part in her terrible behavior, but I can't deal. I know they miss Kayo, but I refuse to have them around him and his bitch. I don't give a fuck if it is court ordered. I make sure they are always gone to my mom's house when Kayo tries to get them.

"Go pack your clothes so that you all can go to granny's house."

"I don't wanna go over there. It's boring, and all granny wants to do is pray and make us watch church TV," Paree replied, stomping up the stairs of our new seven-bedroom home.

"You need Jesus. Stomp again, and I'm gone break your back!"

I PULLED up to my mother's house, and she was already on the porch with open arms. My mother is so beautiful, and I thank God every day for helping her find her way in life. I still can't believe how far she has come, but I'm glad she found herself. I watched London run up the stairs while Paree slowly walked. I swear this lil girl is gone be the death of me. I got out and hugged my mom. I peeled her off a few hundred dollars for food and snacks for their movie night before hopping back in my white BMW M3 and speeding off to my laundromat.

I was extremely busy. Between my businesses and the streets, I barely had time for myself, but I wouldn't have it any other way. I was making triple the money by myself than I was with Kayo. All I need is for Rio to come home, but the judge went hard on my boy and sentenced him to twenty years, but he's only serving half of that. I make it my business to keep his books full and am present on every visiting day. All he talks about is killing Neka and Kayo, so I know when he does touch down, there's going to be an all-out war. Kayo is on his way to the bottom anyway. The deal I set up with him and Waun went just as planned, so I know his money is real tight right now. Kayo and I haven't seen one another since the divorce. He stayed clear of me, and I did the same, but I know it's only a matter of time before we cross paths.

I turned my music up and did the dash. There were a couple of urgent documents that I had to fax over to my lawyer tonight. Otherwise, this shit would've waited until tomorrow. I pulled in front of the laundromat and killed the engine while looking around to make sure it was safe before I hopped out. The usual alcoholics and crack heads stood a few doors down, but other than that, the coast was clear. As soon as I stuck my key in the door, I felt someone breathing down my neck. My heart started racing as a million thoughts ran through my mind.

"What do you want? I don't have any money on me. It's in my car!" I said, trying to see what they wanted.

"That's bullshit, I been watching you. Bitch, unlock the door, hurry up! I swear to God I will slit your throat," They said, now pressing a knife to the side of my neck.

I fucked up and hopped out the car without my purse, which held my gun. I could kick my own ass for this fuck up. I was about to unlock the door when I heard, *POW*. One single shot went off causing whoever was behind me to fall to the ground. I immediately turned around and looked down at one of the local crackheads who was about to rob me before locking eyes with a kid who looked to be every bit of twelve years old, holding a smoking gun still aimed at the lifeless body he had just killed. I quickly walked over to him, took the gun, and put in the trunk of my car. I put him in the passenger side before speeding off as the sirens got closer to us. Murders were normal in this area, so I knew it wasn't going to be an issue. Just another dead nigga in the hood.

"You hungry?" I asked, breaking the awkward silence.

He just nodded his head up and down without looking at me. He looked like he was homeless and hasn't eaten in days. I instantly felt bad for him when I looked down at his clothes. Here I was spending hundreds even thousands of dollars on one outfit when this kid has nothing. He wore an oversized hoodie and pair of jeans that had holes at the knees. First thing tomorrow, I'm taking him shopping for new everything. I knew I couldn't take him home, but I will do everything I can to give him a better life because he saved mine.

"What's your name?" I asked with a smile, but he didn't budge. He just looked down.

"Ok. Well, from now on your name is Young Goon, YG for short, ok?" He finally smiled and shook his head in agreement.

NINETEEN
KAYO

My mind has been all over the place since Kyana showed her true colors. I want nothing but the worst for her. I jumped in my truck and decided to ride with no destination in mind. It's crazy how fast my life changed. I wanted to reach out to Rio, but I know I'm the last person that nigga wants to hear from. I let this bitch Neka shake my life up, and now I have no one except her dumb ass.

My cell phone vibrating in the cup holder pulled me out of my thoughts. I picked it up and saw Waun's name flash across the screen. Ever since he dropped the dime on Kyana, he's been a part of my team. He handled a couple of situations in the streets for me, but I mainly pay him to work with Kyana and keep me updated on her every move, so I know he's calling with some information.

"What's up, my nigga?" I spoke into the phone.

"Aye, who lives in this little blue house in Oak Park?" Waun asked.

"Nigga, I don't know. I pay you to find shit out, not the other way around," I replied clearly annoyed by his dumb ass question.

"Naw, I was asking because I was riding past, and I thought I saw your little daughter's outside playing in the yard."

"What's the exact address?"

"126 Madison Street."

"Good looking, bro."

"Yup," he replied, ending the call.

I flew to the address Waun had just given to me because I haven't seen my girls in months. Kyana completely went against the court orders for my visitation rights, but there was no way in hell I was running to the police for help, so I just took it for it was. I turned down a quiet block and had to take a double look as I watched my twin daughters playing in the yard of a nice little house. I can't believe how big they have gotten. I knew it didn't belong to Kyana because it was too small for her liking, and Waun would've known whose house it was. She only leaves the girls with one other person, her mother. I never got a chance to find out where she lived because she was still living with us when Kyana found out about Neka.

I pulled up in front of the house as the girls looked at my truck. London took off running toward the truck while Paree looked at me like a total stranger when I climbed out of the driver side. I knew Kyana had brainwashed my babies, but I also know they love me regardless. I walked around the car and scooped London up in my arms, planting kisses all over her little face. I placed London on the ground and reached for Paree, but she didn't budge. I kneeled down and put her hands in mine.

"What's wrong, baby girl? It's me, daddy."

"We're not supposed to talk to you."

"Who told you that... mommy?"

"Yes, and granny says you're the devil, and I'm afraid of him," my baby said, causing my heart to ache.

"Baby, I'm not the devil. I'm your father, and I love you. Go wait in the truck, and I'll go talk to granny, then how about we go get some new toys?" I replied. A smile spread across her face, and then she joined her twin in the truck.

I walked up to the door and twisted the knob. As soon as I walked in, the smell of freshly fried chicken hit my nostrils causing my

stomach to growl. I walked in the direction of the loud gospel music
and knew that's where I would find Ms. Shelly. Just as I thought, she
stood near the stove stirring something in a pot with her back turned
towards me.

"It smells good in here, what's for dinner?" I said, startling her
causing her to drop the spoon she was holding in her hand. She
turned around, placing her free hand over her chest.

"How did you get in my house and what do you want?" she asked
clearly frightened.

"I'm the devil. I let myself in," I replied with a chuckle.

"That you are. Where are my grandbabies? I swear to my heav-
enly father, I will kill you before I let you take those girls away from
here," she said trying to walk past me. I stepped in front of her stopping her dead in her tracks.

"My kids are outside waiting on me to come out. Why are you
and your daughter filling their heads up with that bullshit? I don't
appreciate that shit not one bit," I said.

"Watch your mouth in my house!"

"Shelly, please. You must've forgotten where you came from. I
know you remember when I use to slip you bags just so that I could
spend the night with Kyana and fuck her in your house all night," I
replied, tracing my hand over her old but pretty face as tears formed
in her eyes.

"KAYO, GET THE HELL OUT OF MY HOUSE NOW
BEFORE I CALL KYANA! BASTARD!" she yelled.

"That's the Shelly I know. I have something good for you. Something I know you miss because you two were once in love," I replied,
reaching into my pocket and pulling out a bag of pure cocaine.

I waved the baggy in front of her face, but she turned her head
and prayed at the same time. I opened the bag, dipped my finger in
and forced it into her mouth. Just like that, I woke up dope fiend
Shelly. She looked up at me and reached for the bag. I gave it to her
and watched as she wasted no time running over to her table. She
grabbed a piece of paper and rolled it up before filling her nostrils

with the powder. She leaned back in her chair, looked at me with a set of red, glossy eyes and smiled with powder covering her nose. I reached into my pocket before leaving and tossed an eight ball on the table.

"I'll take my kids off your hands while you reunite with an old friend."

TWENTY

KYANA

"Hello ma'am, my name is Kya-" I started to introduce myself to the woman standing in front of me with a cigarette hanging from her mouth.

"What do you want? I don't have any money to pay whatever this little fucker stole from you," she said, cutting me off in the middle of my sentence.

I looked down at YG as he stood there looking nervous. I could tell he was clearly living in a broken home, and he wasn't the only one. There were about five other children that looked to be years younger than him. I placed my arm around him as he stood there with both of his hands filled with bags from the shopping spree I took him on. I made sure he had everything and then some.

"He didn't do anything. He's a good kid. I was just making sure it was ok with you if he can keep the things I brought him today."

"We don't take handouts. Give her that shit back."

"NO!" YG yelled, and I looked at him shocked by the sound of his voice.

"Look, ma'am. It's ok. I don't brag about the things I do. No one will ever hear about it."

"Yeah, that's what they always say. Thanks, but no thanks. Get off my porch and take that shit with you," she said, pointing at the bags as YG gripped them tighter.

Kyana, don't beat this lady in front of her son, I coached myself before I ended up beating the shit out this bitch. I knew she had to be on some type of drugs because she was scratching and looking around. I have sold enough drugs in my time to know the symptoms of an addict. I couldn't help but flashback to the days when I was in YG's shoes. I see the same pain that I used to carry around when my mom was an addict. I remember being the butt of all the crackhead jokes. I refuse to let him go through that shit.

"YG, go inside with your things," I said. He did as he was told and pushed past his mother with his bags.

"Get yo ass back out here, muthafucka! And who the fuck is YG?"

"Listen, bitch. I tried to come at you as a woman, but I guess you don't want that. Apparently, you can't provide for that boy, and I'm trying to help him, but you want to refuse that too. I don't understand you, but then again, I'm not trying to. I will be here every week with new things for him, and if I find out you sold anything that I have purchased with my money, I will make a special trip over here to beat yo ass up and down this block," I said. She just looked at me along with all of her nosey ass neighbors.

"YG, I'll be back Friday!" I yelled before turning to leave.

I will never understand how a woman could not want the best for their children. Speaking of children, I've been so wrapped up with YG that I haven't checked on the girls today. I pulled my phone from my purse and dialed my mother's number. It rang about five times before going to voicemail, which was weird because my mom always answers her phone. I called a few more times and then decided to drive over to check on them.

I pulled up to her house and noticed her car was still parked in the same spot from earlier. The house looked dark with the exception of the porch lights that I had installed along with the cameras around the perimeter. I walked up to the porch and didn't have to use my key because the door was unlocked. I instantly pulled my gun from my purse because something didn't feel right. I maneuvered my way through the pitch-black house. I could hear a scratched gospel CD playing throughout the house and felt slightly relieved. It wasn't until I entered the kitchen that my heart dropped to my feet. Cocaine covered my mother's kitchen table and face. I threw my purse off my shoulder and ran over to my mother, who had a single self-inflicted gunshot wound in her head. I bought my mother a pistol in case of an emergency.

"Mommy, wake up! OH, GOD! PLEAASE HELP ME! MOMMA!" I yelled, but her face was turning dark purple.

I dialed 911 and ran through the entire house searching for my kids, but they were nowhere in the house. I ran back downstairs to my mother, and she had a piece of paper folded in her hand. I took it and stuffed it in my pocket just as the police rushed in. I watched the EMT's checked for a pulse and pronounced her dead at 6:45 p.m., and I was just stuck. I stepped to the side and pulled the paper from my pocket to read it.

Kyana,

I never meant to hurt you. I'm not as strong as you are. Kayo came here, and he brought a demon with him that I couldn't resist. He took the girls and left me here to fight a battle that I couldn't win. I chose to take the easy way out because I can't put you through this struggle again.

Please forgive momma. I love you so much, baby girl. Kiss my babies for me!

"NOOOOOO, MOMMMMMAAAAA! I will go through it again with you! MOMMA PLEASE, WHY DID YOU DO ME LIKE THIS?" I yelled with tears falling from my eyes.

I stuffed the note in my pocket. My heart has never felt pain like this. I would do anything to bring her back, and I definitely would've taken that ride again. I stuck around while they investigated and removed her body. I walked over and kissed her cheek one last time. As soon as some of my family arrived, I was out the door. I hopped in my car and did the dash to my old address as warm tears ran down my face. I ran every light and stop sign until I got there.

I saw both Neka and Kayo's cars parked in the driveway. Even better, I can kill two birds with one stone. I jumped out, ran up the stairs with a pistol in hand, and banged on the door. Neka opened the door with a stupid ass smirk on her face, but I was not here to play games. I wasted no time hitting her in her dick kissers with the butt of my gun. She fell back as blood gushed out her mouth. I walked through the house like I still lived in it, checking every room for my kids. I went to London's old room and found them playing with some of their old toys that were left behind. I knew Sincere wasn't home because I checked his room first. It was just like her trifling ass to drop the boy off to anybody so that she could follow behind Kayo's ass.

"Get up... GET YOUR BEHINDS UP NOW and go to the car!" I yelled. They instantly started crying and running down the stairs.

"Where the fuck are you, KAYO?" I yelled, making my way back downstairs while Neka stood back and watched my every move.

A few seconds later, Kayo came walking from the back of the house on his cell phone, wearing a white V-neck t-shirt and a pair of gray jogging pants. He had the nerve to smile at me and put his index finger up to tell me to hold on. I looked to the sides and behind me to make sure this bitch ass nigga was talking to me before pointing my gun at his head. Whenever I aim my gun, I shoot with no hesitation. I let off a shot, but Neka ran and pushed me, causing me to lose my balance, but the bullet still ended up hitting him in the left leg. He fell back and yelled out in pain as I finally got a hold of Neka's ass. I climbed on top of the bitch and delivered blow after blow to her face and body. She threw a punch and connected to my face, causing me to fall back, but I was too quick for her. I jumped up, ran over, and kicked her so hard in the ribs that I could hear them cracking. She laid down in pain, and I then stomped her ass for old and new. I looked over at Kayo and aimed my gun at him, sending one last bullet his way. I hit Neka with the butt of my gun twice and walked out never looking back.

TWENTY-ONE
KAYO

I tried to open my eyes, but it felt like someone had bricks sitting on top of them. I knew the bed I was lying in was way too comfortable to be a hospital bed. The smell of Asopao, a gumbo made with chicken, filled my nostrils. I knew there was only one person that can have a place smelling this good, and that was my MaMa. I tried my eyes again. This time opening them completely but quickly closing them because the sunrays blinded me. I looked around the room and noticed I was laying in my California king sized bed, which meant my mother was in the states to reign havoc. I have no idea how or when she got here, and I don't even know what today's date is, and it feels like I have been asleep for years. I tried to lift my head, but it was too heavy. I cleared my throat and got the attention of Santana, who was standing in the window resting his head on his arm. He immediately grabbed a chair and slid it next to the bed. I tried to speak again, but no words would come out, and I was thirsty as hell. He snapped his finger, and a beautiful young maid came with a glass of water. I knew she had to have come with my mother because I didn't have a maid. Santana took the glass and helped me take a sip.

"You're finally awake, sleeping beauty," he said while smiling. I cleared my throat and prepared to try speaking again.

"Fuck you. How long have I been in this bed and please tell me MaMa came here in peace?"

"Whoever shot you left you and Neka in here for dead without a leaving a trace of evidence. You were shot twice once in the leg and once in the head. Thank God the bullet grazed you and didn't penetrate, but you lost a large amount of blood and slipped into a deep coma. MaMa has been waiting on you to wake up so that she can take care of the people behind this," he replied, capturing my undivided attention.

"Where are Neka and Sincere?"

"They're here. She loves Sincere, but she doesn't care for Neka one bit. I'll go get her," he replied, and I let out a sigh of relief knowing my son was here.

He came back a few seconds later with Neka. She walked over and tried to kiss me, but I turned my head. I hated the sight of this woman, but I know she loves me more than life itself. She wanted to be Kyana so bad that it was killing her. I still can't believe my mother is in the states, let alone my home, but my mother's family means the world to her, so I know it's about to be chaotic in Chicago.

Do I save Kyana's life even though she tried to take mine? I have a million thoughts running through my head.

"Hola, my sweet baby," I heard the most angelic voice say as my mother appeared in the doorway, and Santana stood to his feet out of respect.

"Hola, MaMa," I replied. She walked over and kissed my forehead.

My mother is just as gorgeous as she was in her twenties. At fifty-two years old, she would give a younger woman a run for her money. Her body was still top notch, and she dressed in nothing but women's designer suits and dresses. Kyana reminds me so much of her it's scary. I knew the sweet talk would only last for a moment before she got down to business. I know if I tell her that Kyana shot me, my children will be motherless by midnight. I have to think and think fast.

"So tell me, my son, who's behind you lying here so helplessly?" she asked while looking into my eyes like she was searching my soul.

I took a minute before I answered her, but I knew better than to look away because that's a sign of weakness.

"My friend Rio, he got upset because he was busted with a shipment and got sentenced to ten years. He called the hit from behind bars, but I will handle him when he's released, MaMa," I lied. Then Neka bucked her eyes and cleared her throat. I wanted to slap the shit out of her.

Santana looked at me in disbelief.

"Nonsense, I would've had him handled tonight if you were telling me the truth. I won't pressure you, but I know you are protecting someone. Where is Kyana? You have been talking about her in your dreams," she said, catching me and everyone else in the room off guard.

"Kyana...I messed up, MaMa. I had the perfect woman in life, but I slipped up and cheated on her with her best friend," I replied, lowering my eyes in shame.

"Neka?" she asked, piecing together my wrongdoing and looking at Neka in disgust.

"Yes, but it was a mistake. I don't regret my son, but I miss my family."

"A mistake, huh? Fuck you, Kayo! I'm taking my son, and I swear you will never see him again!" she yelled, tears falling from eyes.

"Try it, and you won't make it out of this house alive. You're more than welcome to leave, but the boy stays. How dare you act like those words hurt you? You slept with your best friend's husband and got pregnant. You are a whore. You will never be accepted into this family, so you are wasting your time hanging on to Kayo. You're in love with a man that is loving someone else. It will never work. Excuse yourself," my mother said, reading Neka like a book. Neka wiped her tears and stormed out.

"This Kyana is a strong woman because if it were me in her shoes, I would've made sure I killed the both of you. I see why she shot you," she said, turning her attention back to me and letting me know she knows exactly who shot me.

"MaMa, please don't hurt her. I've done enough. I can't watch my kids lose their mother at a young age."

"I will do no such thing. Those girls carry my name and blood, I know you care a lot for her, but I promise she's going to be the death of you. A scorned woman is very dangerous. Get some rest, my boy. Santana, I need to speak with you," she said, kissing my forehead and walking out with my brother in tow.

It's sad, but I don't believe a word that just left my mother's mouth. I know how she operates. I don't give a fuck about Kyana trying to kill me. I just can't see myself sitting watching as a hit is placed on her head. I know I can be killed for going against my family, but I will take that chance. Maybe if I save her life, she will forget about all of the bullshit I put her through and fix our family. As much as I wanted to hate Kyana for the shit she pulled, I just can't.

I tried to sit up, but my body said no. I finally swung my legs off the bed and ran my finger over the healed bullet wound in my leg. My legs felt like noodles as I tried to stand up. I kicked in place to get my blood flowing properly. I slowly walked over to my dresser to see if I could locate my cell phone. I had no luck and no way of reaching Kyana. I knew my mother was about to pick Santana for all of the information she wanted from me. I banged my fist on the wall, and I heard a glass shatter behind me, causing me to turn around instantly. The beautiful young maid was kneeled down placing the broken glass on her serving platter. I swear I don't remember the help being this sexy. I tried to kneel down and help her, but my sore body declined.

"I'm so sorry, Mr. Castillo. I'll clean it."

"It's ok, sweetheart, and please call me Kayo," I replied. She smiled and turned red in the face from blushing.

"I'm Silvia," she said in a heavy Spanish accent.

"Ok Silvia, I need a cell phone," I said, making the phone gesture with my hand. She hesitantly went into her apron pocket and pulled out a flip phone.

"It's ok. You won't get in trouble. Thank you," I said. She nodded and walked out.

TWENTY-TWO
WAUN

I haven't heard from Kayo in over a month. I called his phone, but it was going straight to voicemail. I guess the nigga went into hiding from Kyana since she popped his ass. I rode pass his house a few times and saw his car parked in the same spot, but there was no life inside the house, so I didn't bother getting out of my car. I have stirred up so much shit between the two of them. I sent those niggas to chase Kyana and lead her straight to me a while back. I set the carwash on fire, and I sent Kayo to Kyana's mother's house on purpose, may she rest in peace, and I'm just getting started.

I pulled right behind her car and turned my ignition off before taking a shot of the Patrón I had in my glove compartment. I exited my car, walked up to the house, and rang the doorbell. Kyana snatched the door open a few seconds later with her cell phone resting between her head and shoulder, wearing an ankle-length black silk robe. I couldn't help but watch her ass as she gave me a head nod. I followed her to the kitchen where she ended her call, placed her phone on the counter, and told me she was going to hop in the shower. I thought this would be the perfect opportunity to get rid of her because I knew she wouldn't have her gun on her. I waited until I heard her bedroom door close before I started walking toward the stairs, but I stopped and turned around at the sound of her cell phone vibrating. I walked over, picked it up, and noticed she had a few missed calls and a text from a weird looking number, so I decided to read it.

787-321-9877: Kyana this Kayo, this is not a social call. I'm just warning you, my mother is in here in Chicago and is looking to speak with you about the shooting. As you know my mother doesn't talk, she's a killer. Please just chill until I can find a way to dead this shit. I'm not mad at you for shooting me. Just be careful and watch your surroundings.

Me: Kayo, fuck you and your mother. She's a killer, and so am I. I don't need your warning. Tell her I said come and see me. I'll guarantee her body will be sent back to Puerto Rico in a bag. Have a nice day.

I instantly placed my gun back on my hip. Hell, I can kill two birds with one stone. I was about to place her phone back on the counter when another text came through. I knew it was Kayo responding, and just as I was reading the message, a light popped on in my head.

787-321-9877: Kyana, I know you're upset, but I need you to listen to me this one time. I don't want anything to happen to you or the girls. Just trust me on this one.

Me: Trust you Ha! Fuck you. I don't need your warnings. You fear your mother, not me. I have no problem talking to her. Matter of fact I'll reach out to her, have a nice one!

I erased the messages, placed the number on the block list, and put her phone back on the counter. This shit is too easy.

I took a seat at the island and browsed the internet trying to find all the information I could on Kayo's mother. The way he spoke of her in the message I knew there had to be something I could find to lead me to her in Puerto Rico. I Googled the last name Castillo, and I'll be damned. The Castillo Cartel is one of the most notorious cartels in Puerto Rico ran by a woman named, Amelia Castillo. I clicked on images and watched as a million photos appeared. Some included Kayo at a young age standing alongside his mother and brother.

I know if I can reach out to the cartel and tell them that I have a direct address on Kyana, they would come and do all of my dirty work, and I could walk away with clean hands. I just need to figure out a way to contact someone connected to that cartel. I know this is not going to be easy because they don't trust anyone, and I'll be damned if I get myself killed trying to set another motherfucker up.

I quickly exited the browser when I saw Kyana coming down the stairs in a skintight red dress and a pair of tall heels to match. Her honey blonde hair matched her skin perfectly giving me an instant hard-on. Kayo has to be the dumbest nigga in the world to lose a bitch like Kyana. I thought about fucking her and killing her at the same time, but the sound of her voice pulled me away from my devilish thoughts.

"How do I look?" she asked, spinning around.

"You decent," I replied, laughing.

"You so petty. Sounds like a hater to me," she said, balancing her weight perfectly on the heels.

"I'm just playing. You look good, boss lady. What you got a date?" I asked slightly being nosey.

"I wish. You know the grand re-opening of the carwash is tonight. The reconstructing took forever, but it's finally done. I thought I told you about it," she replied, never looking up from her phone.

"You probably did. Shid, you know I smoke a lot, but aye, I want you to meet the Ricans I get my work from so can ditch that weak ass, Cuban nigga, you been dealing with. They are charging you way too much for the shit so don't freak out and start shooting muthafuckas if you see me pull up with a group of Puerto Ricans."

"I swear I needed to hear that because I don't know what the fuck is going on with my connect. You know I don't conduct any business where my children lay their heads so if you pull up here with anyone, consider yourself and them dead," she said, finally looking up from her phone and locking eyes with me.

"Yes ma'am," I replied, throwing my hands up in the air as her cell phone vibrated in her hands.

I got nervous as hell because I just knew it was Kayo calling from a different number, but the nervousness quickly went away when I saw all thirty-two of Kyana's teeth while she spoke to the caller and twirled her hair like a teenager in love.

"You so silly, I'll talk to you later," she said, ending the call.

I wonder if Kayo knows about this shit. He's going to flip the fuck out when I tell him. I swear working for both Kayo and Kyana had my bank account sitting pretty, but I know it's only a matter of time before Kayo bitches up and tells Kyana everything, so I have to start making moves fast...I need to meet this Amelia Castillo.

TWENTY-THREE

KYANA

"Kayo please, I don't need your help, I'm good. I can drive myself to the hospital."

"Kyana, you're shot. Let me help you."

I felt my chest, and it was soaking wet. I looked down at my hand expecting to see blood, but it was sweat. This was the third night in a row that I had a dream about being shot, and Kayo being a part of it. I fell back on my pillows and stared up at nothing in particular. I always get a gut feeling when something is wrong, but I always figure it out when it's too late. I kept an ear to the streets, and I knew Kayo didn't die the night I shot him, so I know he's probably waiting on the perfect opportunity to seek revenge.

I heard him, Neka, and Sincere have been M.I.A, but I know better. Kayo has never been the type to run from a fight, so I know if he did leave Chicago, he'll be back soon, and I'll be waiting. My girls haven't spoken one word about Kayo since the tragedy happened with mom a few months ago, and I'm fine with that. I told them he moved on with his other family. My girls are at that age where I can't sugarcoat shit with them anymore. I told them they are not allowed to contact Kayo under any circumstance.

I just don't understand why he can't move on and be happy with his family, I have. I haven't been thinking about Kayo. I forgave him a long time ago, but I will never forget all of the pain he has brought upon my life. I would've never thought I would have to bury my mother, divorce the man I once loved, and become a single parent all before reaching thirty. It once felt like I couldn't catch a break, but through prayers, I made it out.

My phone started ringing under my pillow pulling me out of my feelings. I looked at my lawyer's name flash across the screen and prayed she had some type of good news for me pertaining to Rio. My boy has been locked down long enough, and I paid this bitch top dollar to work her number.

"Hello," I sang into the phone.

"Hey Kyana, you have a minute to talk?"

"Sure do."

"Well, I have some good news that should make your day!"

"Good I could use something positive in my life," I replied, sitting straight up in the bed.

"Ok, well as you know Mario was supposed to be sentenced at his upcoming court date. Well, I reviewed the surveillance cameras from your car wash multiple times and spoke with the arresting officers. They had no probable cause for pulling Mr. Wilson over in the first place. With that being said all charges will be dismissed, and he will walk away a free man," she said.

"Are you serious right now? What about the shit, I mean the drugs he was caught with?" I asked.

"Well, that doesn't matter because that had no right to pull him over. Of course, they won't release the shit back to him, but he walks away a free man. I will say this, though. When he gets released, he better lay really low because they want him bad."

"I bet they do, but I'll make sure he stays out the way. Thank you so much!" I replied, smiling from ear to ear.

I know for a fact that shit is about to get crazy because Rio's coming straight for Kayo and Neka, and I'm gone ride with him, so they might as well get ready. I personally want to put a bullet in Neka's head, not over Kayo, but just off the strength of crossing me. I loved the girl like she was my blood sister, and for some reason, I thought she would be right by my side when I had to bury my mother regardless of the shit she did, but she didn't even call and send her condolences. So, she's dead to me. All I have in this world is me and my girls, and I swear I will kill the whole city or die in the process before anyone ever gets the chance to hurt us.

I can't believe my lawyer pulled this shit off. I have to grab her Gucci bag or something for the miracle she pulled off. I knew she was the best, but damn. I just knew he was gone be gone for the next decade, but God saw differently. I stacked all of his bread back up like I promised, so as soon as they let my mans go, he can pick up where he left off.

I decided to grab YG and go to the mall. I have to grab the girls and Rio some new shit anyway. YG has really grown on me. I love the lil nigga like he's my own. I even stepped in and helped his mother get her shit together after I almost had to beat her ass. I paid for her to go to rehab, and she completed the program with no relapse. I brought her a four-bedroom townhouse in Oak Park just to get her away from the hood. YG is the most laid back lil nigga I have ever met. He's very mature and different from other kids his age. I know he's going to be something else when he gets older. He has too much potential.

I wrapped up the call with my lawyer and took it all in before flipping my covers back and walking over to my closet. Summer has finally made its way to Chicago, and I couldn't be happier. That snow shit is for the birds. I grabbed a pair of white shorts, a tank top, and a pair of Gucci sandals because I knew I was going to be in the mall for hours messing with YG. I hopped in the shower and combed my hair down from the wrap that my scarf was holding in place. I put some MAC lip gloss on and popped my lips in the mirror before grabbing my purse and keys then heading out the door.

I decided to drive my new Benz since it was nice out today. I let my garage door down, hopped in, and hit the e-way. I decided to ride through my old hood to see who was out. I hadn't been back on my old block since I moved my mother from over there. I was riding down 16th street when I spotted Kayo's truck. I instantly pulled over to watch and see what he was doing in the area. I sat there for about twenty minutes watching him talk to random people. I was about to pull off when I saw a familiar car pull up. I immediately killed the engine and shifted in my seat. I couldn't believe my muthafucking eyes. I watched as Waun hopped out of his Tahoe and walked over to Kayo. They shook hands and did a bro hug before stepping off to the side to have what looked like a deep conversation. I might not be the smartest bitch in the world, but I know if a nigga sold me some stepped-on dope for two hundred sixty thousand dollars, I would have nothing but a bullet for his ass. I mean, these niggas were standing here talking like they have been friends for years, laughing and shit.

I started my car and pulled off with a million thoughts running through my mind. I thought about turning around and killing them both. I guess I was put on this earth to be fucked over by everyone I come in contact with, but I'm in bullshit mode now. I have to figure out what's to Waun and why he's talking to Kayo. I'm not really worried about Kayo because Rio is going to handle him. I'm not gone say shit to Waun. I'm gone play right along with these niggas and may the smartest muthafucka win. I knew that if anyone had some information on this nigga, it would be his baby mama.

TWENTY-FOUR

KAYO

"Santana, I need you to warn Kyana about MaMa. I can't let her hurt Kyana. I tried, but she won't listen to me," I whispered to my brother as he sat at my kitchen table cleaning his pistol.

"You're paranoid for no reason. MaMa doesn't want to hurt Kyana. She actually thinks Kyana never intended on killing you. She was simply warning you. Look, you need to get your shit together. I'm going back to PR with MaMa," Santana replied without looking up.

"Why? That's some bullshit!" I yelled slamming my hand on the counter as my mother walked into the kitchen, speaking Spanish through her cell phone.

"KAYO, yo, I need to holler at you," Waun said power walking into the kitchen but stopping dead in his tracks because everyone, including my mother, was aiming a pistol in his direction.

No words left my mouth, and this stupid muthafucka stood there speechless. I wanted to kill him right in the middle of my kitchen for walking up in my house unannounced. I just shook my head while my mother looked at me crazy and waited for justification.

"Is this how you conduct business? Your operation is very sloppy.

If it's this easy to walk into your house, it's way easier to kill you. Who is this?" she asked never lowering her gun.

"I'm sorry, Ms. Amelia Castillo; I didn't mean any disrespect. I'm Waun," he said, removing the Bulls fitted hat from his head as a sign of respect and extending his hand.

"No disrespect taken. You didn't walk into my house, or you would be a dead man. How do you know my name?" she replied, lowering her gun and looking down at his hand that was still extended towards her.

"Everyone knows your name. You are a well-respected woman and believe me I meant no harm walking in here like I did. I just wanted to speak with Kayo," Waun said never lowering his hand.

This nigga is a natural. He knew all the right things to say and do to stay alive when dealing with a cartel, let alone the head of a cartel. He never lowered his hand, and he's lucky he didn't because she would've definitely killed him. I watched as he made direct eye contact with her, and she sized him up then finally shook his hand. Once she shook his hand, Santana and I lowered our guns. My mother never responded to his last statement. She just walked out and left us standing there. I walked to the office with Waun in tow. I looked behind me to make sure no else was following us.

"Nigga, what did I tell you yesterday when we met up? I said to call me after you talked to Kyana. I told yo ass not to come to my house because my mother is visiting. You damn near signed your own death certificate," I said, pouring two shots of Hennessy from my mini bar that sat in the corner.

"I know but nigga, I had to come and tell you this shit face to face before I even got a chance to even tell her what you told me to. She ordered a hit on you and your family. She said something about you sent a text talking about what your mother is going to do to her, so she called a mandatory meeting and put the hit in order," Waun said, taking a sip from the glass I had just handed him.

I looked at Waun as he spoke and something about this nigga isn't sitting well with me, but I can't put my finger on it. I listened to the bullshit he was telling me, and it sounded nothing like Kyana. She wouldn't put a hit on me. I know Kyana like a book and if anything, she would try to kill me herself like she did in the first place. I'm gone to have to watch this nigga extra close.

"Ok, since the bitch wants to be tough, I'm gone give her what she's looking for. I tried to warn her dumb ass, but she wants to play big boy games and put hits in motion, huh? Ok, cool, I'm gone get to the bottom of it," I replied, pacing the floor like what he said really had me heated.

"And she's fucking with some nigga from out west on Chicago Avenue. The nigga be all up in her crib cooking bacon and shit like he lives there, and then she got your kids calling that nigga daddy. He called her ass the other day while I was there and nigga he got her ass wide open," Waun said, leaning back in his seat while I registered the words that just left came out this nigga's mouth.

I saw my office door slightly open, and Neka walked in wearing a fitted tank top and a pair of leggings that showed her big round ass. I watched Waun's eyes follow her ass as she walked over and handed me a duffle bag that I had her to pick up from one of my workers. She hasn't really been fucking with me over the last few weeks. Everything has been strictly business with her. I don't give a fuck one way or another, though. Waun licked his lips as she threw her wide hips and bounced right back out of the door. If only he knew that bitch was up for grabs, and he could take her ass right out the door with him when he leaves.

"So, what you want me to do, boss man?" Waun asked once Neka was out of sight.

"It's not serious. Kyana is just trying to get over me. That nigga doesn't stand a chance. Just keep playing your part. I'm gone handle this bitch myself."

TWENTY-FIVE

WAUN

"So, when are you gone pack yo shit and move in with a real nigga?" I asked jokingly.

"Now you know you and I can't be together. This is just fun fucking," she said, laying across my chest asshole naked and passing the blunt back to me.

"So, I'm just a piece of dick, huh?" I replied, taking a long pull from the blunt and letting the smoke fill my lungs.

"In a perfect world, I would love to be with you, but I know Kayo will kill us if he finds out about this," she said, making me laugh and choke at the same time.

I knew I had her ass right where I wanted her after her last statement, and now I'm about to go in for the kill.

"Mannnn, Neka. I'm gone keep shit funky because I like you, but that nigga doesn't give a fuck about you. He was the one that gave me the ok to fuck you in the first place. He told me to shoot my shot, and he didn't lie when he said you got the best head in the city, but you my baby," I said, rubbing her head before she sat up and looked at me.

"Really? So this shit is just a game?"

"You're the one that just said it's fun fucking but now you mad at me?" I replied, pulling her toward me, but she pulled back and looked down as tears started falling from her eyes. I sat up and wiped her face, which made her cry harder.

"Come here, man. Don't do that," I said, wrapping my arms around her and lifting her head.

Even though I made all that shit up, I knew I said all the right shit to get her to turn on Kayo. I liked this bitch, and her sex is A-1, but I will never trust a bitch like her. She's a straight dog. I have been fucking this girl for almost a month right up under Kayo's nose. Shid, sometimes in his bed, and she gives zero fucks. If she crossed her best friend, I know it wouldn't be shit to do me in. What I am gone do is continue to fill her head with bullshit and use her to my advantage like I'm doing everybody else around her.

I got up and walked to the bathroom to get her towel to wipe her face. I laughed to myself because I ain't shit. I put the towel under the water and stared at myself in the mirror. I was looking at the devil in disguise, and I'm cool with that. I wasn't always like this. I left Chicago years ago to keep from turning into the nigga that I see in the mirror, but trouble just seems to follow me.

I walked into the bedroom and wiped her face as she sat on my bed Indian style. Her eyes were red and swollen. I laid back down and pulled her back on my chest. There was an awkward silence between us like we were both in deep thought. The sound of my cell phone vibrating pulled me out of the trance. I looked down at the screen and smiled because Mena's name appeared, alerting me of a text.

> **Mena: Have any plans today?**
> **Me: Only if they include you.**
> **Mena: I'll hit you back with a location.**
> **Me: Please do.**

TWENTY-SIX

KYANA

I know my face was the only face Rio wanted to see sitting outside of the county when he walked out of those doors, but I had business to handle, so I sent one of our old friends to pick him up.

We pulled up five cars deep. I stepped out of my car as my workers crowded around me to listen to my instructions, which were rather simple.

"Knock on every fuckin door on this block until y'all find out who Tasha is. Do not pull any weapons. Two people to a house, we don't want to draw too much attention. When you find her, call my phone, and I'll come to you."

I made sure they were all carrying either a case of pop or water for the kids on the block since today was the annual block party. We needed to throw off the nosey ass old people who've been living here since I was a kid. I walked in front with the guys in tow. They respectfully spoke and sat the drinks down before breaking up into pairs as instructed. I walked over with open arms to one of my mother's old friends, Ms. Ann. She's a hot mess but sweet as pie.

"Heyyyy Ms. Ann, how are you?" I sang as she hugged me tightly.

"Hey, baby. How you been holding up?" she asked, referring to my mother's tragedy.

"I've been good, just taking it one day at a time. How about you and little man?" I asked, referring to her little grandson that she's raising.

"Oh honey, I'm ok. After I buried Tanya, my oldest grandson, Tyjuan, moved back to Chicago to help me out with their little brother. He's been a big help, but I worry about him. He and his sister were very close, and he took her passing really hard. Here let me show you a picture of my baby," she replied, pulling her phone out while looking over her glasses and trying to pull the picture up.

I really felt bad for her and her family. I followed Tanya's story after I saw it on the news a while back. I still don't understand the reason behind her death, but from what I hear, she was a good girl. I hope whoever did it dies a slow death. I can't imagine losing one of my girls at the hands of someone else. There would be hell to pay.

"Ok Ms. Ann, excuse me for one second," I said, answering my ringing phone. I knew it they had to have found the bitch.

"Yeah," I spoke into the phone.

"Yo, boss lady. There is no Tasha on this block. Somebody is lying," one of my workers informed me.

"Fuck, ok. Y'all can go," I disappointedly said as I walked back over to Ms. Ann.

"Ms. Ann, did a girl named Tasha move off the block recently?" I asked.

"Baby, ain't nobody new been on this block since you were a kid. Ok, this is my oldest grandbaby Tyjuan. He should be here in a little bit. Maybe I could introduce you two," she replied. I made a mental note of her response and smiled as I took the phone from her hand.

I looked down at the phone and immediately felt sick to my stomach because I was staring at a picture of Waun. I had so many questions running through my head. I quickly passed the phone back to Ms. Ann and told her I forgot to pick the girls up from camp. I looked down at my watch and rushed off. It was the first excuse that popped up in my head, so I went with it. Why the fuck would this nigga lie and say his baby mama lived over here and not his grandmother? I have to think and think fast because this shit isn't making any kind of sense to me right now. I need answers ASAP.

TWENTY-SEVEN

NEKA

"Ok, baby, momma is gone put a little of this eyeshadow on you to make you look pretty. Remember what I told you. When he comes in here, you do what I showed you on those videos. Don't be scared. It's only gone hurt in the beginning, and then it's gone feel good. You are such a good girl," my mother said, scratching her arms while I sat there scared shitless in an oversized panty and bra set.

"Momma, I'm scared," I replied.

"You are twelve years old, and it's time to become a woman and start making some money, I can't take care of you forever. I know you're scared, but this is easy money. All you have to do is lay there. I'll go get him," she said, walking out and returning with a tall, skinny guy.

The guy wasted no time unzipping his pants as my mother took some money from his hand and walked out, closing the door behind her. I used my hands to slide back on the bed away from the man, but he kept coming closer. In a matter of minutes, he was butt ass naked. He came and stood in front of me and then placed his private part near my mouth. I remembered what the lady in the video did, so I did the same thing. I hated it, but he seemed to be enjoying it. He stopped me

and told me to remove my clothes. I did as I was told, revealing my
small but growing breasts. I used both hands to cover my naked body
as he told me I was beautiful. He pushed me back and used his tongue
to lick all over my body. He was very nice and gentle, but I really
didn't want to do this. He eventually found his way to my private part,
and I wanted to take off running, but I knew my mother would only
make me come right back, so I laid there as he pushed himself inside of
me. A few tears fell from my eyes, as he did his business. All I could
think about was running to Kyana when I got a chance to tell her what
happened to me.

I snapped out of the flashback of my fucked up childhood and
decided enough is enough. I need my friend back, and I will do whatever it takes. I fucked up our friendship, so I have to fix it because she
was the only person who genuinely loved me for me. I took another
drink before dialing Kyana's number.

"*Hi, you've reached Kyana. I'm not available right now. Please*
leave a message, and I'll return your call at my earliest convenience."

I sat in the middle of my hotel bed and turned the almost empty
fifth of Hennessy bottle up. I killed the rest of the liquor while
waiting for the beep on Kyana's voicemail.

"Kyana it's me, Neka. I know I'm the last person you want to
hear from, but I need to tell you some things before I do what I'm
about to do. Kayo loves you wayyyy more than he will ever love me,
and I'm so sorry for breaking up your happy home. I don't deserve to
live, but before I leave this earth, I'm gone kill Kayo for hurting us.
Remember when we were all we had? I fucked up, and I miss you.
I'm sorry about your mom. I wanted to be there, but I was scared,
scared of how you would react to me. I need you to be careful out
here. You know that guy Waun that you sent to Kayo has been
working for him to spy on you, and he tells Kayo your every move.
Yeah, I fucked him too, just watch yourself. I know you probably
won't call back, but I love you Kyana, and I'm sorry for everything.
Kiss Paree and London for me," I said, slurring every other word
before hanging up.

"Fuck, I shouldn't have called her!" I yelled, hitting myself upside the head as my phone started ringing.

"Somebody called Kyana?"

"It's me, Neka."

TWENTY-EIGHT

KAYO

"I have to go back to Puerto Rico, my boy. I have a business to run. I wish you would come home with your brother, but I know you are still that hardheaded bull you've always been. Remember what I told you about Kyana. I have been watching her, and she reminds me of myself. Don't go after her. You might not be as lucky as you were this time. If it's meant to be, she will come to you, but don't underestimate her. I know women because I am a woman, and trust me my son. A broken woman is more dangerous than any weapon. Stay out of her way," my mother said, speaking nothing but the truth.

"I know, but that's easier said than done. I still love her, but I will stay away," I replied, trying to lie with a straight face. I love my mother, but I swear I am so happy to see her leave. I have been on pins and needles since she's been here, but I'm ready to get back to business.

"Better alive than dead, and sometimes love hurts. Just listen to me and stay away from that puta Neka. She's no good just like that Waun guy. Use your instincts. It's in your blood," she replied, patting my cheek and walking out with Santana in tow.

I locked the doors after watching my mother's driver pull out of my driveway. I can't believe Santana left me in the states. I walked back inside and sat down on the couch. I laid my head back and replayed the memories of my fucked up life. I haven't heard from Neka in days. The bitch hasn't even called to check on Sincere, but it's cool. It's been peaceful without her anyway.

"Sin!" I yelled out for my boy, and he ran from his room at top speed.

I couldn't help but smile because he's the spitting image of his sisters and me. They all look more Puerto Rican than black. My girls are just as beautiful as their mother. I miss them so much. I really wish I could have all of my kids under one roof, but I have accepted the fact that I may not ever get to see my girls. I know Kyana can't keep them away forever. I just hope they don't forget about me.

"What up, pop?" he replied, dribbling his ball on the hardwood floor, causing the chandelier that Kyana loved to shake.

"You want to go over your cousin house, or you want to stay in the crib? I'm gone be out for a while. I understand if you scared to stay in the crib by yourself," I said jokingly.

"I ain't scared of nothing; I'm just like you. But, I do wanna go to Malik's house, so we can play the game, and can you buy us some pizza because they always make us eat noodles?" he said, throwing the ball up in the air.

I chuckled and shook my head before grabbing my phone to follow his request. Sincere ran to his room and was back in no time with a gym bag full of clothes and his PlayStation.

"I'm ready," he said. I stood up and stretched before walking to the door.

We hopped in the car and headed out west to grab his food. We both bobbed our heads to his favorite rapper Lil Wayne's song, "A Milli" and rapped along. I turned the music down a little when I saw one of my informant's name flash across my cell phone screen. I normally wouldn't talk business around Sincere but shit, he might as well get used to it because one day he's going to be taking these same calls in front of his kids.

"Yo," I said over the music and my rapping ass son.

"Aye, you sitting down for this shit?" the informant asked.

"What you find, nigga?"

"Yo, that nigga Waun is a dirty ass nigga. He's been plotting to fuck you and your family's lives up because you killed his sister. All this shit was a game. He played his part with you and your baby mama, but we on his ass. He just pulled into a bar, and it looks like he's waiting on someone. That nigga grandmother stays right off Sixteenth Street. You want mufuckas to grab her? I got niggas in the area," he replied. I replayed all the bitches I murdered in the past and tried to pinpoint who he was talking about.

"Yeah, grab the old bitch, I'm about to drop my son off. Y'all bring her to the trap, and I'll meet y'all there. Matter of fact, don't take her from her house. Send me her address. Y'all stay on his ass and keep me posted on that nigga's every move," I replied.

A text came through my phone two seconds later. I knew it was the old lady's address, so I didn't bother looking. I pulled up to Sincere's cousin house and threw the car in park. It looked like something was bothering my boy, so I went into parent mode.

"You ok, son?"

"If you and my momma dies, who is gone take care of me?" he asked without looking up.

"Hold ya head up. Never look down that's how people get caught slipping. Don't talk like that. I told you I would never leave you out here by yourself. I will always be here. Your mother loves you. She just needs some time to herself. You know women stuff. I swear as long as I got a breath in my body, you good!" I replied, putting him in a playful headlock as he fought to get loose.

"Aight pop, but let me get some money for Malik and me tomorrow. I'll pay you back from my stash at home," he said, causing me to laugh at his independence.

I reached into my pocket, peeled off two crispy one-hundred-dollar bills, and handed them to my son as he hopped out. His overly excited cousin greeted him, and he handed him his hundred-dollar bill.

"Aye!" I yelled as they both ran back to the car.

"What's up, pop?" Sincere asked.

"Malik, give this to your mom," I replied, peeling off five more hundred-dollar bills because she always looked out for Sincere.

"I love you, son."

"Love you too, pop. Bye," he said, running off.

I blew my horn and waved before pulling off and heading to the address that was texted to me. I pulled up on the block where I used to pick Kyana up years ago and caught a park. I noticed a few people standing around on the block. I hopped out and joined the small group of niggas standing near the lady's house. I wasted no time walking up the stairs and ringing the doorbell. I was greeted by a chubby little boy who was around Sincere's age. He stood there and sized me up before yelling to the woman.

"Who are you and what you want?" he asked.

"My name is Kayo, and I need to speak with your grandmother," I replied, making sure I made direct eye contact with the lil nigga.

"Grandma... some nigga at the door," he said as the woman walked up and popped him upside the head.

"You better carry your little ass on outside before I beat you. I'm sorry, how can I help you, honey?" she asked while the little boy pushed past me and ran outside to play.

"I wanted to know if I could have a word with you about your granddaughter," I said as two of my workers stood at the bottom of the stairs and watched the surroundings.

"Tanya...well, I'm sorry to tell you honey, but she was murdered a while back," she said as sadness covered her wrinkled but pretty face.

I almost felt bad, but that shit quickly went out the window when I thought about all of the shit Waun called himself doing to get revenge on me. I guess losing a sister wasn't enough, sometimes you have to hit a nigga where it really hurts. Everybody knows niggas love their grandmothers.

"I know she passed because I killed her," I said, and her eyes grew to the size of golf balls.

She tried to force the door closed, but I kicked it, causing it to hit her directly in the face and blood to gush from her nose. I backed her into the house while they stayed on the porch and looked out. I told them this would only take a minute before I closed the door behind me. I walked into her house and saw plants and pictures everywhere.

"I hate that I have to do you like this because I was taught to respect my elders, but you see, this is the consequences behind your grandson having the audacity to fuck with me and my family. So now I have to fuck with his... again. Please have a seat," I said, but she stood there, scared to death and holding her bloody nose.

I walked over, looked at a picture of Tanya, and smiled before turning to her grandmother.

"She was really a good girl, but her mouth always got her in trouble. You know she was carrying my baby when I shot her," I said, smiling and twisting the silencer on my pistol.

"Please don't do this! It's ok baby. I forgive you. God forgives you," she said with pleading eyes.

"I wish your grandson was as forgiving as you are, beautiful," I replied, sending three bullets into her body before walking out and never looking back.

TWENTY-NINE
KYANA

I listened to the voice message Neka left on my phone a million times before I decided to call her back. She begged me to come and get her from her hotel so that we could talk. I have no intentions on reconstructing this friendship, but I did what she asked me because she was drunk as hell and she sounded suicidal, and that was the last thing I wanted her to do. We came back to one of my nice ass trap houses. I made sure they all had top-notch furnishings and soundproof basements for business. I stared at the girl I once loved to death before my emotions hit me, and I kicked off the long overdue conversation.

"Neka, what did I do to deserve the shit you did to me? When everybody in the world was against you, I was for you. You really fucked me up. I thought we were sisters, and you broke my heart," I said, resting my hands on my knees as tears flowed freely from my eyes.

"I know, Kyana, and I am so sorry. I don't know what the fuck I was thinking. I was jealous of you, and I wanted everything that you had. You didn't have to sell your ass to provide for yourself. Your mother wasn't passing you off to different men every night. I wanted your life!" Neka replied, trying to talk in between crying.

"Neka, I don't wanna hear that sob ass story because you didn't have to fuck for anything. We were good, and we made sure one another was good. You had everything I had, but that wasn't enough. You had to have my dick too. How is it? How do like my life?" I asked, awaiting a response.

"Kyana, Kayo is the devil. I take my hat off to you for staying with him as long as you did. I haven't smiled in months. I lost myself. I wish I would've listened to you and stayed with Rio. Now I have destroyed everything around me. I lost you, and Rio's in jail because of me," she replied, wiping her face.

"What do you mean Rio's in jail because of you? Neka, please tell me you had nothing to do with that shit," I said, fucking with her head. I just wanted to hear her say it.

"Yes, Kyana. It was my idea to set him up and take his money. Kayo just made the call to tell him to move the shit. I called the police and told them there was a drug deal going down in my neighborhood, and I gave them a description of Rio's car. I moved all of his money from his account to a joint account I set up for Kayo and I. Now he's gone because of my selfish ass, I wish I could just visit him and tell him I'm sorry," she replied.

I was starting to get a headache sitting here playing this dumb ass forgiving role with this nothing ass bitch. I had no intentions of letting her talk for as long as she did. I only went and got her for one reason and one reason only.

"You can apologize to him now," I replied. Her head snapped in the direction that my eyes were in while I wiped the fake ass tears I had been dishing out.

Rio walked into the living room with pure hate in his eyes as Neka looked from him to me. I sat back in my seat and gave them the floor.

"Rio? How? When did?" Neka tried to ask before two of my

workers came walking full speed from the back of the house, grabbing her as she kicked and screamed.

"Take her ass to the basement," I yelled. I stood to my feet, knocked the wrinkles from my skin-tight pencil skirt, and followed them to the basement.

I had been planning on getting Neka snatched off the streets soon, but she reached out to me first, which made the process that much easier. I have no love for a bitch that clearly had none for me, and I'm excited to see the damage Rio is about to do to the bitch. I carefully walked down the basement stairs in my stilettos as one of my workers grabbed my hand to assist me. I took a seat in a chair nearby and gave Rio, who was standing near a tied up Neka, a head nod.

Rio wasted no time wrapping a metal link chain around his hand and drawing back, hitting Neka across the knees. She screamed out in pain, and she locked eyes with me. I didn't have one sympathetic bone in my body, so I blew her a kiss. Rio swung the chain a few more times, hitting her in the same spot and officially breaking her kneecaps. I held my hand up just as he was about to swing the chain again.

"You are taking it too easy on this bitch, Rio," I said, standing up and walking over to the cabinets I had built.

All eyes were on me as my heels clicked across the floor. I opened the cabinet, took out a razor blade, and grabbed the bottle of bleach out of the corner.

"Kyana, please don't do this! I am so sorry. Please, what about my son?" she said, pleading and I let out a loud laugh.

"What about him? You didn't give a fuck about him when you were around this bitch doing dumb shit to make sure Kayo was happy. Where is your knight in shining armor now? Probably somewhere finding your replacement and telling your son to call her momma! Sincere is better off without his bitch ass parents, but don't worry, Kayo will be joining you in hell soon. I promise you that. Y'all were made for one another, nothing asses," I replied, swiftly running the blade across her face, opening it completely up.

I repeatedly cut her in the face and different places on her body before twisting the cap off the Clorox bleach bottle. I held the bottle over her head and let it run down her face and body as she shook uncontrollably in pain. I stepped back making sure bleach didn't get on my heels. The cuts turned pure white as the bleach burned through her flesh. Some of my workers turned their heads in disgust. I stood there and looked at her while she became visibly unnoticeable and flashed back to the day I overheard her talking to Kayo. I remembered the pain I felt as my heart broke into a million pieces. That thought alone made me want to bring more pain to her. I wanted her to feel what I felt. I slipped on a pair of black leather gloves and blacked out. I started connecting blow after blow to her already fucked up face. I yelled out everything I wanted to say that night they hurt me. It wasn't until I felt a hand grab my arm that I stopped swinging.

"She's dead. It's ok. It's over now," Rio said. I collapsed into his arms and cried like a baby.

"Clean this shit up," I said, wiping my face and walking upstairs with Rio in tow.

"You cool?" Rio asked, stepping in front of me.

"Yeah, I'm good, I'm just tired of losing. I wanna be hap..."

Before I could finish my sentence, Rio kissed me. My mind told me to pull back, but my body wouldn't allow me to. He finally stopped and looked down at me with the sexiest facial expression I had ever seen on a man. I couldn't even look him in the face, so I looked down. He placed his hand under my chin and lifted my head up. Shit, for the first time in my life I didn't know what to do, so I just stood there and gave him the floor.

"Thank you, Kyana. You stuck with me when I was at my lowest point. When I thought I had nobody in my corner, you came through. I will spend the rest of my life trying to pay homage to you. You didn't have to do half of the shit you did for me," Rio said with nothing but sincerity in each word he spoke.

"Rio, you don't have to thank me because I know if the shoe was on the other foot, you would have done that and then some to make sure I was good. I told you a long time ago my family is everything to me."

"After I kill Kayo, I'm making you mine," he replied as I blushed and slightly laughed.

"Listen, Rio. I think you are one hell of a man, but I could never go behind Neka, that would make me a nasty bitch just like she was," I replied.

"I can respect that," he said as I pulled my ringing cell phone from my bra.

"Mena, Mena talk to me," I spoke into the phone, taking a seat on the couch.

Mena is one of my good girlfriends, and she's the true definition of a boss bitch. She's book smart, street smart, and last but not least, a stone-cold killer. I needed someone to vent to about the fuckery that's been going on in my life, without thinking twice, she got on business with Waun. She followed him as soon as he pulled away from the laundromat. I told her needed all of the information she could possibly get out of this nigga because I didn't believe shit that came out of Neka's lying ass mouth.

"It's a go. I'll have him singing like a bird before the sun sets."

"Good because I plan on killing him before the sun rises."

THIRTY

WAUN

I stood in front of the mirror hanging behind my bathroom door, thanks to my granny. She came and decorated my entire apartment when I came back to Chicago because if it were left up to me, I would have a bed and a flat screen. My granny and little brother is all I have left in this fucked up thing called life since I don't fuck with my mother at all. She gave me to the streets a long time ago when she found out I was selling drugs, and I haven't spoken to her since. I didn't even acknowledge her presence when she stood over my little sister's casket.

I made sure I put on my best fit to meet with Mena. I still can't believe she hit a nigga up out the blue earlier. I immediately dropped Neka's ass off to her hotel when I got the text and came back to get fresh. I decided to rock an all white Ralph Lauren Polo shirt and a pair of all white Gucci jeans with the belt and sneakers to match. I know I have to bring my A-game when it comes to a female like Mena. She's a top-notch woman. You can't be anything less than a boss to fuck with her. I'm glad I got a fresh haircut yesterday because I'm pressed for time. I have to meet her at some restaurant called, Wishbone downtown in about in forty-five minutes, and I refused to be late. I threw on enough diamonds to blind the blind before grabbing my keys and hopping in my Benz.

I made it to the restaurant in record time. I pulled up and saw a Maserati that hadn't even made it to the streets yet, and knew I was going to be out of some real bread after paying for dinner at this place. I looked down at my watch and noticed it was almost five, so I decided to shoot her a text to make sure we were still meeting.

Me: I'm the restaurant, pretty lady.

Mena: Me too, I'm sitting in my car wrapping up a call. I'll meet you by the door.

I flipped my mirror down and looked at myself to make sure I didn't have any flaws on my face. I made sure to power my phone off because I didn't want any interruptions. I was about to step out of my car, but I was caught off guard. I noticed it was Mena stepping out of the Maserati. I watched her as she composed her weight on the heels that looked impossible to walk in, while her long hair blew in the wind. I swear I'm gone go broke fucking with her. I felt my dick rising in my jeans as I made my way toward her. She handed valet her keys and pointed her finger at him, warning him not to fuck up her car. I swear I don't even want to fuck her. I would just eat her pussy all night if she let me.

I waited until she was in the door until I walked up and entered. She was seated at the bar with her ass hanging halfway off the seat. I adjusted my dick in my pants before walking over to join her. I lightly tapped her shoulder, and she spun around in her seat and stood up to hug me. I wrapped my arms around her waist and inhaled her perfume. I was praying I could hold my composure. We sat down and ordered drinks before she kicked off the conversation.

"Soooo handsome, what brings you to the slums?" she asked, slightly resting her head on her wrist that was covered by a gold Rolex watch.

"Well beautiful, I had no intentions on ever move back to this fucked up city, but tragedy hit home, and I had no choice," I replied, taking a sip of the Patrón and lime juice that the bartender had just sat in front of me.

"I'm sorry to hear that, sweetie. What happened if you don't mind me asking?" she asked, sipping her margarita.

"Well, my sister was murdered by this weak ass nigga. She was a good girl but got tied up with the wrong type of nigga."

"Noooo! I am so sorry, sweetheart. Give me a hug!" she replied, removing her hand from over her heart and walking up to hug me.

"It's ok. I know exactly who did it, so I feel somewhat at ease," I said, taking a shot and chasing it with my original drink.

"Oh really? Well, if you need any assistance let me know. I only told you part of who I am. I want to help you. Who's behind it anyway, if you don't mind me asking?" she asked, replacing her look of sympathy with a look of slight anger that turned me on.

I was hesitate to tell her, but for some weird ass reason, I felt like I could trust her.

"This nigga named Kayo."

"Kayo Castillo? His wife name is Kyana Castillo?" she asked, rolling her eyes and folding her arms across her chest.

"Yes, ma'am."

"I had a few run-ins with Ms. Kyana, and I can definitely assist you. I just need to know your plan, and I'll follow your lead," she replied, climbing back on her stool.

"I've been on their asses since I found out Kayo was behind it. He took my baby away from me, so I made a vow to bring nothing but pain to his entire family, and that's just what I've been doing. Everything bad that has taken place in their lives, I've been behind it. Once I found out they were divorced, and Kyana hated Kayo, I slid right in and started working for her. Kayo reached out to me for some bricks, and I agreed to meet with him. Kyana mixed a little cocaine and a lot of drywall together to make these "bricks", but I dropped a dime on her ass and started working for Kayo to watch her every move. I've been sparing them because the money I'm making between the two of them is crazy, but I'm tired of playing with these muthafuckas. I need closure," I replied, finally sharing my motive with another human being. I didn't mind telling her though, because like I said, I feel like I could trust her.

"That's a clever ass move, but I don't know if I would've been able to hold out that long. I would've been dropping bodies left and right. I know being around them is killing you on the inside. I'm surprised you held it together this long. You seem like a hot head. So my question is what you want me to do?" she asked, making direct eye contact with me, which let me know I made the right decision by telling her.

"I calmed down a lot. I just go to my sister's grave when I feel myself about to do something crazy, but it's all good baby, this is some shit I have to do on my own. That's the only way I'm gone get past the death of my sister, but thanks for listening to me," I replied slightly bumping her.

"No problem. I'm just a phone call away, love. Well, I better get going I have to make a few stops before I head home. Remember, if you need me I'm here," she replied, standing to her feet and adjusting her skin-tight jeans over her ass.

We walked to the door and waited for the valet to bring the cars around. They pulled up with hers first.

"By the way, nice whip."

"Thanks, love. See you later, and thanks for the drinks," she replied before stepping into her car and pulling off.

I stood there for a few seconds and took it all in as the valet pulled up with my car. I couldn't stop smiling if I wanted to. I powered my phone back on, and the messages started coming through nonstop. I knew something was up when I answered the call from my little brother's phone and heard my mother's voice.

"There's been an accident at your grandmother's house," she said, trying to get her words out.

"Is granny ok?" I asked as she said absolutely nothing on the other end of the phone, causing my stomach to turn.

"IS SHE OK?" I yelled.

"NO! She's been killed, and it's probably your fucking fault!" she screamed into the phone.

Everything she said after she's been killed fell death on my ears. I dropped the phone into my lap while she ranted on the other end. I tilted my head back and banged on the steering wheel as tears fell from my eyes.

"FUCK! FUCK! FUCK!"

I started my car with a face full of tears and did the dash to my granny's house. I ran every light until I reached her block, but the police had it blocked off. Once I saw the red tape, I felt my body shutting down. Every news station in Chicago was on the scene along with what looked like a million nosey ass people. I finally forced myself to get out my car and walk toward my mother who was making a fool of herself as usual. The bitch never came to check on her mother but have the nerve to play hurt. I was only concerned about my little brother. I could care about how my deadbeat felt.

"It's his fault my mother is dead! I know you had something to do with it, fucka!" my mother yelled while some random ass nigga hugged her from behind.

"Fuck you! You didn't give a fuck about my grandma. All you did was chase niggas, have babies, and drop 'em off at her doorstep. The only time you pop up is when you think an insurance check is about to be cut. You pulled this same stunt when Tanya died. Fuck outta here," I replied, pushing past her and walking over to my little brother, who was talking to a detective.

"You cool, Tremell? Can I have a word with my brother, officer?" I asked. The detective sized me up before walking off.

"Yeah, I'm cool. I know the code; I didn't tell them nothing, but I know who hurt granny," he said, looking up at me. I pulled him further away from the detectives.

"Who?"

"His name Kayo."

TANYA Wilson
Jan 12, 1988- June 12, 2006
Loving Granddaughter and sister.

I STOOD over my little sister's grave while another funeral took place directly on the side of her. I watched them for a minute as a nice ass solid gold casket sat in the middle of the small crowd waiting to be lowered into the ground. I knew their pain too well, and I knew that in a few days I would be in that same position once again when I buried my granny. I watched a woman, whose face was covered in a black veil, cry her eyes out and lean on a guy's shoulder. I instantly felt sorry for her.

I turned my attention back to my sister and let the tears roll from my face to the grass. She and my granny were the only two people that understood me in this world and that nigga Kayo took them away from me. My granny was the most beautiful woman in the world. She stepped up and took care of all three of us when my mother ran off with different niggas. When I got old enough, I robbed, killed, and sold drugs to make sure they wanted and needed for nothing.

I looked down at my sister's picture, embedded in her tombstone, and cursed myself for not being there. She was the sweetest person in the world, and I would've never thought in a million years she would die such a horrible death. I still don't understand how she even got tied up with a nigga like Kayo. She barely left the house unless she was going to school. The last text messages in her phone were messages between him and her, leading up to her death, which led me straight to him. What really fucked me up is the autopsy confirmed she was carrying a baby that was his, which is why I'm killing his entire family.

"I swear to God... I'm gone make that nigga feel my pain, T. I know it wasn't supposed to end like this, baby sis. You're not alone anymore. Granny is with you," I said, speaking to my sister because I just knew she could hear me.

I replayed my little brother's story. He told me word for word about the nigga that knocked on the door and that nigga Kayo was bold enough to tell him his name just so that it could get back to me. I could see nothing but red as I pulled out my phone and called Mena.

"Hello," she answered in the most angelic voice.

"Mena, that nigga killed my grandmother, I'm killing all of them tonight. I might need you. I'll call you when I leave the cemetery," I said, taking a seat on top of my sister's grave.

"Ok," she replied, ending the call.

I immediately jumped to my feet when I heard footsteps behind me.

"Man, she had some good pussy. It was to die for."

THIRTY-ONE
KYANA

I knew if anybody could get the job done it was my bitch, Mena. She called me earlier after her date with Waun and told me some shit that blew my mind. I'm so disappointed in myself. I could've been killed along with my children. I have never been on to get caught slipping like this. I have really been dancing with the devil, but it's my turn.

Ms. Ann's homicide was on every news station in Chicago, and it had Kayo's name written all over it. He always was reckless with his shit. This would've been so simple if Waun would've just killed Kayo when he first found out he killed his sister. Why come for me? Now I have to sit here in this hot ass black dress to attend my last funeral of the year. Mena didn't even have to tell me Waun would be at the cemetery because I do the same thing when shit gets too real, I run straight to my mother's grave. I was already one-step ahead of the nigga, though, and if my instincts are correct, Kayo will be joining us shortly.

I leaned over on Rio's arm and forced myself to drop a few fake tears while I kept my eyes on Waun as he talked to his sister's grave. I wanted to pull my gun out and get him out the way, but fuck that, he's going to die a slow death. I listened to him pour his heart out and talk about how he was going to kill all of us tonight, but that's bullshit. Rio slightly elbowed me to alert me of Kayo's presence as he walked up behind Waun, causing him to hop to his feet. I felt Rio about to stand up, but I pulled him closer to me. It wasn't time. I wanted to see just how far they were about to go. From the looks of it, Waun wasn't strapped because without thinking twice, he swung on Kayo, causing him stumble back into one of the guys that was with him.

"Grab this muthafucka!" Kayo yelled, and the guys did as they were told.

Kayo walked over to Tanya's grave and did the unthinkable. The nigga unzipped his pants and pissed all over her grave while Waun tried his best to break loose from the guys. Kayo laughed loudly and put his dick back in his pants, not giving a fuck about our fake ass funeral.

"So, you came for my family because of this bitch, huh? She wasn't as innocent as you think. She could suck some of the best dick. You know I use to bust nuts all over that pretty little face of hers. I fucked up that last time though and didn't pull out. You know I wasn't going to kill her? The lil bitch wanted to run to Kyana though, and I couldn't let that happen."

"Fuck you, bitch ass nigga! I hope somebody fucks your daughters and gives them AIDS. That's why you still ended up losing yo bitch. She's more of a boss then yo weak ass. I hope she kills yo bitch ass. You're a snake ass nigga. You and that bitch Neka set yo right-hand nigga up, and you call yourself a real nigga? Nigga, you a hoe! Put yo gun down and fight me!" Waun yelled, and Kayo laughed once again.

I still didn't move because I was finding out all kind of shit from their conversation.

"FUCK ALL OF THOSE MUTHAFUCKAS! I'm in this shit by myself; I don't need nobody. Just like I'm gone kill you right here, I will kill them too. Don't no nigga or bitch put fear in my heart!" Kayo yelled.

I had heard enough. I stood to my feet while Rio and the eight niggas behind me all pulled their guns out, immediately taking out everyone except Kayo and Waun as instructed. Once the smoke clears, I want it to be me against them so that I can end this shit once and for all. The look on Kayo and Waun's faces were priceless, Kayo tried to run. Two of my guys caught him and tackled him to the ground. As the others grabbed Waun and walked him toward his casket, I walked behind them, and he didn't put up a fight. I want to see if he still plays this tough ass role when I'm done with him.

"You see what happens when you cross me Waun, and to think I liked you. I know you heard the saying, "If you live by it, you die by it." You lived your last days trying to put my family and me in a casket, so that's where I'm going to put you."

"Man, look. Kyana, if you're gone kill me, do it. I'm not about to stand here and go back and forth with you," Waun replied, looking me dead in the eye with no emotion.

"I will do no such thing. That's way too easy. You know in order to destroy someone, you have to find their weakness, and from the looks of it, you loved your sister with all your heart, so I wouldn't dare separate you two. You will have all the time in the world to get reacquainted with your sister, and the rest of your new neighbors. GET IN!" I said, opening the casket.

"I'm not getting in, shit. Like I said kill me Kyana, that's the only way I'm getting that box. I don't have shit to else to live for anyway, that bitch ass nigga took it all," he replied, pointing back at Kayo.

"You know, Waun. You're not as smart as I thought you were. You would've probably had a chance to kill me if you hadn't poured your heart and plans out to my good friend Mena. You really put a lot of time and effort into signing your own death certificate. Y'all put his bitch ass in that box!" I ordered as they fought to get him in the casket.

Waun kicked and screamed like a little bitch when they duct taped his hands, and feet together before finally stuffing him inside. I was so shocked to hear tough ass Waun bitch up, but I guess I would too if I was being left to die with a bunch of dead muthafuckas.

"Stop that nigga from yelling. It's disrespectful to the deceased."

"Mena? Wait, Kyana. I just wanted that bitch ass nigga to feel my pain. I knew he loved you, so I came after you. I'm sorry for sending him to your mother, and I'm sorry for burning down your carwash, I was seeking revenge on the wrong person, and I fucked up. The nigga paid me to keep tabs on you. Please just hear me out!" he yelled.

"Shut him up. I don't want to hear his voice!" I said, looking over at the next victim.

Rio hit Kayo with the butt of his gun as he stood over the other guys as they held Kayo down. I could hear Waun trying to scream while they removed the wooden sticks and lowered him into the ground. I made my way over to Kayo.

"So, this is what it comes down to huh, Kayo?" I asked. He chuckled and looked up at me.

"You're so sexy when you're mad, Kyana. You couldn't kill me if you wanted to because whether you want to admit or not, you still love me," he replied.

"Bullshit! I stopped loving you a long time ago. I should do you how I did your bitch and send you to your maker. I have every reason in the world to kill you, especially after what you did to my mother, but you know what... I'm gone let Rio handle you because he has unfinished business with you. I'm gone collect a fat ass insurance check off yo ass, baby daddy," I said, leaning over kissing his forehead before stepping back letting Rio handle his business.

Kayo turned red in the face and tried to get up.

"You dirty bitch, I made you! Look, whatever you gone do, nigga, do it because you know ain't no bitch in me, Rio. And if you don't kill me, you already know what's gone happen!" he yelled.

"Nigga, this is me you're talking to. You already know how I move. I hope all that shit you did to me for that bitch was worth your life. What happened to the code, my nigga? You let a bitch turn you against me. We all know your weakness is pussy, which is why you're a pussy ass nigga!" Rio said before shooting Kayo in the chest.

I knew, at that moment, I had no love left for Kayo anymore

because I watched his body shake as each bullet hit him with no type of remorse. For some reason, I felt like a burden had been lifted off my shoulders. I knew Neka had family that would take care of Sincere, so the least I could do is send a check every month from a distance. I grabbed Rio's arm as the rain started to fall and walked away from my old life, looking forward to my new one.

"Let's let these niggas rest in peace, Rio."

THIRTY-TWO

KAYO

"Let's let these nigga rest in peace, Rio," was the last thing I heard as I laid there and pretended to be dead. These dumb muthafuckas didn't even check for a pulse to make sure I was dead. I opened my eyes slightly as raindrops fall on top of me. I could see them walking away with no worries, thinking they put an end to Kayo Castillo, but I was far from dumb. I waited until all of their cars were out of sight before I sat up and pulled my hoodie over my head. I looked down at the holes in my bulletproof vest before removing it. My body was sore and swelling up from the impact of the bullets, but I'm good. I managed to stand on my feet and walk toward my car. I know Waun is down there scared as hell right now. I have to give it to that bitch Kyana that was some clever shit. I would've never suspected it was them sitting around that casket. I know one thing, though, this time around, I'm gone do shit a lot different. I'm gone lay low and raise my boy because this shit here was a close call, but this shit is far from over. I know how to play Kyana. She's smart, so I have to watch how I move. It's the end to them, but the beginning for me.

UNTITLED

"When you become a parent remember, Don't allow anything in your life that you don't want reproduced in your children. Always remember the apple doesn't fall too far from the tree and time waits for no one!"

THIRTY-THREE

LONDON

Present day, June 2018

"Turn around, let me look at you," I heard my mother say standing in the doorway of my bedroom.

I did a cute spin on my six-inch Louboutin's. Today is me and my identical twin sister Paree's early graduation party and one of the happiest days of my life because not only did we finally get our driver's license this morning, but our mother promised us a car. My mom had this thing where we both had to have a license before she would buy us a car, which I thought was the dumbest shit ever. We could clearly use one license. I wasn't worried though because we've always got what we wanted, which is why she let us plan the biggest graduation splash bash ever. Not to mention we didn't have a budget, but that was no surprise because my mother made sure we had the best of everything.

"See what you cursed us with?" I said to my mother as my twin walked into my room looking stunning.

My mother truly marked us with the wagons we were dragging behind us, at the age of eighteen we were built better than most women twice our age. Paree and I were impossible to tell apart. If you didn't know us, the only thing that distinguished us was a beauty mark that was on Paree's left cheek. People often said we put them in the mind of the singer Christina Milian because of our high yellow skin complexion and naturally curly hair. Having perfectly shaped bodies were a gift and a curse because we weren't allowed to do regular "teenage" things with our friends without her watching us like a hawk. She made sure we were safe at all times by having her people to look after us, everyone knew we were not to be fucked with.

"Well hell, now y'all see how I felt growing up. Y'all can thank me later," she replied running her hands over her perfectly shaped ass before flopping down on my queen-sized bed.

"But for real ma, can you let up on us a little bit," I said, looking over at my mom.

"Right, we're eighteen. We not fucking," Paree chimed in as I snapped my head around in her direction.

"PAREE, watch yo fuckin' mouth! Yeah, you're eighteen, but I will still beat yo ass," my mother yelled.

"Sorry ma, but she's right. We've done everything you asked of us. We're graduating in a couple of weeks, and we're virgins. You don't get that too often in this day and age," I replied, laughing and high fiving my sister.

"Yeah, I know, and I'm proud of you two. I just want y'all to stay focused. I have never hidden anything from you all, and I never will. Eventually, the two of you will be running the business, and I need y'all to be headstrong. This is a dangerous game and only the strong survive. You two are all I have, so I need y'all to listen to me and listen to me good. I will not be here forever, all you two have is each other, and don't ever forget that. Let nothing and no one come between that. Remember you were born together and if push comes to shove y'all better die together," our mother said as every word hit me straight in the heart.

"Mommy, stop talking like that. You gone be here forever and a day," Paree replied on the verge of tears.

"She's right, Paree. It's us against the world," I said as we all hugged, and my mother walked out with tears rolling down her face.

I loved my mother with everything in me, but I really wish my dad could be here to see us shine. Don't get me wrong my mother did an exceptional job raising us, but it's just certain things I really needed him for growing up. I mean we had our Uncle Rio, but I longed for my real father. My mom and dad were teenage lovers, and at the tender age of nineteen, she had us. Together they started one of the largest drug organizations in Chicago, making them multi-millionaires at an early age. They were the modern-day Bonnie and Clyde, and everyone knew Kayo and Kyana Castillo. Their names still ring bells all over the city. My father is deceased and is still the man.

I remember my father being handsome, mixed, slightly built and standing around six feet. I like to think we got our hair and skin color from him. Being mixed with majority Puerto Rican he was quite the lady's man, but he was all for Kyana. When my mom found out about an affair that my father was having with her best friend, my mother, being the boss that she is, took his ass to court and took everything he owned and some. I will never forget that day because it has replayed in my mind every day since it happened.

We were not allowed to speak a word about our dad under any circumstances, which I thought was selfish and unfair. My mom would flip out any time we brought up his name or the subject. She destroyed every picture leaving us with nothing to remember him by. My mother lied to us for a long time saying he was killed in a crossfire before finally telling us the truth. It broke my heart when she told us Rio killed our dad because I had dreams of one day finding him and picking up where we left off. I knew that if he were alive, there would be nothing and no one that would be able to keep him away from us. My mother always said, *"Never dwell on the past because it could come back and bite you in the ass,"* but I wish my dad could come back. I was mad at my mother for a long time when she told us what went down at the cemetery when my dad was killed because she could have stopped it. I never looked at Rio the same after finding out he killed my dad. Paree, on the other hand, was fascinated with the story. She thought it was the coolest shit ever.

"Bitch, you ready?" Paree asked, pulling me out of my trance.

"Yeah," I replied, applying my lip gloss.

"Don't tell me you're thinking about pops foul ass," Paree said with her hand on her hip.

"Bitch, you only know mommy's side of the story, so you don't know who's foul. Nobody's perfect. I just wish he were here to make this shit right. I thought family was forever. I know you think about the 'what ifs'," I shot back.

Paree would believe the sky was green if my mother said it, but I know there is more to the story than what we were told. My dad loved us. The majority of my childhood is a blur, but I remember his hugs and kisses. I just don't believe he did half of the shit I've been told over the years. Everyone that I have crossed paths with had nothing but great things to say about my father, and I believe it.

"I don't think "what if" shit because that's his loss. We haven't missed out on shit. He cheated on mama with her best friend. I wish I could've gotten my hands on that bitch. I would've beat her ass bloody. Mommy did what any real bitch would do...bread up, kill anybody that gets in the way, and never look back!" she replied as she walked toward the door. I just shook my head because she actually had a valid point.

WE WALKED down our winding staircase and was met by at least a hundred of our peers and family members. We had the biggest smiles on our faces as everyone yelled "Congratulations!"

My mother really went all out for our big day, our dresses alone were two thousand dollars apiece, and we were only wearing them for a few minutes.

We made our way to the backyard, and it was beautiful. Our party planner made every vision we had a reality. Everything was pink and purple, and even the pool water was dyed pink. There was a huge congratulations banner with our picture on it hanging over the brick balcony overlooking the backyard. The picture man and DJ were in the far back of the yard, but the music was blasting. Our guest didn't have to bring anything. We provided swimsuits, trunks, and towels. We had three different restaurants catering everything from seafood to Mexican food, and my mother also had the grills going. Waiters were walking around wearing custom made shirts with our picture on the front passing out virgin drinks, well virgin for now.

We took a few pictures in our dresses before changing into our bathing suits. It was early June and hot as hell. I wore a two-piece that was way too small, but I was on a mission. Jason Green was supposed to be here, and I needed his undivided attention. Paree and I had our belly buttons pierced a few weeks ago, and I loved it. She walked up and smacked my ass, causing me to jump and knock her hand away.

"Yo dick, I mean friend just walked in," Paree whispered, looking toward the gate.

"How do I look?" I asked quickly fixing myself up.

"Like you ready to fuck," she replied, laughing while him and his friends walked in our direction.

Jason was the star basketball player at our school North Lawndale College Prep, and every bitch wanted to be his girl. He was dating this hood bitch named Cami on and off, but I'm gone put an end to that shit real soon. She had the entire school afraid of her because she had a huge family, but that shit meant nothing to me. She tried everybody in school except for me but made it clear to everyone else she hated me. I didn't give a fuck as long as she stayed in her lane.

"Damn look at the Castillo twins, all grown up," one of Jason's friends said, hugging us.

"I been grown," Paree said, sipping her drink and seductively sucking her straw.

"Paree, you looking real..." one of Jason's friends started to say before she cut him off mid-sentence.

"Thanks, but you know I like the same thing you like...pussy," Paree replied slightly embarrassing him and causing all of us to laugh.

"London, let me holla at you," Jason said, walking off to the side.

"How the fuck you even know them apart, nigga? Shit, I be guessing," another one of his friends said.

"You're funny as hell. Paree has a mole on her left cheek, dumb ass," Jason replied, causing me to blush because he actually knew the one thing that told us apart.

I felt like I was about to throw up. This man has never said more than two words to me, and here he is pulling me to the side. I knew he could have any bitch he wanted, but he was checking for me. I'm standing here nervous as hell, and this is my damn party. Paree saw how slow I was walking and pushed me. I looked at her and rolled my eyes as I made my way over to Jason. I swear my twin is a bad influence on my life. She's always pushing me to do shit I don't want any parts of, but I don't mind this time.

"I know you're not acting shy, popular girl," he said, flashing a million-dollar smile as the sun shined off of his diamond earrings.

Jason came from a wealthy foster family and was a privileged kid. He was the only nigga at school driving a Benz. Hell, we didn't have cars yet, but everybody knew we were holding on the money side. I heard his mother owned a funeral home and his dad was a music producer, but who knows how true that is. They don't stay too far from us. I always wondered why he went all the way over there to school. Hell, we practically begged our mother not to make us go to one of those uppity ass private schools.

"No, I'm just shocked you said more than "Hi" to me and even more shocked you that showed up. You walk past me in school, give me a simple head nod, and keep it moving," I replied, smiling.

"Fuck outta here, you don't fuck with me," he replied, handing me a Tiffany box.

"Wow and he comes bearing gifts," I said, taking the box from him.

I opened it and looked up at him. Did this nigga just give me an empty box?

"What the fuck is this supposed to be funny? You can go now." I said, turning to walk away as embarrassment spread all over my face.

He grabbed my arm and pulled me close to him. His Armani cologne filled my nostrils, and I couldn't resist him. I turned around and stood face to face with him. I wanted to lean in and steal a kiss, but I'm not no hoe. I turned my head to avoid making eye contact with him.

"Chill, brat. I got it right here, and I just wanted to put it on you," he said as turned me around and put the most beautiful necklace with an "L" charm hanging from it around my neck.

I was living in that moment when I heard one of his homies say, "Aww shit, Jason."

I turned around and saw Cami and her friends walking through my party swinging that cheap ass weave like it was theirs. I watched as she looked around trying to find Jason. Paree came and stood next to me. I looked over at Jason as anger covered his face.

"I'll handle it," he said.

"You better because I will not play with her," I responded as she spotted us and headed in our direction with her girls in tow.

"So, you not answering your phone because you got yo face all in this bitch's ass. You got me fucked up, Jason," Cami said, pointing at me.

"Watch that bitch word. That's your first and final warning," I said, shifting my weight to one side.

"Fuck this! Man, get these hoes up out my crib before they get carried out, Jason," Paree said, sitting her cup down on a nearby table.

"Cami, get the fuck on before they beat yo ass. You know you can't fight, and I ain't breaking shit up," Jason said, causing me to chuckle.

"These hoes know better than to fuck with me. My people will shut this bitch down," she replied, causing her sidekicks to laugh.

"Cami, you couldn't pay yo people to fuck with us. You better listen to Jason and get the fuck on while we're giving you a chance to leave," Paree replied.

"Shut yo carpet munching ass up. I'm talking to MY man!" Cami spat, turning her attention back to Jason.

Paree and I looked at each other, and without saying a word, we started swinging and slinging bitches in every direction. We didn't play that disrespect shit. I had Cami beating her face like a piñata. Jason wasn't lying. The bitch couldn't land a punch to save her life. Every punch I threw connected. I was trying to kill this bitch. I looked over and saw all of our cousins running in our direction. They put hands and feet all over the girls. My mother stood there with a smile on her face and watched us work those hoes out for a few minutes before breaking it up. My mother always told us if one fights we both fight, right or wrong.

"On my momma y'all just fucked up. We on y'all asses!" Cami yelled, power walking towards the gate.

"Fuck you and yo momma, bitch. I dare y'all to come for us. Shit gone get real!" Paree yelled.

"Let's go, Jason!" Cami said when she realized he wasn't walking with her.

"He ain't going nowhere, now get the fuck on," I replied while fixing my bathing suit.

"Really Jason? This is how you doing me?" she asked as she gave him the death look.

"Man, slide," Jason finally spoke.

"You a bitch ass nigga!"

"Bye Lance," Paree said, quoting the little boy off of the movie The Player's Club.

Cami looked like she wanted to break down and cry as Jason's friends laughed, but instead, she nodded her head and walked out. We picked up right where we left off. We all partied and bullshitted for the rest of the night. I was in heaven. I got my man, and Paree and I got matching Mercedes AMG's. Mine is white, and hers is black. Life is great!

THIRTY-FOUR

PAREE

I will be glad when this prom and graduation shit is over. I'm ready to start getting money like my OG. I plan on being the best queen pin in the game and make my momma proud. She's been running this shit for a long time, and she's getting old. Our mom gave us the option to go to college, but fuck that high school was enough. Besides, we don't need no degree to sell drugs. London and me gone run this shit, but I want the entire city on lock, not just the west side, which means I'm coming for everything and everybody. I know London and I have the power to take over Chicago together.

London and I swerved through the Holy City in our Benz's with music blasting. I swear Chicago summer days brings the whole city out. We were on our way to Douglas Park to watch Jason play ball. He and my sister have been inseparable since our party, and they even decided to go to prom together. My black ass still doesn't have a date, and it's two weeks away, I just want to take a badass redbone bitch with me. I know my momma gone be mad as hell if I take a female, but she's gone have to get over that shit. Don't get me wrong. I like niggas too, but I haven't met a guy that can hold my attention longer than two minutes. So until that day, I'll be chasing bitches.

I put my blunt out as we turned into the parking lot. I grabbed my Gucci bag and sprayed myself with my Burberry Weekend perfume. London pulled on the side of me and hopped in my car to re-light the blunt I put out, as I looked myself over in the mirror. I wore my hair in a high curly ponytail with blonde streaks. I flipped the mirror up and noticed Jason walking toward my car with a wife beater and basketball shorts on with two niggas that looked like they stepped straight from heaven to earth.

"Who the fuck is them niggas walking with Jason?" I asked London quickly before they approached the car.

"I don't know, but they both fine as fuck, damn," she replied, dropping the blunt out of the window.

"Well, I bet I know who they are by the end of the night," I said, meaning every word.

"Aw shit, Paree is checking for a nigga. You ok?" London replied, laughing and placing her hand on my forehead to see if I had a fever.

"Bitch, I like niggas too. I just haven't come across none that look like that in a while," I replied, laughing. I pushed her hand down as they walked up.

London hopped out and hugged Jason as he gave me a head nod. I couldn't keep my eyes off this nigga as he leaned on the hood of my car. It feels like I know him from somewhere. I got out and walked in front of him and shifted my weight to one side before asking

"So, you just gone lean on my shit without introducing yourself?"

He didn't say a word as he stood straight up wearing a white V-neck and a pair of Nike sweatpants. Seventy-five percent of his body was covered in tattoos, and his yellow complexion matched mine perfectly. I could easily tell he was also mixed with something as he sized me up.

"Sincere," he replied, focusing his attention back on his phone as his friend introduced himself as Malik.

I instantly turned my attention away from Sincere's rude ass to Malik. He was the sexiest dark skinned skinny nigga that I had ever laid eyes on and not to mention he had a perfect set of teeth. He had his dreads twisted neatly to the back with a fresh lining. No words would leave my mouth, and that was a first. I was stuck in a trance as he smiled at me and extended his hand. It wasn't until our friend Taylor walked up and spoke, which brought me back down to reality. Taylor has been our friend since our freshman year, and the three of us are thick as thieves. They often called us triplets because her body and beauty matched ours to a tee, but she was one ghetto ass bitch. Taylor had no filter and was always looking for a nigga to finesse. I couldn't help but notice the way Sincere stared at her. I ain't no hater though. Maybe she's more of his type.

"I'm...I'm Paree." I finally spoke, shaking Malik's nicely tattooed hand, which I didn't want to release.

"Damn Paree, I've never seen you lost for words. Hey Malik and Sincere, I'm Jason's girlfriend, London," London said, causing everyone to laugh and me to turn red.

"Don't put my girl on the spot," Malik replied, winking at me. I instantly felt my panties getting moist.

"Well, excuse me," London said, walking off with Jason with Taylor and Sincere in tow.

I couldn't believe those bitches left me alone with this nigga. I didn't know the first step on talking to a guy being that I never gave the lames that came at me a chance. I guess it's true that there's a first time for everything. Besides, it's something about him. He came and leaned against my car as I tried my best not to look nervous.

"What's wrong? You look scared as hell," he asked.

"I'm not. I'm just kind of shy," I lied.

"You didn't come off as the shy type. Who whip you stole? This bitch is nice," he asked, touching the hood of my car.

"Thanks. It was a graduation gift, but I'm very outspoken. You just caught me off guard. I've never really "talked" to a guy."

"So, you like females?"

"Yeah I do, but I like niggas too, and for some reason, I really like you."

"I like you too, and I'm gone turn you all the way straight," he said, smiling.

"Boy bye, good luck. I probably get more pussy than you!" I replied, laughing.

"That's cold," he said, shaking his head.

I knew in the back of my mind that he had the power to fuck me right now if he wanted to, but I'm still a virgin and scared of dick. I fucked with a few studs in my time, but I didn't play that strap-on shit. The thought of penetration had me scared shitless. From the outside looking in, you would've thought we had known each other for years, instead of a half an hour. Malik put his arm around my neck as I hit the alarm on my car, and we headed toward the park.

THIRTY-FIVE
SINCERE

"Yo pops, where you at?" I yelled as I walked through our mini-mansion.

"In my office," he replied.

I walked in and saw my father sitting behind his cherry oak wood desk looking like a boss on a business call. I took five stacks of hundred-dollar bills from the bag that I was carrying and sat them on the desk. My father nodded.

"Is it all there?" he mouthed to me as he picked the stacks up and placed them in the locked drawer on his desk.

"Hell yeah, fifty-thousand even. Niggas know not play with me," I replied, meaning every word.

I started working for my pops doing small shit. I caught my first body at sixteen, and the rest is history. Now I'm eighteen and running shit, I'm an only child, and my mom was murdered years ago. My dad raised me by himself and did a hell of a job. I salute him. It takes a real nigga to step up and raise a child. Niggas usually run from parental responsibilities. It was just us in this big ass house until he moved his girl in a couple of years ago. I didn't mind because she was appealing to the eyes, and she was a few years younger than him.

Chanel was a badass redbone who didn't look a day over twenty-one, but thirty-two looked good on her. She would easily put you in the mind of that Boo Boo Kitty bitch off that show *Empire* because she was short and rocked a short hairstyle with a dope ass body. She's super loyal to my pop.

"Chanel, step out let me talk to my boy," my father said as she hugged me and did as she was told.

"What's up, pop?"

"Nothing much, young buck. What's up with you? I barely see around the crib."

"You keep me busy," I said, causing him to chuckle.

"You know you don't have to work if you don't want to, but you have always been the type that doesn't want handouts. Even as a kid you wanted to work for your allowance and toys. The shit always amazed me. I always felt like I owed you because your mother isn't here."

"It's cool, pop. You don't owe me nothing. You've done enough," I said, cutting him off because I didn't like speaking about my mother.

"I know it's a touchy subject for you, but I want you to know she loved you. I know you don't remember certain shit. I'll tell you the story behind her death when I think you're ready." he said, looking up at nothing in particular.

"Pop, I can handle it. That shit doesn't bother me like it did when I was a kid."

"I hear that, but just know jealousy is real and unlike men, women work off emotions. I know you're young and probably got a bunch of lil females on your heels, but don't follow my footsteps. Be a better man than me, son."

"That's why I don't do relationships. I talk to a couple of chicks, but nothing serious. I stick and move with no strings attached," I replied, rubbing my hands together and making a face like the reality TV star Stevie J.

"Just stay strapped. I'm too young to be a grandpa," he replied, laughing.

"Always," I replied as I walked out to answer my phone. I smiled as Taylor's name flashed across the screen.

It was something about this bitch that I liked. It was probably the fact that she fucked the shit out of me in my car after we left the park the other day. My dick got hard just thinking about her lil thick ass. We're all supposed to meet up tonight and chill. The twins are cool, but I have to watch they ass because I have an eerie feeling when I'm in their presence, especially Paree.

"Yo," I answered the phone.

"Girl, his dick was so big, and yes I fucked the shit out of him after they played ball. This nigga got real bread, and he drives a 750 BMW. I'm gone tear them pockets down. He's definitely the new member of "Taylor Gang!"

"YOOOO!" I yelled into the phone, but she couldn't hear me because she pocket dialed me.

Just like a hood bitch, thinking she came up. I listened to her rant for a few more minutes to whoever she was talking to before I ended the call and dialed her right back.

"What's up, baby?" she answered on the first ring.

"Text me yo address. I'm about to come get you," I said, hanging up before she had a chance to respond.

The text came through within seconds. I loved when a bitch thought she was gone get over on me. The crazy part is I liked the lil bitch, but she just fucked up. I'm a young nigga but very mature for my age, and this is the main reason I never fucked with bitches my age. I always went after the twenty-one and older hoes.

I hopped on the expressway and pulled up in front of a run-down court way building. I watched my surroundings because I wasn't from the area, and I knew how out west niggas operated. I waited for about three minutes before Taylor came walking toward my car with a dress that looked painted while smiling as the other ghetto bitches turned their noses up at her. I can't lie she's badd, and the pussy was A-1. I thought about fucking her one last time, but fuck her.

Jason shot me a text and told me he got a suite at the Marriot by

Midway Airport. This was perfect. I just hope it was some other bad bitches coming so that I could teach this gold-digging bitch Taylor a lesson. We walked into the hotel lobby and straight to the elevator taking it straight up to the top floor. I could hear Future playing from the hallway as we approached the door. I walked in first, and my eyes got big as I saw asses bouncing everywhere, I forgot Taylor was behind me until I heard her say, "Thanks for holding the door, Sincere."

I ignored her as I made eye contact with a sexy ass female with fire red hair. She wasn't a stripper, but her body would easily fool you. She was giving me the "come fuck me" look, and I knew she was the one I was leaving with tonight.

Taylor walked over and joined London as she uploaded snaps with stacks of hundred-dollar bills in her hand. I guess her twin sat this one out because she wasn't here. I walked over to the dice game and pulled a wad of cash out. I peeped Taylor smiling and watching me out the corner of my eye, and it was time to act a fool. I got my hand on the dice and took all that shit walking away two thousand dollars richer. I walked out on the balcony, lit my blunt, and took a cup of Hennessy to the head. I let the smoke fill my lungs and take control of my body. I felt a pair of hands rub the front of my Gucci t-shirt as I leaned over the banister. I already knew it was Taylor. I took a long pull from the blunt and turned around, and to my surprise, it wasn't Taylor. It was the redhead from earlier. Bitches are bold as fuck these days. I hate if Taylor were my lady or else it would've really been some shit. I didn't even bother looking to see where Taylor was because I didn't give a fuck, and clearly she didn't either.

"I want you," she said, taking the blunt from lips.

"Is that right, what's your name?" I replied licking my lips and running my hands over the True Religion jeans that covered her ass as her hair blew in the warm Chicago wind.

"Brandy...come here," she said, pulling my shirt until my lips were close to hers as she gave me a shot gun with the smoke in her mouth.

"Get your shit, you leaving with me," I replied, popping her on her ass.

"What about your girlfriend? Never mind fuck her."

"You funny as hell. If that were my girl she would be out here beating yo ass, but that's not my bitch, let's slide," I said, walking in first holding my pants up by my Gucci belt.

I shook my homies hand and knocked one last cup back as Taylor stood there looking at me with a face full of rage and on the verge of tears from embarrassment. I looked her dead in the eyes and smirked at her while reaching into my pocket handing Brandy all the money I won in the dice game. I bet I'm the last nigga she tries to play. Brandy and I walked out without looking back.

Taylor: U a weak ass nigga... on my mama, u can't come back out west. I'm gone have my brothers to fuck u up and hit them pockets.

Me: Bitch, don't send no threats because I'm still in the area, and if yo gold digging ass wasn't trying to "tear my pockets down" I wouldn't be about to tear her pussy down. Now find you a new recruit for "Taylor Gang" Hoe.

THIRTY-SIX
PAREE

"Paree, what are you doing, sewing the damn outfit yourself?" I heard London yell from downstairs.

"I'm almost ready," I shot back.

I walked over to my full-length mirror and smiled. I'm a bad bitch. I decided to switch shit up tonight and dress like a real girl and not my regular fitted shirt and sweatpants. I went shopping earlier and grabbed an all black Chanel bodysuit with the gold double C chain belt and a pair of low top Chanel sneakers with the purse and shades to match. I let my bone straight wrap fall to my ass, flipped my shades down, and walked out of my room. I walked downstairs, and London's mouth fell wide open.

"Damnnnn twin, don't fuck 'em up like that," she said, covering her mouth with her fist.

"Gun in my purse, bitch I came dressed to kill!" I replied, quoting a Nicki Minaj verse.

"Ohhhh I know what you on, operation Malik."

"I'm on that nigga heels, Ooooooooouu," I replied, impersonating the rapper Young MA.

"Do ya thang, baby. We're taking yo car. I ain't got no gas."

"Damn Paree, where you going? You know you almost look as good as I did in my prime," my mother said, walking into the kitchen as her Tom Ford stilettos clicked across the marble floor.

"Out, see you later mommy," I replied, pushing London toward the door before she started going down memory lane.

"Ok, I love y'all!" she yelled.

"Love you too," we said in unison.

We made it to Hillside Bowling Alley in less than thirty minutes. We beat everyone else there, so we sat in the car and smoked a blunt. We were almost done when three foreign cars turned into the parking lot, causing our windows to rattle from the sounds coming from their trunks. A smile spread across my face when I saw Malik step out of his Infiniti Q7 truck dressed in a fitted Gucci t-shirt, a pair of white Balmain jeans, and a pair of all white Gucci sneakers. I had never wanted a man this bad, but I had to have this nigga. I was smiling until I saw a stiletto touch the ground from the passenger side of his truck. I guess London saw the salty look I had on my face and told me to play it cool. I hadn't talked to Malik since that day at the park. She didn't have to tell me to play it cool because once the girl stepped out, I was smiling harder than I was before. I could easily forget a face but an ass, never. I knew exactly who the girl was that was with Malik because she was just eating my pussy last week. The bitch he's toting around was just crying because she's in love with me, which is why I put her ass on the block list along with the other thirsty bitches that wanted me to wife them. London looked back and forth from the girl to me and shook her head.

"Tell me you don't know this bitch," London said, shaking her head.

"Ohhhh I know her very fucking well, that's my hoe," I replied, stepping out of the car.

"Don't start no shit, Paree. We too cute to be fighting."

"I ain't on shit. I'm chilling."

We walked in the bowling alley right behind Sincere and some thick ass girl with some fire red hair. I'm guessing this is the girl he stunted on Taylor with. Malik and shorty were getting their shoes to bowl when we walked up. We hugged Sincere and spoke to everyone else. As soon as Malik turned around, he locked eyes with me before undressing me with his eyes, totally disrespecting the girl he had on his side. I smiled slightly before speaking, and as soon as the girl heard my voice, she snapped her head in my direction.

"Damn Paree, so you put me on the block list?" the girl snapped, going straight in.

"Woah chill, ma. Ain't you on a date?" I shot back as everyone focused their attention on us.

"No, I'm not on a date. I'm just outside chilling. Had you not put me on the block list, I would've been with you, and you know that."

"Nah you good, continue chilling how you be chilling, and umma do the same," I replied, turning my attention in every direction but hers as she stood there staring at me.

Malik looked at me and gave off the sexiest grin followed by a head nod. I winked at him and walked toward the lanes that were assigned to us. I didn't come here to bowl. My mission was to let Malik know what he could have if he plays his cards right. I sat there and watched them bowl forgetting all about shorty as I became Malik's personal cheerleader. I think I saw steam coming from baby girl's ears as she burned a hole in the side of my head. It wasn't until I felt my face stinging that I acknowledged her presence. It was like the sound of her slapping me echoed through the entire bowling alley, and everyone stopped to see what was going to happen next. Before I could even react to the bitch, Malik had his hands wrapped around her throat as she fought for her life. Sincere and Jason didn't budge as London swung around Malik trying to hit the girl. I snapped out the astonishment I was stuck in and got Malik to release her. She immediately fell to the floor, trying to catch her breath. All I saw was people pointing and laughing. I walked over, kneeled, grabbed her hair, and whispered in her ear because I didn't want to act a fool in the bowling alley and get us put out.

"You got two seconds to get yo dumb ass up and get the fuck out of here before I beat yo ass into a coma. You're working off yo emotions right now, and that shit is gone get you hurt."

I stood up and spit dead in her face as she scrambled to get up off the floor with tears falling from her eyes. I didn't feel a lick of remorse for the hoe because she knew better than to put her fucking hands on me. I wanted to bug up on her ass, but I'm gone give her a pass because Malik choked the life from her ass.

"How am I supposed to get home, Malik?" she asked wiping her face.

"You would've had a ride if you knew how to fucking act. You better call an Uber," Malik replied, walking over to Sincere.

"You can wait outside, fuck out of my face," I said as she stormed out.

I sat back down as London asked was I good. The truth is I was more than good. The way Malik stepped in and handled her before I had a chance to react made me like him ten times more. He is definitely bae ass. I shifted in my seat as Malik walked toward me, and London walked off.

"You the man, I see. What you do to her?" he asked, smiling and sitting down next to me as I inhaled his cologne.

"Shit, I ate the box a few times," I replied, causing him to bust out laughing.

"You lying, that bitch wouldn't even let me touch the pussy."

"I told you I probably get more pussy than you."

"I see. I hope this shit turned you straight."

"I'm not gay; I'm bi. So that's you shooting yo shot or nah?"

"Hell naw. I ain't shooting no shot. I just helped you fight. We go together now."

"You didn't help me do shit, but as you can see people can't take Paree," I replied, laughing.

"I'm not *people*, baby. Paree don't bother me."

"Say no more."

THIRTY-SEVEN
LONDON

"Man, Taylor, leave that shit alone bro. That shit is old. You act like y'all went together or something, damn."

"I don't give a fuck. He thinks that shit is over because I let a few weeks pass. He got me fucked up. I told my brothers what he did, and they still gone fuck him up period. He bet not come out west," Taylor replied, sounding dumb as hell.

Sometimes she made me want to beat her ass. I told her she acts just like them nothing ass bitches from her neighborhood. She was salty because Sincere started bringing Brandy everywhere we went. Paree and I didn't have beef with her, and she's actually a dope lil bitch. Taylor tried her best to be into with the girl, but she was unbothered by Taylor, and I liked that about her.

"Yeah, ok. You know Sincere is that nigga too, fuck around and start a war," I replied, meaning every word.

Truth is I don't know much about Sincere, but everywhere we went, niggas were walking up to him like he's a celebrity and asking if he's good. Jason told me his dad is a straight killer and the apple doesn't fall too far from the tree. I watched how Sincere moved, and everything about the boy screamed killer, from the way he observed everything around him to the .9mm he carried on his waist. Just like him, I watched everything and everyone that was in my presence.

"Girl bye, his south side ass will get killed fucking around. He's too pretty to fight, my brothers gone make him bitch up, watch!"

I didn't respond to her last comment. I just maneuvered around my room looking for the perfect outfit for tonight. I planned on officially becoming a woman tonight. The last month Jason and I have become best friends. We killed prom and attended each other's graduation. His parents loved me, and my OG approved of our relationship, so life was good. We had so much in common, especially the fact that both of us lost some people that we loved. He opened up to me and told me about his fucked up childhood and how his real mother didn't want him and a bunch of other tragedies that he went through at an early age. I was kind of sad because he decided to go out of state for college. The man got a full ride to any school of his choice. He chose to attend Duke University in North Carolina, so we were going to make the best out of the time we have before he leaves. I was slightly nervous about tonight because I didn't want things to change between us.

I walked over to my closet as Taylor filled her bag up with shit that I didn't wear anymore like she did whenever she came over. I wanted to look real sexy tonight, so I pulled out an all white Chanel dress with the entire back out that hugged every curve on my body with a pair of red pointed toe stilettos and clutch to match. I sat down at my vanity and lightly beat my face. I completed my look with a high ponytail that stopped right above my ass slightly covering the small butterfly that was tattooed on my lower back. I sprayed myself down with my Juicy Couture perfume, and I sprayed everywhere I thought he was going to kiss. I grabbed my keys and headed out the door with Taylor in tow. She threw her two bags full of my shit in her backseat, chucked the deuces, hopped in her Dodge Avenger, and sped off with the music blasting.

Everything about tonight felt sexy down to the warm wind that blew across my skin. I pulled into Jason's driveway. His parents went away for a week to celebrate their anniversary. They had a beautiful house from the outside. It was slightly smaller than ours was, but it was nice. I stepped out, ran my hands over my dress to knock the wrinkles from sitting out, and walked up to the front door. I stood there for a half of a second before the door swung open and Jason stood there in a pair of all white fitted True Religion jeans, a white V-neck t-shirt, and a pair of white Louboutin high-top sneakers. The diamonds that cover his body instantly turned me on, as he leaned in and kissed my lips. I could smell his cologne mixed with the candles that his mother had around the house. I followed him to a secluded dining area where he had a candlelit dinner prepared. Even though I knew it was takeout, it was so romantic.

"You look, beautiful baby," Jason said, pulling my chair out.

"Thanks. You clean up nice as well."

"I didn't know what you wanted to eat, so I ordered everything," he said, causing me to laugh.

"You trying to make me get fat. You not slick!" I replied, filling my plate up with food.

"The way you slamming I don't have to try hard, lil fat ass," he said as I gave him the side eye and continued to stuff my face.

We sat and talked for a while before we headed upstairs to "relax." I walked into his bedroom, which looked like a mini apartment. His closet looked like it belonged to a celebrity. He had more shoes than I could count, and I was really impressed at how neat it was. A huge king-sized bed sat in the corner of the room with a black and gold comforter set to match the black paint that covered the walls. There was a door right next to the closet that led to a full bathroom that was also decorated in gold. I looked at the pictures of him, Malik, and Sincere that sat on his trophy case and smiled.

"I love how close y'all are, but why is that nigga so serious all the time?"

"That nigga is always serious, but he's low key funny as hell. Them my niggas though," he said proudly.

"I see, come here." I said lying across the bed as Dej Loaf's "Hey

There" came through the surround sound speakers instantly putting in the mood.

Jason walked over and joined me on the bed. He climbed right next to me and just stared at me. He looked at me like he was trying to solve a puzzle in his head. I tried to turn my head to break the eye contact, but he leaned in and traced lining of my lips with his tongue, causing my breathing to pick up. I was nervous as a hooker in church on first Sunday. I took a deep breath and tried to calm down as he ran his hand over my thick thighs. After a few more minutes of kissing, I was for sure ready to take the next step. I had no clue what to do, so I kept my hands to myself and let him lead. My body was so tense that you would've thought he was forcing himself on me. I tried my best to loosen up and go with the flow as I ran my hand across his freshly cut hair.

"You sure you want to do this, baby? I want you to do it when you ready."

"Yeah, I'm sure, I love you," I replied with sincerity.

"Yeah, me too."

He had me to stand up as he helped me step out of my dress. I stood there wearing nothing but a red lace thong. I covered my body shyly as he removed his clothes now wearing nothing but a pair of Versace boxer briefs and his jewelry. This man was beyond sexy as stood in front of me sizing me up and licking his lips. The waves that flowed through his hair were even sexy to me right now. I felt the goosebumps growing all over my body as came closer. I looked down at his semi-large manhood, trying to escape his boxers and got nervous all over again.

"Don't be scared, baby. I promise to take my time with you and if it hurts I will stop," he said, laying me down on the bed.

"Ok," was all I said.

I laid back as his tongue explored my neck. I let out a soft moan as he made his way down to my small swollen breasts. He took his time and licked my nipples, making sure he showed both equal atten- tion. I grabbed the back of his head as he went further south and stopped right at my pussy. He pushed my legs up towards my shoulders and dived in head first, licking around my clit. I masturbated almost every day, and it felt nothing like this. I couldn't control myself as he locked on to my shit and tried to suck the soul out of me through my vagina. I felt my legs starting to shake uncontrollably, as I tried to keep up with his tongue. I grabbed the back of his head and grinded my pussy on his face barely giving him air to breathe. I don't know what came over me, but I couldn't control myself. I felt my pussy get extremely wet, and I knew what was coming next, but I was super ready. He came up and wiped his mouth with his hand before removing his boxers. I looked down at what looked like eight inches and wanted to get up and run as he ripped a Lifestyle condom open and put it on.

"You ok?" he asked, as I shook my head yes.

He climbed on top of me and rubbed the tip across my already swollen clit. I ran my nails across his back as he found my opening. I took a deep breath and prepared myself. He slipped his tongue into my mouth and pushed his dick in inch by inch. I felt myself ripping as he took my innocence, replacing it with nothing but pleasure. Once it was all the way in, I felt like I was going to cry because I had never experienced anything that felt this good. I dug my nails into his back as he made love to me hitting every beat of Bryson Tiller's song "Don't". I was officially a woman.

We were about to go another round when we heard loud noise and glass shatter outside followed by a car alarm. We both jumped up and ran to the window, which was right above the driveway. I saw my entire windshield smashed in as Cami and two other girls looked up and begged me to come out. I was far from a scary bitch, but smart enough not to try and fight all three of these bitches. I grabbed my phone, called Paree, and told her to get here ASAP as I threw on a pair of Jason's basketball shorts and a wife beater. I looked at Jason as he shook his head and started going off.

"I'm about to beat this bitch's ass!" Jason yelled as his voice echoed through the empty house.

"Nah, it's cool. I got her!" I said as she smashed my back window out.

"Bring yo badass out here, London!" Cami yelled, pointing the bat up at the window.

I stood there as they sabotaged my car. Once I saw my sister's car pull up, I hit the stairs. I grabbed one of Jason's dad's golf clubs that I noticed when I first walked in and ran outside. Cami was on top of Paree as she reached into her back pocket and grabbed a blade to cut her with. I swung the golf club with all my might and hit her across the back. She yelled out in pain and rolled off Paree. Paree jumped up and started stomping the shit out of Cami as I swung the golf club getting her friends off of Taylor. Me, Taylor, and Paree together have always been an ugly sight. Jason tried his best to break it up but made sure to stay clear of me and my swinging. I hit Cami a few more times, and she was now begging for us to stop.

"Bitch, you asked for this. You wanted this shit! I told you to stay the fuck away from me, I told you!" I yelled, connecting my foot to her face as bloodshot from her nose.

"Come on bae, fuck her. Cami, bitch, I hope you learned yo fucking lesson. That shit we had is over and done. Stay the fuck away from my crib and my girl. Come on. I'll get yo shit fixed in the morning!" Jason yelled, wrapping his arms around me from behind and pulling me toward the porch.

"Ok, please just let me leave," she managed to say between cries as Paree hit her upside the head.

"Bitch, you bet not come nowhere near my sister again because next time, I'm gone kill you, and I mean that shit. Call me later, twin," Paree said as Jason pulled me inside.

We talked and laughed about the shit that just went down before fucking the rest of the night away.

THIRTY-EIGHT
PAREE

I woke up sore as hell from fighting them bitches last night. I flipped the covers back and grabbed my phone as it vibrated and alerted me to a text message.

Malik: GM beautiful

Me: GM handsome

Malik: Breakfast??

Me: I got a date with my OG and sister...but dinner??

Malik: Wherever you wanna go...just HML

Me: Bet

I couldn't help but smile. I really like this boy. I got up, washed my face, and brushed my teeth before busting into London's room and jumping into bed with her. She flipped over and faced me with the biggest smile and glow on her face.

"Ohhhhh you fucked him! I should've known when you had on his clothes last night. Come on. Fill me in, did it hurt?" I asked curiously.

"You're so silly. Yeah, it hurt when he first put it in, but the fore-play had me hot and ready. After he finally got it in, it felt so fucking good, bitch. I can't wait until we get done with mommy today. I'm getting some more tonight."

"You crazy I'm scared of that shit, but I really like Malik, sister. I haven't even thought about fucking with no hoes. He's all I think about."

"Aww my baby is falling for a real nigga, that's what's up though. I like him for you."

"Shid, me too, bitch. Bet you didn't know Sincere and Malik are real cousins on their mother's side," I replied, laughing.

"I didn't. I thought they were lying," London said, laughing.

"You a clown."

"I heard that name Sincere somewhere before," she said, trying to remember.

"Yeah bitch on the movie *Belly*.

"Fuck you, come on let's get dressed before mama start tweaking," London replied, climbing over me.

I walked to my room and flipped through my clothes before grabbing a pair of skin tight white ripped up jeans and a white halter to match. I pulled my hair up in a high bun, I love my hair, but it's too hot for this shit to be on my back. Once I got out the shower, I was dressed and ready to go. I walked into London's room and stole some perfume. They were already downstairs waiting on me as usual. I slowly walked down the stairs because my damn body was sore.

"Both of y'all sore huh, fighting and fucking will do that to you. I need to speak with you later, London," our mother said, catching us both off guard as we looked at each other.

I don't know how she always knows what's going on with us, but we can never get shit pass her. We didn't even bother replying, we just followed her out the front door. I hopped in the back seat of her Bentley and let my body sink into the soft leather. I was trying to figure out how she knew every damn thing, I knew she was the man, but damn. She turned on her favorite song and every other old person song "Good Kisser" by Usher, and we were in the wind. I planned on leaving this damn mall with a bunch of shit. We always had a mother-daughter day at least once a month because she was always super busy. We were halfway to the mall when her phone started ringing through the speakers in the car. She answered from the steering wheel.

"We got them niggas."

"Handle it. I got my kids with me.

"We caught Ken too, boss lady."

"I'm on my way!" she replied, ending the call.

My body shifted to the left as she turned her car around and headed to the 290 expressway. She was doing at least ninety as she came up at Independence. I don't know what this Ken nigga did, but I feel sorry for his ass. I was excited to see my mama work. She never let us see her work or get anywhere near the "business." She always said once you're in, ain't no easy way out. I knew she was gone try to make one of her workers take us home, but I'm not going this time. We pulled up to a nice two-flat building, and she killed the engine before turning to look at us, shocking me with her words as a smile spread across my face.

"Let's go. I can't leave y'all out here. It's too dangerous."

We wasted no time hopping out and following our mother into the house. Everything about our mother screamed boss bitch, from the honey blonde twenty-eight inches of hair that swung as she walked to the six-inch stilettos on her feet. I have never seen her wear a pair of sneakers unless she was working out. She threw her Chanel purse over her shoulder and walked up the stairs with us in tow. The door swung open before she could even touch it, and a huge black nigga with dreads welcomed my mother and sized us up. I believe she called him Bear. This was one nice ass trap house, and you could easily tell a woman was running it. My mother had it fully furnished with top of the line furniture including a sixty-five-inch TV hanging on the wall. The police themselves would walk in this bitch and take their shoes off at the door.

"Y'all have a seat. I'll be back. Do not move, Paree!" my mother ordered.

"But, I wanna come with you,

Ma, we ready!" I blurted out.

"NO! If you come downstairs, you might as well get ready to put in work, and no, you all are not ready yet. Now stay here until I come back up." she replied, walking toward the back of the apartment.

We sat there for about two minutes. I looked at London and gave her a head nod. She shook her no as I stood up and started walking toward the back. I looked back, and London was right behind me, I knew if I walked first she would follow me, even if she didn't want to. We walked down a long hallway before stopping at a cracked door. I peeked in and saw a dark stairway. I opened the door and tiptoed down with London right behind me. I stopped dead in my tracks as the smell of fresh flesh hit my nostrils, but for some reason, it smelled like fresh roses to me. I heard London gag, which caused my mother and everyone else in the room to look in our direction. I elbowed her as she stood up straight. Our mother stared at us with a steel bat in her hand standing in front of a man who was tied up to a pole in the middle of the floor.

"So y'all disobeyed me, right? I guess that means y'all ready. Come here," she said pointing the bat in our direction.

We did as we were told and stood right next to our mother as all twenty of the men in the basement looked at us with lust and respect. There was one guy who stood out from the rest. He was dressed in Versace from head to toe with enough diamonds to light up a dark room and the only nigga sitting while everyone else stood up. We stared at each other a little longer than we should have. My attention was directed back to my mother when she yelled my name.

"Y'all these are me and Kayo's twins, Paree and London. They are next in line to be your bosses. They are to be given the same respect you give me; I will not play about my kids. Bear, you are now their head bodyguard, so protect them with your life. Now that that's clear, Ken here thought it was a smart move to run and tell another muthafucka how I run my business. I guess you thought the shit wasn't gone get back to me, but I run this muthafuckin' city! I can't believe you of all people let another nigga get in yo head to go against me after I took care of you. It's greedy niggas like you that make my job harder than it should be. I had no plans on killing a muthafucker today, but here we are. Let be an example to the rest of you, if any of you niggas think about crossing me, don't! Y'all use that bat on his ass!" my mother ordered as I took the bat from my mother's hand and Bear handed London his.

I lifted the bat with no hesitation and connected it the middle of his face, causing his head to fly back and blood to cover his once white shirt. I immediately took matters into my own hands after London just stood there taken back by the way I was connecting this bat to his ass.

"Bitch ass nigga you thought it was sweet, huh?" I spat as I hit him directly in the neck with the bat instantly breaking it.

"Now that's how you handle a bitch ass nigga, welcome to the business!" my mother said proudly as London stood there in disbelief. I knew she would eventually come around because it's definitely in our blood.

THIRTY-NINE

SINCERE

"I swear to God bro Paree's gone be my main bitch," Malik said as we rode down Lake Street.

"You like her, huh?" I asked rhetorically

"Yeah, she's cool as hell, like one of the guys but sexy as hell, and she got her own bread."

"Right, they lil asses do be holding, and they spoiled asses don't work."

"Yeah, Paree said they OG has her own business."

"That's what's up, but umma tell you like I told Jason ass, make sure they ain't nothing like they weak ass friend Taylor. I got a feeling I'm gone have to open her head up. She thinks shit is sweet."

"They ain't like that ghetto ass bitch, and I heard she put a hit out yo ass," Malik said as we both started laughing.

"Fuck that hoe. I ain't dodging shit. Man, where the fuck is this park at tho?"

"Over there where all the cars and hoes at."

I made a left turn and pulled into the first park I saw. It was packed. I got out and leaned against my car as Malik shook up with some of his peoples and all the hoes looked in my direction. I let this nigga talk me into coming up to some park called "The Circle." It was cool. All the niggas had their cars out showing off their paint jobs and rims that they saved all winter to buy. I wasn't really picky when it came to females, but these out west hoes were too thirsty for me. I kept catching this same group of niggas looking at me, but I paid them no mind because I wasn't from out here, and I know for a fact they don't know me. I put my phone in my pocket and felt my .9mm as they walked in my direction.

"What kind of car is this, my nigga?" one of the niggas asked.

I didn't say a word. I just pointed to the BMW emblem attached to the front of the car.

"Damn bro, you can't talk."

"What up, man? You asked a stupid ass question, nigga. You clearly see the "BMW" emblem on the front of this car," I replied, standing up to face the niggas.

"What you standing up for?" he asked as his homie stared at me like he was trying to figure out if he knew me.

"Yo chill, I know this lil nigga. His pops is..." his homie semi-whispered trying to pull the nigga in the direction they came from.

"I don't give a fuck who his daddy is!" his homie said, cutting him off before he could finish his sentence.

Before I could react, Malik swung and knocked the nigga out cold. His homies rushed us, and we were exchanging blows left and right, and all of a sudden they stopped swinging long enough for me to get my hands on my gun. I looked around and noticed my pop and Chanel standing in front of his Rolls-Royce Phantom with at least twenty niggas with guns in their hands. The shit shocked me because my father never came out west. He was a real low-key cat.

"I heard you say and I quote "I don't give a fuck who his daddy is" now either you really don't give a fuck, or you have no idea who the fuck I am," my pop said to the nigga as he looked down the barrel of my gun.

"I told yo dumb ass," I heard his homie mumble.

"I didn't know who you were sir, but he played my sister. I

thought he was just a regular nigga," the trembling nigga said as his once white jeans turned yellow from the piss that covered them.

I instantly knew who the nigga was when Taylor's bomb ass came running through the crowd begging me not to shoot her brother. Oh, I'm killing this nigga on today's date, and she better hope I don't shoot her ass too. I can't believe she's still mad about that hotel shit. That's what I'm talking about. These out west hoes are something else.

"Now it's sir; you're confusing me. Son, you make the decision. He disrespected you not me because he calls me 'sir'," my pop said as he chuckled.

Without saying another word, I put a single bullet in his head as my father's people collected every cellphone they saw recording.

"NOOOOOOOOOOO!!" Taylor screamed as she leaned over her brother's limp body.

"From now on when you muthafuckas see him, know that's mine, and I have no problem killing parents, kids, or old people. Please don't fuck with mine, and I won't fuck with yours!" my pop said as he pointed at me and every set of eyes in the park focused in on him.

I could hear the police sirens coming our way, but I wasn't worried about it because more than half of CPD was on my father's payroll. This body might not even make it to the morgue to be identified by the family.

"Now send the rest of them niggas you were talking about at me, bitch," I said as walked toward my car.

"I hate you! Umma see yo ass about this!" she yelled through her tears.

"Fuck you, Taylor." I shot back with my back turned to her.

I sat on the bathroom floor beside the toilet where I had been for last hour because it was something I ate or that shit I saw Paree do to that man had me sick to my stomach. I couldn't keep anything down, and I felt light-headed. I was about to get up, but I as soon as I stood to my feet, my mouth started watering, and I knew I was about to vomit again. I got on my knees and put my head over the toilet. I heard a knock on the door before I saw Paree stick her head in.

"You okay, twin?"

"No bitch, did you get the Pepto? My shit is fucked up."

"Yeah, here," she replied as she slowly turned to walk back out.

Paree handed me a bag from CVS Pharmacy. I looked inside it with a stale face once I realized she had purchased a pregnancy test along with the medicine. There was no possible way I was pregnant because Jason and I used protection every time we had sex. I put it back in the bag and opened the Pepto Bismol, taking it to the head. I conjured up enough strength to get up off the floor and walk to my bed. I opened the drawer on my nightstand and placed the test inside. I laid back and turned *Martin* on, but I couldn't get into it because my mind was in overdrive with the "what if" thoughts. I flipped the covers back, said fuck it, and grabbed the test before heading to the bathroom.

I sat on the toilet and waited on my bladder to release and hit the stick as I held it under me. I wiped myself, set it on the counter, and waited for a minute before I looked. My eyes damn near popped out of my head as two lines appeared without hesitation indicating I was indeed pregnant. I don't understand. We never had unprotected sex. I sat there and took it all in before tossing the empty box in the trash and sticking the test in my bra.

I sat on my bed and tried to figure out how I put myself in this predicament. How I'm gone, tell my momma, and most importantly, what are Jason and his parents going to say. I wasn't worried about the baby needing anything because we are both well off, but the thought of bringing a baby into this crazy world was enough to scare anybody. I grabbed my phone off the nightstand and shot Jason a text.

Me: Baby, we need to talk.

Jason: What's up stink, you ok?

Me: No, I um, I need to tell you something.

Jason: What London, just tell me, baby.

Me: You said it "BABY" Jason I'm pregnant, I've been sick all day. I thought it was something I ate, but my sister went and bought a test, and it came back positive. I haven't told anyone except you. Please don't be mad at me. I'm scared.

Jason: You serious right now? We having a shorty?

Me: Yessssss, are you mad?

Jason: Hell naw, I'm not mad. You're my baby, and we gone do what we gotta do. I gotta call my people and tell 'em.

Me: Wait don't tell them, I'm scared. What if they get mad?

Jason: Either they gone be happy or not, either way you keeping my shorty.

I fell back on the bed with and cried tears of joy. I can't believe I'm having a baby. My bedroom door swung open, and Paree stood there with her arms folded across her chest. I looked over at her as an angry expression spread across her face. I instantly sat up and looked at her with a confused look on my face.

"What's wrong with you?" I asked as she shook her head in disgust.

"You pregnant, ain't you?"

"Yes! You're going to be an auntie!" I replied.

"So, you're keeping it? London, how are we supposed to run the business with you being pregnant, and you tripping? He's just trying to trap you! You're going to have to go through the whole pregnancy alone. He leaves for school in a couple months. Use your brain, London. Now is not the time. You're too young!" she spat, cutting me off in mid-sentence and instantly hurting my feelings.

"I don't believe you. If anybody was going to be happy for me, I just knew it would be you, but I guess not. All you care about is this fucking business, and that's cool. You just like rest. Fuck out my face, Paree," I said with tears falling from my eyes.

"I'm just trying to give yo smart dumb ass some advice, but you too dumb to take it. You haven't even started living your life, and you want to have a child. I bet you think it's gone lock that nigga down, but that's bullshit. You need to think and hard before you fuck up your life dummy. I don't know where the fuck you came from, but you're weak," she replied, walking out as I slammed the door behind her.

FORTY-ONE
PAREE

I walked downstairs with a wife beater and a pair of yoga pants. I made it to the last step and heard a couple of male voices along with my mother's. I tilted my head around the corner without being noticed, and my heart rate instantly picked up. That fine ass nigga from the basement was sitting at our kitchen island eating breakfast as if he lived here along with Bear's ugly ass. I jetted back up the stairs to my room snatching my bonnet off in the process. I pulled off my house clothes and replaced them with a love pink sports bra with the leggings to match and lightly beat my face before hitting the stairs for a second time. I turned the corner and once again, we locked eyes, but he quickly looked away. I made sure I bounced my ass past him extra hard as Bear wasted no time greeting me with his thirsty ass. He didn't try to hide the fact that he was obsessed with me from anyone.

"Hey, Paree."

"Sup," I replied as my mother introduced me to dude.

"Paree this is YG, my right-hand man, and your business partner, YG as you already know this is one of my twins and the nutty one Paree."

He looked up with a sexy smirk and gave me a simple head nod. I returned the head nod with a smile. This man was so sexy. He looked to be about twenty, light-skinned, medium built with tattoos covering his hands and forearms. He had a fade with enough waves to make you seasick. I mean this nigga was God's gift to women. He would simply put you in the mind of the rapper, The Game. I couldn't take my eyes off the man, and I think Bear noticed it because his cock-blocking ass broke my trance with his next sentence.

"You look beautiful today, Paree."

"Thanks, Bear," I dryly replied as London turned the corner.

"Bear, leave my baby alone," my mother said in a playful tone.

London walked in clearly unbothered by the sexiness that sat at the island as she brushed past and fixed her a plate of the breakfast our mother prepared. I watched as YG watched London's every move. I had to catch myself a couple of times because he was about to blow me. She stood by the refrigerator pouring a glass of orange juice in a pair of basketball shorts, an oversized t-shirt, and a messy ponytail.

"YG, that's my other baby London," my mother said as London smiled and waved.

"What's up Ms. London, nice to meet you," YG replied, causing my head to spin around at the sound of his voice.

Ain't that a bitch. He gave me a weak ass head nod but verbally spoke to this bitch. London and I haven't spoken to one another in a few weeks since she called herself "checking" me, but I guarantee I will have the last laugh, I could've easily went and told my mother her secret, but I had a better idea.

"Hi, nice to meet you also," she replied, smiling as she grabbed her plate and headed back upstairs.

I watched him watch her until she was no longer in sight. I noticed she left her orange juice sitting on the counter, so I decided to be nice and take it up to her. I grabbed the glass and went upstairs, stopping in my room first. I had been trying to figure out how to put my plan in motion, and this was the perfect opportunity. I walked over to dresser and grabbed a small Zip-lock bag that contained a single that pill I paid one of my home girls to get for me. I dropped the pill in her glass and waited a couple of minutes for it to dissolve before walking towards her room. I lightly knocked before pushing the door open.

"Here you left your juice downstairs," I said, handing to her and turning to leave.

"Thanks, twin, wait," she replied, causing me to turn and look at her.

"I'm so sorry for blowing up on you like I did, and I know I hurt your feelings, but you hurt mine too. I just thought you would be just as happy as I was, but I understand where you were coming from. I promise the baby will not stop me from handling business. I love you, and I can't take us walking past each other like strangers," she said.

"It's cool twin, I thought about it, and I was wrong. I'm happy for you. I just hope you don't forget about me when you start your new family. When do you plan on telling mommy?" I asked, trying my best sound like I gave a fuck.

"I will never forget you Paree. You're my other half lil sis, and I don't know, but I have a feeling she knows already. I mean I am going on four weeks," she replied, calling me lil sis because she was a minute older than me.

"Yeah, you gone be big in a minute," I replied, rubbing her semi-flat stomach.

"I know right."

"Well y'all finish eating, I'm going to take a nap. Call me if you need me," I replied as I walked back to my room. I had about four hours before show time.

I climbed into my bed and texted Malik until I couldn't keep my eyes open any longer. I drifted off into a deep sleep. It wasn't until I heard London screaming my name at the top of her lungs that I jumped up smiling. I ran to her room doing top speed as I heard my mother and the guys hit the stairs. I busted in the door and saw London lying on the side of her bed in a fetal position with blood surrounding her.

"My baby Paree, help me!" London said as she cried.

I almost felt sorry for her when I saw how hard she was crying, but that shit quickly went out the window when I saw YG run over and scoop her up off the floor like he was her baby daddy. I just rolled my eyes in disgust as Bear pulled out his phone and dialed 911. My mother looked at me with hurt and anger in her eyes as she wasted no time questioning me about what was going on. I had no problem telling her little miss perfect was carrying a whole baby that she knew nothing about.

London was always the apple of everyone's eyes, and she could do no wrong. Sure, I stayed in trouble for dumb shit, but damn. It's true what they say. There's always a good and a bad twin. I guess that's me but whatever. I love my sister to death, but I'm tired of living in her shadow. We are two different people, and hopefully, my mother can see that after this.

"Paree, what the fuck is going on?" my mother yelled.

"She's pregnant ma, and from the looks of it, she's having a miscarriage," I replied sarcastically.

"PREGNANT?! YG put her in the car. Fuck the paramedics. My baby could bleed to death waiting on them. Let's go!" she said as she stormed out behind YG with us in tow.

"Mommy, I'm sorry. I'm so sorry. Please don't let my baby die," London cried as YG walked her down the stairs.

"It's ok baby, just breathe for mommy," my mother said trying to keep her calm.

I couldn't believe that was her only fucking response. I wanted to curse everybody the fuck out. I jumped in the truck with Bear, as he pulled off behind YG's car. I shot Malik a text and told him to let Jason know what was going on. I was trying my hardest not to cry as my thoughts got the best of me. One lonely tear managed to escape my eye, and I quickly wiped it away. I know Bear probably thought I was crying because of London's situation, but the truth is I was crying because no matter how hard I tried to love my twin, there was a small part of me that hated her. We are identical, but it seems like she's prettier than me, smarter than me, and always manages to outshine me effortlessly. I noticed Bear looking back and forth from the road to me.

"You cool?" He finally asked.

"Yeah, I'm good. I just have a lot on my mind."

"You can talk to me, I'll listen," he replied, sounding just like the rapper Biggie as he moved his dreads out of his face.

"Appreciate it."

"Why you act so hard? I see right through that shit. Even the hardest niggas need a lil love, Paree," he said, causing me to smile as we turned into hospital parking lot.

I watched as two nurses ran out with a stretcher as YG laid her down. I walked in right behind my mother as she gave them all of London's information. We tried to follow the nurses to the back, but they stopped us at the double doors as they wheeled London back. We stood there until she was no longer in sight before joining YG and Bear in the waiting room.

"YG, I'm good. You all can go ahead and leave. I'll call you when I'm ready," my mother said, looking down as she paced the floor.

"Naw, umma stay with you," YG replied as he stretched his legs out in front of him.

"How did it get past me?" my mother mumbled to no one in particular.

"Your little princess popped her pussy for a real nigga, and this is the outcome!" I said sarcastically.

Before I could blink, I felt my mother's hand connect to the left side of my face. I balled my fist up and drew back, but Bear quickly grabbed my arm. I wanted to fight her like she was a bitch on the streets. I felt the tears forming in my eyes.

"Release her arm, Bear. I wish like fuck you would. Show me you bad, Paree," my mother said, stepping so close to me that I could feel her breath on my face.

Everyone in the waiting area looked in our direction. At that moment all the love I had for her ass left my body. From this moment on, I'm all for Paree. She thinks she can treat everybody like those niggas on her team that bow down to her, but not me. I will respect her as my mother, but I will never bow down to her. I watched my mother punk some of the toughest people while growing up, but there is no punk in me! I was about to speak my mind, but a petite nurse followed by a doctor called for the family of London Castillo. My mom instantly shifted her attention to them and off me. I walked over to hear what the doctor had to say.

"Hi, I'm her mother Kyana Jones, please tell me she's ok," My mother said.

"Hi, Ms. Jones, your daughter is fine. She lost a tremendous amount of blood, but we were able to stop the bleeding. We had to sedate her to keep her calm after giving her the news of losing her child. We want to keep her overnight to run a few tests, but she'll be good to go if everything comes back ok. You can come up when you're ready. I'll give you all some time to process everything," the doctor said, turning to leave.

"Damn it, my baby," my mother said walking to the reception desk to get a visitor pass. I just rolled my eyes. I'm over this entire night.

"Bear, please take me home," I said, shifting my weight to one side and folding my arms across my chest.

"Yeah Bear, please get her the fuck out of my face. She's just like Kayo's selfish ass. You most definitely have Castillo blood flowing through your veins!" my mother spat, cutting me with each word.

"I'd rather be like him than anything like you, ma. You've always loved London more than me anyway," I replied as I headed out as Jason and Malik rushed in.

"Right Paree, leave while your sister is laying up in a hospital!" my mother yelled. I didn't reply. I just kept walking.

"Where my babies at, are they ok, Paree?" Jason asked damn near out of breath.

"Nah the baby didn't survive like this weak ass family won't," I replied as he damn near broke down.

Malik rushed out the door behind me and grabbed my arm. I had tears running down my face. I didn't want to talk. I just wanted to go. Bear walked out and looked at Malik and me from a distance.

"Baby, come here and talk to me," Malik said, grabbing my arm.

"Malik, please just let me go. I'll call you later," I said, trying to push past him, so he wouldn't see the tears that were now falling freely from my eyes.

"Man, calm down. You always wanna be tough. It's ok to cry, bae," Malik said as I collapsed into his arms and cried.

I felt someone grab my arm and spin me around. I stood face to face with Bear.

"You, ok?" Bear asked, sizing Malik up.

"Man, watch out. She's good," Malik answered before I had a chance to.

"Paree, I'll be in the truck when you're ready," Bear said without taking his eyes off of Malik.

"Nah, she's cool, bro. I got her. Thanks for yo services," Malik said, dismissing Bear.

"I'll see you at the house, Paree. Call me if you go elsewhere."

"Ok Bear, just go."

FORTY-TWO
SINCERE

I sat at the of the long table that sat in the middle of our conference room at home. At least fifty others were present for this mandatory meeting my father had called. The only time he called these meeting was if money came up short, or we were about to go to war with someone. I strolled through Facebook until I saw him walk in with Chanel right behind him. My pop wore nothing but custom-made suits. He unbuttoned the buttons on his fitted suit jacket and walked around the entire table making sure everyone was present.

"Can anyone in this room tell me why I had to postpone my day to call this meeting?" my father finally spoke as everyone looked around like they were searching for a clue.

"Business purposes we're assuming," this goofy nigga named Boo said with a chuckle.

"Yeah Boo, you right. Come here. Come stand next to me," my father said as he motioned for Boo with his hand.

Boo's smiled instantly faded away as he stood to his feet. I could tell from the look on his face he regretted opening his mouth. My father hated for someone to play with him when he was serious. He smiled as he wrapped his arm around Boo's neck, and with one swift move, he snapped his neck. My father is a six foot even, swole body ass nigga, so breaking this lil nigga's neck was a piece of cake. I didn't budge. I just watched his limp body fall out of my father's arms as he stepped over his body and continued his meeting.

"Does anyone else wanna get their Kevin Hart on, or can I continue?"

No one said a word they just gave him their undivided attention, I looked around the room and shook my head. I could never fear another man like these niggas feared my pop. I leaned back in my chair and listened as he broke down what I already knew. We were definitely going to war to take over the blocks out west. My eyes grew wide when he put me in charge of the hits. I was already putting in work but now is my chance to show my father how I really get down. He laid out all of the information on our rivals from the boss down to the workers. I looked down at the pictures in front of me, and couldn't help but notice how beautiful the leader of this operation was. I mean this bitch didn't look like she could hurt a fly. My father made it very clear that she was a dangerous ass woman and not to be played with. Listening to my father speak so highly of her, she had to be a real threat. He also made it clear he didn't want anyone else involved, but they were to watch my back at all times, so I knew I had to kill her myself.

"Everyone is dismissed. Son, stay," my father said as everyone exited the room.

Once the room was clear, he dismissed Chanel. I saw her cut her eyes at him as she turned to leave. He came and took a seat next to me running his hands over his face. I could tell something was bothering him, but I knew if I asked he wouldn't tell me what was wrong, so I didn't bother asking. We sat in silence for a few seconds before he finally spoke.

"You think you can handle this?"

"I know I can, pop. I'm good with the tool."

"It's more to it than being good with the tool, son. Anybody can shoot. I need you to hit the range and get your aiming on point. This is not a regular hit. If you slip up at any point, she will kill you no questions asked. You need to give yourself time to learn her every move. You can't kill her overnight. It's not that easy. You need at least a month or two to do it right, but stay clear of her. She knows you."

"She knows me? Who is this lady, pop?"

"She's the woman that killed your mother," he replied as I took in the words I've been waiting years to hear.

"Why now though after all of these years?"

"I wanted to wait until you were old enough and ready. You need closure, and that's the only way," he said, sliding his chair back and walking out the door.

FORTY-THREE
LONDON

It had been a month since I lost my baby and fell into a deep depression. Jason and I constantly argued because he slightly blamed me for miscarrying. I was staying in a hotel because I didn't want to be around anyone. I had really lost myself. I knew Jason was cheating on me with someone, but I didn't even bother to speak on it because he would just deny it. In a way, I was glad he was leaving for school next month. I had lost so much weight from stress that I could no longer fit into my size ten clothes. I had to be a cool size eight now. I still had my ass, but my waist was way smaller.

I stood in the bathroom, looked myself over in the mirror, and shook my head. My hair was all over my head, and I had heavy dark circles under my eyes. I hopped in the shower and got out. I refuse to sit in this room and mope around one more day. I need a new wardrobe anyway. I slipped on an oversized Bebe sundress and pulled my hair up into a high ponytail. I grabbed my purse and car key before heading out.

I didn't really feel like driving, so I opted on North Riverside Mall even though I hated this ghetto ass mall. I knew it was going to be overly packed, especially by it being the Fourth of July weekend, but it was the closest one to me at the moment. I walked in praying I didn't run into anyone I knew because I didn't feel like talking to anyone. I just wanted to shop and go.

I walked into Jimmy Jazz to grab the new fall jacket since fall was approaching. Just as I was walking out the store, I spotted one of Paree's talkative ass friends named Netta. I saw her look in my direction, but I made a swift turn and quickly walked into Foot Locker. I grabbed a few pairs of sneakers before hitting a few more clothing stores and stopping at Auntie Anne's Pretzels, grabbing me a cinnamon pretzel.

I made it all the way out to the parking lot without talking to anyone. My luck quickly ran out when I heard Netta yell my name. I tried to ignore her as I tossed my bags in the trunk of my car, but this ghetto bitch walked up and tapped me on the shoulder. I rolled my eyes and took a deep breath before turning around with a fake ass smile.

"What's up, girl? I thought that was you going into Foot Locker, big money," she said, smiling.

"What's up Netta, how you been?"

"Girl, I'm good ready to drop this load," she replied, rubbing her protruding belly.

"I bet," I said, looking away quickly before I got emotional.

"Speaking of loads, how is Paree doing? Did she go through with the abortion pill she had me to get for her? That girl is crazy talking about she had to get rid of the baby before y'all mama found out about it," Netta said unknowingly dry snitching.

Everything she said after abortion pills fell death on my ears, I felt sick to my stomach and light headed. I couldn't believe what I was hearing. She can't be telling me what I think she's telling me. I quickly pulled myself together before she switched the subject. I needed more, and I had to hear it one more time.

"She's fine. I'm guessing she took it because she's definitely not pregnant. When did you give her the pill?"

"Girl, that was a while back maybe like a month ago. She gave me five hundred dollars for that pill, so I know damn well she took it. But let me go before this baby daddy of mine causes a scene. Put my new number in your phone and tell Paree to call me," she said as I locked in her number.

"Bye girl," I said, climbing into my car.

I sat there for at least ten minutes trying to process all of the information that just fell into my lap. I cried until I didn't have any tears left in my eyes, I wanted to kill Paree with my bare hands. I started my car and headed straight the house. I did the dash making it home in less than twenty minutes. I walked in and yelled out Paree's name, making my way to the kitchen. I was beating her ass on sight. I turned the corner and walked right into Bear sitting at the island looking in his phone.

"Where's Paree and my mama?" I asked, getting straight to the point.

"She just went up to shower, and yo OG just left to go grocery shopping for the cookout. Everything good?" he asked, awaiting an answer.

I was about to snap and tell him hell no, but a light bulb instantly popped on in my head, and this was the perfect opportunity. I immediately changed my attitude and took seat across from him. I snatched the rubber band off of my hair and let it hang freely to give off a more seductive look as I licked my lips.

"Yeah, everything is good. I've just been stressing since the miscarriage, but I'm good. How you been though?" I asked, running my finger over his hand.

"I'm good," he said, trying not to make eye contact with me.

I watched as the sweat beaded up on his forehead. This was one ugly ass man. He looked and sounded just like the late rapper Biggie but with dreads. I knew exactly what to do to make him do whatever I wanted. We all know Bear is totally obsessed with Paree, but he would never cross those boundaries unless provoked.

"I know you don't want me, Bear. You want Paree, don't you?" I asked now standing to my feet walking around the island to his side.

He nodded his head up and down. I knew I was turning him on. I took his hand, placed it inside my bra on my right breast, and let him massage it. I wanted to vomit, but I also wanted to make sure his dick hard as a brick before I made my next move. I took his other hand put it under my dress and let him feel my pussy through my panties. He let out a slight moan, and I knew I had him where I wanted him.

"Bear, Paree is different from me. She likes an aggressive man, and you have to take what you want from Paree. You know how hard she is. If you want that pussy, you have to take it. She'll fight with you, but that's what she likes. Now, she's up there in the shower already wet, so go get yo pussy, baby," I whispered in his ear as he wasted no time standing up heading upstairs to her bathroom.

I walked to the top of the stairs as he entered her room, I waited for a few minutes, and then I heard her scream. A smile spread across my face as I heard Bear's moans mixed with her screams. They were knocking shit over in the bathroom, and it sounded like some good rough sex.

"I heard virgin pussy is the best pussy, checkmate bitch," I said as I put my headphones in my ears and walked back down the stairs to the kitchen.

FORTY-FOUR

PAREE

It's the fourth of July weekend, and I can't wait to eat. My mom and Rio went to store to grab the stuff for the cookout. I invited Malik and some more of my friends over, and my mom had a DJ coming through and plenty food and drinks. Everyone knows how lit our cookouts be, so I'm sure we're going to have a full house. I finished cleaning the greens for my mom as Bear sat at the table strolling through his phone. I told him I would be back down. I was going to get dressed before the guest starts arriving.

I climbed into the shower and let the hot water make love to my body, all I could think about was last night with Malik. He had officially turned me straight, and now I know why London had that glow when she lost her virginity. I can't believe I waited this long for some dick. Malik made love to every part of my body, better than any female could ever do. I can't lie though that shit hurt like hell, I'm still sore, but I can't wait to be with him again.

I wanted to tell London about it so bad, but that abortion pill shit was weighing heavy on my conscience, but I'm definitely taking that shit to the grave. London hasn't been herself since the baby died. She barely comes home, and I heard that bitch ass nigga Jason's been fucking with somebody else behind my sister's back, but I'm just waiting to catch it. In a way, I'm glad I saved her from having a baby with his weak ass.

I felt a cool breeze travel up my body as I washed the remaining soap off of my body, it couldn't have been anyone but my momma because London wasn't here, so I didn't bother looking.

"Ma, that's you?" When I didn't get an answer, I turned the water off and snatched the shower curtain back. My eyes grew to the size of golf balls as I came face to face with Bear while he stood there with his dick in his hand as he rolled a condom on. I didn't know what to do so I screamed in hopes of someone hearing me as I climbed out the tub and jetted for the door. My hundred and thirty pounds were no match for his three hundred. Bear slung me around the bathroom like a rag doll, I fought with everything in me, but I knew I had lost when he bent me over on the sink and pinned me down with his arm. I was still fighting to get loose, it wasn't until I felt something heavy go across the back of my head I stopped, and everything went black.

I FELT a soft touch go up my arm to my head as they rubbed my hair. I tried to open my eyes, but it felt like they were glued shut. I felt a warm towel go across my eyes as I slowly opened them. I looked up and instantly wished they were really glued shut as I looked into Bear's eyes. I jumped so hard that I almost fell off the bed. I looked around and realized I was lying in my bed, I tried to get up, but Bear pushed me back down. I said a silent prayer because I just knew he was about to for round two. A nervous feeling filled my body, but I tried my best to act tough and show no signs of fear.

"Get the fuck away from me, fucking rapist. Maaaaaaaa!" I yelled at the top of my lungs.

"She can't hear you over the music, and I'm not a rapist Paree. You wanted this. I see how you look at me and every time I turn around you are bouncing around in some tight ass pants, shirts with no bra, and little ass shorts, so don't play stupid. I just needed that extra push that London gave me," he said, running his fingers through my hair as I turned away.

"Fuck you, you fat sick fuck! You're a liar. My sister has nothing to do with this shit. Wait 'til I tell my momma what you did to me. You a dead man and you know it!" I said as he put his fat ass finger up to my lips shushing me.

"You know you're nothing but a fucking tease. I work for you and London, so I had to do as I was told. And one more thing, I'm not afraid of your mother. I will kill your mother. I know you don't want that, so your best bet is to keep this shit between us. You're my bitch now."

For the first time in my life I wished for my father's presence, I wanted him to help me. I was truly scared, I felt like shit. I was waiting on someone to shake me and wake me up from this bad dream. I couldn't help but wonder why London would do me like this. I knew for a fact she knew nothing about me putting the pill that I put in her drink because it would've been known. I didn't believe in that Karma shit until this very moment. I wish I hadn't put that pill in her drink, I wish I weren't scared to move right now, and most all I wish God would help me. I looked up at the monster standing over me and wanted to curl up in a ball and die. I have never felt so violated and disgusted. I'm glad I gave Malik my virginity last night because this fat bastard would've ripped it away from me today.

"I'm gone have Malik to kill yo ass, and you don't have enough balls to fuck with my OG!" I spat.

"Malik who, that lil bitch ass "boyfriend" of yours? I will cut that lil nigga's head off and send it to his mother's pastor. I'm not to be fucked with. I don't fear a single soul on this earth, now get up, get in the tub, and get dressed before your mother gets back, I'll be waiting downstairs," he said, throwing his dreads back and walking out.

I tried to lift myself up off the bed, but it felt like someone took a sledgehammer to the back of my head and my pussy. I finally forced myself to sit up on the side of my bed as I replayed him busting in the bathroom, I can't believe this nigga raped me, and my own flesh and blood helped him. This man is a real-life monster. I wonder how many other girls have been touched by him. The crazy part is he has two daughters and a wife at home.

I almost jumped out of my skin when my phone started vibrating on the nightstand. I grabbed it and ignored the call as Taylor's name flashed across my screen. I didn't feel like being bothered, before I could sit the phone back down it vibrated again. This time Malik's name flashed, alerting me of a text message.

Malik: What's up baby? Haven't heard from you all day, wyd?

Me: Nothing.

Malik: Damn who blew u, who ass I gotta beat?

Me: Nobody's baby I'm good. Wyd?

Malik: Do I need to bring anything with me?

Me: No, just your appetite.

Malik: Bet.

He has no idea what kind of day I'm having, and I don't plan on telling him, I wish I did have enough balls to tell Malik what happened to me earlier, but I refuse to be the reason behind something happening to him. I knew for a fact Malik was no hoe and had the heart of the biggest lion, but it was something about Bear that didn't sit well with me. He had a fearless look in his eyes. It was a look of death, and the only way to defeat him is to figure out his weakness.

I stood up and slowly walked to my bathroom making sure I locked the door and sat in a tub full of hot water. I sat down and cried for old and new. I feel violated and ugly. I grabbed my towel and scrubbed my body until my skin started to burn, I wanted to wash away Bear touching me, kissing my neck and most of all him penetrating me. I wanted him and London to pay for they did to me, but I knew I couldn't hurt her. I have already done enough to her.

I let my mind go into overdrive and didn't realize I had dozed off until I heard a loud knock on the bathroom door almost causing me to drown. I felt relieved when I heard my mother's voice as she yelled through the door.

"Come downstairs and help me when you get done."

I got out the tub and slowly walked over to my closet and pulled a pair of Nike jogging pants and a tank top out. I didn't want to wear anything too tight or revealing around Bear, I really wanted to stay locked up in my room, but I knew I would have to explain that to my momma. I got dressed, grabbed my phone, and headed downstairs.

I walked into the kitchen and saw London, YG, and Bear carrying stuff out to the backyard. I instantly felt sick at the sight of his ass, and I made sure to keep my distance. I walked into the backyard right pass London and took a seat near the pool. I felt a pair of hands cover my eyes, I quickly grabbed them and uncovered my eyes. I let out a sigh of relief when I looked up saw Malik standing over me looking sexy as hell. I stood to my feet and wrapped my arms his neck as Bear watched from afar. I could see smoke coming from his ears as Malik sat down and pulled me onto his lap. I quickly jumped up when I saw Bear walking toward us.

"You cool, Paree?" Bear asked with no hesitation.

"Why wouldn't I be cool Bear, why does it even matter?"

"Because I'm your bodyguard and it's my job."

"I'm good."

"See you around, Malik," Bear said with a smirk and a head nod.

"I'm right here bro, you can see me now. I'm the wrong nigga to fuck with. Get the fuck on with yo big goofy ass," Malik finally spoke as I grabbed his arm because I know how his temper is.

"Naw, she's the wrong girl to fuck with. See you around," Bear replied now with a straight face before walking off.

FORTY-FIVE
LONDON

I walked out the house feeling great, Paree deserved everything Bear was doing to her conniving ass, and on top of that, it was a beautiful night. I drove with no destination in mind. I ended up turning down Jason's block to see if he was home, so that I could apologize for the way I had been acting. I looked in his driveway and thought my eyes were playing tricks on me, so I circled the block in disbelief as I spotted Cami's car parked next to his car. I hit the corner and pulled up this time, throwing my car in park while watching Jason quickly taking off his sweatshirt, shoving it in his trunk while looking around suspiciously.

He walked over to her car and hopped in. I waited a few minutes before I walked up and tapped on her now fogged up passenger side window. He cracked the window but instantly rolled it back up. My first instinct was to punch to the window, but I knew I would break my hand, so I walked over and picked up a brick out the grass. I drew back and launched the brick with all my might, shattering the window.

I wasted no time swinging, connecting a right jab to the side of Jason's head, causing him to damn near jump in Cami's lap as she scrambled to put her clothes on. I ran around the car, snatched the driver side door open, and pulled Cami out. I connected every punch to her face as she tried to stand up. Jason ran up and grabbed me as I swung wildly. It was at that moment I realized I was making a fool of myself. I was better than this, and I was better than them. I looked at him and then at her. I felt like my chest was about to cave in as I tried to catch my breath. I bent over, put my hands on my knees, and got my breathing under control.

I stood up and looked Jason dead in the eyes. He couldn't even sustain eye contact with me. He just turned his head and looked away. I wanted to kill him and her, but instead I slapped the shit out him and turned to leave as he ran behind me.

"Baby, I'm sorry. I swear to God this shit was an accident. She just showed up. Come on, London. We can fix this," he said, sounding just as dumb as he was looking right now.

"Jason really? I have no respect for you. Out of all of the hoes out here, you run back to that bitch. She can have you back. I don't want you, I'm done. You deserve a bitch a like her. A dog ass bitch for a bitch ass nigga," I replied as tears fell from my eyes.

"Look, I never meant to hurt you London, but you can chill with that "bitch" shit. I apologized now if you don't accept the shit, I don't know what to tell you. I fucked up now either you gone forgive me or keep shit moving," he said as I looked at him with a stale face.

"Do you hear how fucking stupid you sound? There will never be anything between us again. That shit is just as dead as those weak ass lines you just put together. You got me good with this one but I'm good. Love lost is love learned. Bye Jason with yo BITCH ass." I replied as I hopped in my car, leaving him standing there.

"FUCK YOU!" he yelled while raising his middle fingers in the air.

I waited for him walk back toward his house before I broke completely down, I felt like God was whooping me. What did I do to deserve all the things that were happening to me? Every time I love something or someone, it gets taken away from me. I watched as he walked into his house and closed the door as Cami flew out of the driveway. I couldn't help but think about my baby. Maybe it wasn't meant for me to bring a child into this fucked up world with that sorry ass nigga. When I finally pull off from this nigga's house, I'm leaving all of the baggage that belongs to him right here. I sat there and cried for my unborn baby because it had no chance at life, and here this nigga was fucking on the same bitch he claimed to hate. I'm done beating myself up. This moment is the beginning of the rest of my life, and I will carry on as such.

My phone vibrated in the cup holder and scared the shit out of me. I picked it up and saw a new message alert from YG. I immediately opened it. It didn't matter how busy this man was he always checked up on me and my sister. I knew he had a crush on me, but I was too damn loyal to Jason while he was playing house with another bitch.

YG: Yo shorty, you need to double back to the crib ASAP.

Me: Is everything ok?

YG: NO...

FORTY-SIX

SINCERE

I drove to the address my father gave me to scope shit out for the third night in a row to learn how this lady moves, but I must say she had her shit together and her security was on point. I wanted to see what my mother's killer looked like in person. This bitch killed a part of me, so I was itching to put a bullet in her head. I don't know the entire story behind her killing my mother, but it had something to do with my pop. I tried so hard to reflect on my childhood and remember why this lady looked so familiar to me, but the weed had my memory all fucked up.

I had been out here for over an hour, and all I heard was loud music and voices, I'm guessing there's a party going on. I made sure I sat a few feet away from the crib. This lady had to be a real boss because there was nothing but foreign cars sitting in the driveway. I knew her all of her security with the exception of two left around eleven every night, but I could tell this was going to be an extra-long stakeout. I also know some nigga named YG is the muscle behind her operation, so you know what that means.

I dozed off but was awakened by the sound of my phone vibrating. I looked at the private call through my line. I picked it up and put it right back down, before turning my attention toward the house. It looked like the party was finally over and everyone had left. I watched what looked like the last four cars pulled out of the driveway and waited for another hour to let her get settled. Once I saw the lights go off, that was my cue to make my move. I twisted my silencer on both of my pistols before exiting my car. I knew the exact layout of this house so going in should be a breeze.

I tiptoed around the side of the house and entered through a low-key door. The house smelled like fresh flowers, and even though it was dark as hell, I could slightly see that everything was top of the line. I recited the layout in my head and knew a set of stairs were coming up to my left. I slowly made my way up to the second level and down the hall. I stood outside of the master bedroom and looked through the slightly cracked door.

"What the fuck?" I said under my breath as another person dressed in all black with a hood covering their head stood over the bed and let off an entire clip, I tried to stick around long enough to see who it was but just as fast as they went out the window I went back down the stairs and out the door. Once I made it to my car, I pulled my phone from my pocket and dialed my pop's number.

"Hello."

"Pop, somebody beat me to it. Some nigga was already fucking the bitch when I got there, and he emptied all of his kids on her body." I said, referring to the nigga emptying his clip on the woman.

"You sure she wasn't moaning when you left?" he said, asking was she still alive when I left.

"Nah, the dick left her limp. She couldn't move."

"Good, move around. It's takeover time."

My pop was letting this lady run the city and stayed out the way, but one of his informants told my father she was trying to give the business to two new recruits. He never mentioned who these "recruits" were, but he wasn't having that shit, which is partially why he wanted her dead. I couldn't help but wonder how he could allow someone who killed the mother of his child to live this long, but I guess this business shit is more important. I look up to my pop because it takes a strong ass man to lose so much but still manage to be on top. He is one of the realest men I know, and I respect him for that. My whole life he made sure I've never wanted for anything and protected me with his life.

The sound of someone tapping on my window pulled me out of my thoughts. I upped my gun off instinct. Malik chuckled, moving his dreads out of his face. I let the passenger side window down as he leaned down. I laid my gun on my lap before giving him my undivided attention.

"Yo scary ass, what you doing in this area?" he asked, laughing.

"Nigga, fuck you. Shit, I was just around the corner at Jason's crib. I pulled over to call my pop back. What you doing on this block?" I lied.

"Paree lives over here."

"Where nigga?" I asked curiously.

My question was answered when I saw Paree run out the same house I had just left out of screaming. Malik turned around and ran toward her as she collapsed in his arms and cried loudly. I got out and walked over to them just to hear her confirm what I already knew, but I was still wondering how the twins are tied to this bitch.

"BABY, WHAT'S WRONG?!" Malik yelled, trying to make out what Paree was trying to say.

"THEY KILLED MY MOMMA."

FORTY-SEVEN
LONDON

I received a 911 text from Paree directly after YG's telling me to come home immediately. I was already on my way home, but I really didn't have shit to say to Paree. I never thought I would end up disliking my sister, but I do. I still can't believe she killed my baby on some selfish shit. I don't believe in holding grudges because life is too short, but I do believe in forgiving and never fucking with you again. I don't feel an ounce of regret for putting Bear on her. Fuck her and that dirty bitch Cami.

I really don't feel like being bothered if it isn't pertaining business. I've been keeping track of all of the money coming in from each trap house on the west side. I must say I'm good at what I do. As soon as a muthafucka thought they were slick and tried to short us, I was able to pinpoint exactly who it was. In the short time, we've been in the game, I have learned a lot about loyalty and believe me money overpowers it! I'm a fool with the numbers, I often thought about going to college, but I was already making six figures at eighteen, so what did I need college for? I wasn't with the whole getting my hands dirty, so I left that to Paree and the rest of the crew, but I had no problem shooting my .9mm gun my mom gave Paree and me as a welcome gift. I always kept it on me just in case. I thank God I didn't have it in my hands when I walked up to that car because I would've shot them both.

I turned down our block and instantly started shaking as what looked like a hundred police cars surrounded our house. I was holding myself together until I saw red tape with let me know it was something serious. I looked around and noticed Paree crying uncontrollably in Malik's arms. I finally convinced myself to kill the engine and get out. I saw Bear walking toward me as I stepped out. He came and tried to wrap his arm around me, but I was trying to get to Paree. I pushed pass Bear and ran to my sister.

"Paree, what happened? Talk to me."

"Somebody killed her. They killed mommy, London. She's gone!" Paree yelled with every word cutting through my soul.

I knew the words that just left her mouth couldn't have been true. My mother is too smart to get caught lacking like that. For someone to make it inside of the house without her security catching it was hard to believe. It's either one or two things, a lie or a setup, and I'm about to get to the bottom of it. I left Paree there with Malik and made my over to YG who stood as close as he could to the house without crossing the tape.

"YG, tell me this is not happening right now."

"Man, I'm sorry shorty, but it's happening, and shit just got real."

"I just don't understand. There was no beef with anyone. Why would someone come for her? My next question is WHERE THE FUCK WERE Y'ALL AT?" I yelled, walking closer to him as tears formed in my eyes.

"First thing you gone do is lower your voice and act like you have a little sense in the presence of all of these fucking police. Second, don't speak on shit you know nothing about. When you're done speaking with these pigs I'll be waiting in my truck for you and Paree," YG said walking off leaving me standing there.

"FUCK THAT, FUCK THIS, AND FUCK YOU! I want my

momma!" I screamed at the top of my lungs before he turned around walking back toward me, wrapping his arms around me.

"It's ok man, I promise," he replied while allowing me to soak his Gucci V-neck with my tears.

YG DROVE for seemed like forever while Paree and I cried on and off. Even though we had just lost our mother, it didn't take away from the fact that I still wasn't fucking with her because of the shit she did to me. I know at some point we are going to have to come together and figure out what to do next in our lives, but now is not that time. I want to be angry and violent but toward who? We have no idea who is behind this shit. My mother hasn't had an enemy in years, and she treated everyone around her with the utmost respect.

I'm really in my feelings because the police wouldn't even let us see her body before they removed it from the house. They told us we could identify the body at the morgue and handed us a business card before dismissing us. Rio was nowhere to be found, and that alone raised all kind of red flags in my mind because he never leaves her side.

We pulled up to a small two-story home, which I'm assuming is YG's house. I made a mental note to keep a close eye on him. I walked ahead of him as we entered the house my sandals clicked across the floor. It was nicely decorated. I could tell it was a bachelor pad from the black and red color scheme. YG told us to have a seat before he disappeared to the back of the house.

"What the fuck is your problem?" Paree blurted out as I cut my eyes in her direction.

"Stop talking to me. You ain't shit! Momma said you were just like that nigga Kayo, dirty and conniving," I replied.

"Yeah well, Kayo must've been that nigga! I'm sick of your spoiled ass, I didn't do shit to you, and I'm not about to kiss yo ass, the fuck."

"And bitch I never asked you to!" I replied now standing to my feet.

"Fuck you standing up for you ain't gone shake shit," Paree replied also standing.

"Bitch, I'll beat yo..."

"Both of y'all shut the fuck up!" my mother yelled silencing and shocking us both by her presence.

I wanted to run and hug her, but we had clearly pissed her off. She stood near the stairwell looking flawless as usual. She had her signature honey blonde high ponytail, a black bodycon dress that stopped right above her knees and a pair of black pointed toe Louboutin stilettos. Bear came out of nowhere and stood next to my mother, Paree rolled her eyes as we followed our mother to a different room. We all took a seat as Bear eased his way in, I looked at Paree as disgust covered her face. It was obvious she hated him.

"This is a family meeting, why is he present?" Paree asked with no filter.

"Because he's your bodyguard Paree, and you have to learn to trust him. Now is not the time for the stubborn shit, it's too much going on," my mother calmly replied as Bear gave off a devilish grin.

"Naw ma, she's right. I have some personal shit I need to talk to y'all about," I said as Bear shot me a dirty look.

"Ok Bear, I'm sorry, but can you excuse us please," my mother said quickly dismissing him.

He walked out pulling the door up behind him but not closing it. I got up and slammed it closed. Paree slightly smiled at me, but I wasn't returning shit. I was still hot with her ass. I returned to my seat and directed my attention to my mother who was sitting pretty.

"First and foremost, I'm sorry for scaring the shit out of you two, but I had to come to a safe place because as you know, someone wants me dead. I have every ear and eye to the streets, so whoever it is knows my every move. The only reason I'm alive is because I made a run. I would've been lying in my bed."

"Wait, so who was shot if it wasn't you? And where is Uncle Rio?" I asked.

"Right before the barbeque ended Rio's ass got drunk, and I told him to go lie across my bed and sleep the shit off. I fucked up!" She said as tears formed in her eyes.

"Damn ma, I'm sorry," Paree said, holding her head down.

"You ok?" I asked my mother instantly feeling bad for even thinking Rio played a part in this.

"I'll be ok, but it's all a part of the game. Some losses are small, and some are big. This was a big one. I lost my friend. I almost got caught lacking but don't worry that shit will never happen again," she replied, resting her chin on her crossed hands while resting her elbows on the table.

I could see the hurt and pain in my mother's eyes. I watched as she tried to be tough and stop the tears that were in her eyes. I knew shit was about to get real because everyone in the city knew better than to fuck with Kyana. Whoever it is has to be suicidal.

"What's up ma? I'm ready for whatever," Paree said as I loudly popped my lips followed by rolling my eyes.

"What the fuck is going on with the two of you. I'm not too busy to notice when some shit isn't right. You all don't talk nor hang around one another unless I'm present. London, you haven't stayed home since you lost the baby, and I understand you are hurt, but this shit has to stop," my mother said looking back and forth from me to Paree.

"I'm good, ma. I didn't lose my baby it was taken away from me, care to explain, Paree?" I replied, putting her on full blast as my mother shifted her weight and lowered her freshly manicured hands while awaiting a response from Paree.

"Really London? Yeah ma, I paid one of my friends for an abortion pill and gave it to her. I fucked up, and I'm sorry, but I didn't want her to ruin her life, I did you a favor." Paree replied nonchalantly before my mother smacked fire from her ass.

Paree jumped up and ran toward the door, but I grabbed her and hugged her. At that moment, I forgave her as she balled in my arms. She could've easily told my mother what Bear did to her, but she didn't, and I know she didn't say anything because she knew I had something to do with it, I'm pretty sure Bear told her. My mother stood up and made both of us sit back down.

"Paree, you could've killed her. You had no clue how her body could've reacted to that pill. I know I taught you better than that. If you ever do some shit like that again, I will hurt you myself. You hurt those muthafuckas in the streets. You and your sister are all I got, and I'll be damned if I sit back watch you all destroy one another. Make this the first and last time you all go without speaking, I will not tolerate that shit!" my mother yelled with fire in her eyes.

"I'm sorry. I'm so sorry," Paree said, breaking down as my mother walked over and held her.

"Look at me both of you. There is a hit placed on my head, so I know the house is being watched. I want you to listen to me. I know once they find out they missed, they are going to come harder. If they can't get me, I know they will come for you all, and I'm not having it. After we are done here, go to this address. It's another estate I purchased a while back, it's already fully furnished, and your closets are full. You are not to go back to the house. No one except YG and Bear knows about this place, so they are the only guest you should be expecting besides me, and YG has a key. Do not bring anyone to this house, not Malik, not Jason, no one! Stay there and wait for me to contact to you. Keep your pistols with you at all times and do not be afraid to use them," she said in a very low tone.

"But ma we are a part of this business, let us help you. I will not sit back and let these motherfuckers come for you," Paree said as my mother grabbed our hands.

"I said NO Paree, and this is not up for discussion. I can't risk losing one of you. I'll handle it. They can't fuck with me, and they know it. I just need you to follow my instructions. Your cars should be outside by now, I love you!" she said, standing up straight on her heels.

I swear she is so bossy, and the true definition of a leader. She's standing here stronger than both of us with God knows how many people wanting to put a bullet in her head for rank, but you could never tell by looking at her. She still managed to smile just to put us at ease even though I know she's dying on the inside. All I could do was hug her and my sister and follow her directions as we walked toward the door.

I walked out first and caught a glimpse of Bear's fat ass shadow turning the corner, which only confirmed what I already knew. He was definitely listening outside the door probably trying to see if Paree had told on him. I know I fucked up by putting him on Paree, but he won't be around long. He wasted no time asking Paree where she was going like he was her father, but I got his ass right together.

"You work for her not the other way around. Humble yourself, my dude."

"My bad, Ms. London," he replied with a smirk while throwing his hands up in the air.

Yeah, he's gone be the first body I catch.

FORTY-EIGHT

PAREE

The drive to this new house was long as hell. We have already been driving for forty minutes, and my GPS still says fifteen more minutes. I understand she wants us to be safe, but damn, we in the country. Ain't shit out here but trees and gas stations. I don't know how long I can stay out here without going crazy, and I'm too far from Malik.

We finally pulled up to the most beautiful house that I had ever laid eyes on. It made our other house look like shit. When my OG upgraded, she really upgraded. It had to be sitting on at least five acres. I drove up to the gate and entered the code on the back of the paper my mother gave us as London pulled up right behind me.

I was wowed by the huge water fountain that sat in the center of winding driveway. The entire house was lit up, and it was gorgeous. Trees surrounded it, and the neighbor's house had to be at least a half block down. The house was looked like a celebrity resided in it. This was just too much damn space. The grass was neatly cut, and the bushes were trimmed nicely, I can't wait to see what the inside looks like. I put my car in park and got out at the same time as London as she smiled and looked around like a kid in a candy shop.

"This is some shit out of a movie," she said slowly walking toward the huge brick porch that leads up to a humongous set of double doors.

"Hell yeah, but let me holla at you before we go in," I replied as she stopped and leaned up against the banister giving me her undivided attention.

"London, I'm truly sorry about the abortion. I was jealous and selfish. I put this drug shit before you and didn't even care how you felt about it. I just hope you could find it your heart to forgive me. I wish I could take it back; I swear I do."

"Paree, it's cool. It's done and over with. I need to tell you something though, and I hope you can forgive me too. I sent Bear upstairs to bust in the bathroom on you. I'm so sorry. I only did it because I ran into Netta at the mall, and she told me about the pill. I was coming home to beat yo ass, but I ran into him first," she said, confirming what Bear said, but I can't even be mad.

"I will forgive you under one condition."

"What's that, twin?"

"Help me get his fat ass back."

"Aw hell yeah, you know I'm with it. I have one more thing to tell you."

"Aw shit, what London?" I asked curiously.

"I caught Cami and Jason fucking. I should've listened to you when you told me he wasn't shit," she said as sadness covered her face.

"You WHAT?" I asked practically yelling.

"Yeah, after I left the cookout, I rode over there to see if he was home so that we could fix our relationship, and when I pulled up, Cami's car was parked next to his. He was standing at his trunk looking around suspiciously, so I sat there and watched him. Bitch, he got in, and I sat there and watched her windows fog up, so I jumped out and tapped the window. When he wouldn't let it down, I busted it, and there she was asshole naked. I wanted to kill them both."

"You should've, but it's ok. He lost good bitch. You know the best way to hurt a nigga's feelings is to act like he never existed."

Now we have muthafuckin' problem, it's one thing for me to hurt my sister, but them two got me fucked up. My list just gained a couple more people. I didn't want to tell her "I told you so", so instead, I just hugged her as she cried in my arms. We stood there and vented and cried for a few more minutes. We left all of that we did to each other outside as we crossed the threshold of our new home. We wanted nothing but good vibes in this house.

We stood under the biggest chandler I ever seen in my life. Two winding staircases led up to the second level. To the left was a living room and to the right a second living room. We walked through the first level and ended up in the backyard, and it was breathtaking. The pool was three times bigger than our other one, and it had pink lights with a surrounding deck and outside furniture. This is definitely where most of my time will be spent.

We finally made it up to the second level. I couldn't understand why my mother purchased an eight-bedroom house, but hell who's complaining? We went to our bedrooms, which were on total opposite sides of the house. My mother put out names on the door like we were still kids and shit, but it was cute. My mother had already marked her territory, and her bedroom alone was a mini apartment. She had a California king size canopy bed that sat so high up off the floor that you would have to run and jump on it. She topped it off with a custom-made silk bed set with her name stitched on the pillows.

I walked into my room and went straight to the closet. I knew my mom had brought me some dope shit. I swear to God no lie my closet looks like another bedroom. She filled it every designer you could name mixed with my favorite Victoria Secret PINK outfits. She even had my sneaker game on point. I couldn't help but start trying on shit. I played around in my closet until I got tired.

I laid across my queen size sleigh bed and thought about Malik until I dozed off. It wasn't until I heard a loud ass noise that I jumped up. I tiptoed to the hallway, looked over the banister, and didn't see anything. I flew my ass to London's room and pushed her door open, but she wasn't in there. My heart rate instantly sped up as I felt my bra for my phone and dialed London number, but it started vibrating on her bed. I grabbed it and stuck it my bra before creeping back to my room to grab my pistol.

I crept back out and slowly walked down the stairs. I was moving through this big ass house like James Bond in the movie 007. I got close to the kitchen and paused as a glass hit the floor and shattered. I took a deep breath and turned the corner with my gun pointed. I slowly lowered it when I saw YG standing between London's legs as she sat on the counter. I looked down at the pots on the floor and figured out what that loud ass noise was. They were so wrapped up in the spit they were swapping they didn't even notice me standing there. I just smiled and slowly backed out. I'm happy for her. She deserves a good nigga. I just hope I don't have to hurt him for hurting her.

FORTY-NINE
LONDON

I walked downstairs to grab a bottle of water out the refrigerator and heard the front door open. I peeped my head around the corner to see if it was my mother. I almost choked on my water when I saw it was YG/ I tried to make a run for the stairs when I realized I was wearing a wife beater and a pair of panties. I was too slow because he grabbed my arm before I reached the first step as I pulled my tank top down as low as I could trying to cover myself.

"What up? You look like you seen a ghost," he asked, looking me dead in the eyes never once looking down at my body.

"Yeah, I'm good. I just wasn't expecting you to pop up," I replied.

"You want me to leave?"

"NO! Look I like you, YG. I've liked ever since the first day I saw you, but I just knew it could never be shit between us because you work for my mother, so I pushed that shit out my head. But, I'm grown, and I want you," I said, inhaling his cologne as he looked away then back at me.

"I work "with" your mother not for your mother, and I'm nothing like the lil niggas you're used to fucking with. I'm a grown man,

London. I can make you or break you," he replied slightly scaring me while turning me on at the same damn time.

"And I'm a grown woman, YG. I don't act like most girls my age. I'll be all for you if you promise to be all for me," I said, walking up so close that I could smell the Ice Breaker mints on his breath.

"I don't make promises because they can be broken, but I will tell you this. Once you're with me London, you're with me, so I'm gone let you think about it."

"I already thought about it," I replied, tracing his lips with my tongue as he backed me up to the counter and sat me on it.

I can't believe I'm actually in this kitchen kissing this man. Somebody, please pinch me. I don't know what the fuck came over me, but I'm glad it did. It felt like my pussy was gone bust through my panties my shit was throbbing so hard. We kissed for seemed like forever until I finally grabbed his hand and led it to my pussy. This is definitely a man the way he was touching and kissing me. It made me think I was just practicing with Jason. This man was making me cum back to back just by playing with my pussy and talking shit in my ear.

I jumped down off the counter and walked up the stairs with him in tow. Once we reached my room, I stripped down ass hole naked as he stood in the doorway and watched. I walked to him and dropped down to my knees and tried to go for his belt, but he stopped me and pulled me up as confusion covered my face.

"Why you stop me?"

"Because to be honest, I have a million hoes that can suck my dick. I'm on some other shit with you, and besides when I put this dick up in you, ain't no turning back," he said, pulling me down on his lap as he flopped down on my bed and kicked his Christian Louboutin sneakers off.

"Umm ok," I replied clearly salty as hell, putting my wife beater and panties back on.

We laid there talking, laughing and chain smoking blunts, I learned his real name and how he caught his first body by saving my mother's life. I fell in love with his personality. I just pray he doesn't hurt me.

I had the best sleep I had in a long time being in his arms, but when I woke up, the nigga was gone. I mean he didn't leave a note or shit, and this that shit I don't like. I was about to grab my phone and send his ass a dirty text, but Paree came and stood in my doorway dressed in white fitted button up, a black high waist pencil skirt, and a pair of black pointed toe pumps like she was on her way to a business meeting.

"Where the fuck you going?" I asked.

"WE got shit to do. Get dressed, and you need to steal an outfit out of momma closet like I did. Hurry up!"

I have no idea where we're going, but it must be very important for her to be up before nine o'clock and dressed like a girly girl. I showered and walked to my mom's room and slipped on a tight black dress and my Loubs. I pulled hair back into a neat low ponytail and put on a pair black clear lens glasses to give off the teacher look. I walked downstairs, set the alarm on the house, and met Paree in her car.

We rode on the 290 expressway for about an hour before she came up in Central. I was truly confused because we were definitely overdressed for the hood. I was also nervous as hell because we were told not to leave the house. I swear Paree's ass is always persuading me to do the wrong shit.

We pulled up to a nice little two-story townhouse that looked too nice to be in the neighborhood we were in. Paree flipped her mirror down and applied some lipstick before handing it to me. This bitch is really creeping the fuck out now because never in our eighteen years on earth have I seen her wear lipstick.

"Ok bitch, whose house is this?" I finally asked, pointing at the house.

"Bear's, let's go," she replied, grabbing her door handle before I stopped her.

"Why didn't you fill me in about the plot?" I asked totally unprepared for whatever she has up her sleeve.

"This is exactly why I didn't tell you. Just follow my lead and let me talk," she replied handing me my pistol that I totally forgot to grab before we left.

I walked behind Paree as she balanced her weight perfectly on her six-inch heels. She walked right up to the porch and rang the bell. A short petite woman who looked to be in her early thirties answered the door politely as she wiped her hands on a towel. I couldn't help wondering how in the hell this lady ended up marrying that ugly ass man.

"Hello, how may I help you?" The woman asked.

"Hello Mrs. Marks, I'm Monique Jones, and this is my twin sister Domonique Jones, and together we represent "A Reason to Grow" foundation. It's basically something fun and safe for your girls to do over the summer. We do fundraisers, community service, and lots of other fun things. I spoke with your husband Mr. Marks earlier this week, and he told me today would be a great day stop by and go more in-depth with you about the program," Paree replied, sounding like an amateur. If this lady believes that shit, she's a dummy.

"Ok hold on one second. Let me get my husband. Derrickkkkkk!" she yelled out.

I looked at Paree who was holding her composer very well while I started sweating bullets. It wasn't until their daughter who looked like a girl version of Bear walked up and said he was gone, I felt relieved. I let out a sigh of relief as the woman invited us in and just like that, the operation fuck up Bear's life was in full effect.

"So where are your papers and stuff?" she asked, offering us a seat as she sat between her daughters on the couch while sizing us up.

"Right here," Paree said, pulling her pistol from the back of her skirt and aiming it directly at the woman.

The woman didn't scream or anything, but her daughters were screaming and crying as she put her arms around them.

"You can kill me, but please don't hurt my babies. They're just kids. Please don't take their lives," she said with pleading eyes.

"Fuck that, I'm just a teenager, and your husband took my life when he forced himself inside of me. He took from me, so it's only right I take from him," Paree said putting a bullet at a time in each daughter's head as their mother broke down.

"Fuck this, we have to get out of here," I replied, pulling my pistol from behind my back pointing it at the woman with a shaking hand, pulling the trigger as her body slumped over.

We hurried and power walked back to the car before all of the nosey ass people started coming out to see what was going on. Paree turned the car on before pulling a government phone from the glove compartment and handing it to me.

"Text his bitch ass and tell him what's up. It's the 773 number."

Me: There's been an emergency at your house bitch ass nigga.

FIFTY
BEAR

Seeing my wife on that couch with her brains blown out really didn't faze me. My kids, on the other hand, really did something to me. I never wanted the shit I did in the streets to come back on them, but Karma does no fucking around. I was so wrapped up in Paree that I had neglected my wife anyway. I didn't want to touch her anymore; my dick only got hard for Paree. I knew the shit I did to her could cause me to lose my life, but she is my life. I was loyal to Kyana all the way up until the day she introduced me to Paree. I could tell by the way she first looked at me she wanted me in her life, and I will stop at nothing to have her in mine.

I parked two cars over as I watched Paree throw her bags in the trunk of her car, I wanted to jump out right then and there, but it was too many people around. I didn't have to follow her because I knew her every move. I have never loved another woman like I love Paree, not even my wife. I started my engine and pulled out right behind her as she headed towards the 290, I knew it wouldn't be long before she would be pulling over to the shoulder due to the holes I poked in her tires. I followed for about two minutes, and just like that, she pulled over, and so did I. Luckily the sun had just gone down, so it was kind of dark.

I was in a rental, so she had no idea who I was pulling up behind her as she put her phone up to her ear. As soon as she ended the call, I popped my trunk and hopped out. I walked up as she bent over to look at her tire and put a black pillowcase over her head as she kicked and scream. I lifted her up off the ground, carried her to the back of my car, and dropped her in. I didn't want to hit her, but I had to draw back and punch her with all my might to knock her out and make her stop screaming. I made a mental note to apologize to my baby later.

I grabbed her keys and purse out of her car and quickly jumped into my car and pulled off. Where we were going, I wasn't worried about anyone finding us. I knew she killed my wife, so we could be together. Hell, she did what I was about to do anyway. My neighbor told me he saw two beautiful women that looked like twins leaving my house on the day the murders took place, which let me know it was Paree and London. I knew I could give Paree the life she deserved which is why I brought us a house way out with no neighbors to disturb us as we start our new family and life.

I reached into my pocket for my phone to call YG, so I could tell him I'm leaving town to clear my head so that my disappearance wouldn't seem suspicious. I patted both pockets before lifting my body up in the seat to feel my back pockets, but my phone wasn't here. FUCK, I yelled out loud realizing I had to have dropped my shit when I was fighting to get her ass in the trunk. I came up at the next exit and hopped right back on in the opposite direction, and I saw Paree's car parked in the same spot as a smile spread across my face.

By the time I made it back around to her car, London had pulled up along with AAA roadside assistance. I knew I couldn't stop so I said fuck it and kept going. Fuck that phone. I don't care if they know I have her. They'll never see me or her again anyway. I plan on getting her pregnant as soon as possible because I'm ready to be a father again since she took my kids away from me.

I HAD BEEN DRIVING for almost an hour before I heard a loud noise in the trunk, which let me know my love was up and alert.

"Don't worry baby we're almost home!" I yelled toward the back.

I can't believe I finally got my baby to myself. There would be no sneaking, no hiding in her closet to watch her get dressed, no jacking off to her picture, just me and her. I went shopping and got her all the designer clothes that I knew she like, not that she was going anywhere, but I wanted her to be comfortable and feel at home. I even got a couple of extra bedrooms for the kids and a pool in the back. I just want to make her happy. I knew the life she was accustom to, and I planned on picking up right where Kyana left off. Paree will never want for anything because whatever she wants she will get as long as I have breath in my body.

I finally pulled up to our brand new two-story home. I made sure it was equipped with a home gym and game room. I opened my door, and her screams got louder as I moved closer to the trunk. I unlocked it with the key and tried to grab her, but she looked up at me and started kicking and fighting so, I punched her ass again but not as hard as the first time. I picked her up, carried up the stairs, and twisted the already unlocked door.

I walked her up the stairs and took her to our master bedroom. I laid her on the bed and tied her arms to the bed because I knew she would be scared the first few nights until she got comfortable. I stood there and watched my baby as she adjusted her eyes and tried to figure out her location. I made sure the house was escape proof by drilling all of the windows shut and putting skeleton key locks on every door in the house, and I only had one key that I kept on me. I made sure the house was filled with enough food to last us for a while so that we wouldn't have to leave the house.

"Welcome home, baby," I said as she looked up at me with tears in her eyes, but I knew they were tears of joy.

"Bear, take these fucking things off my arms and let me go! Where am I? I wanna go home," she said as she cried.

"This is your home for now until forever so get used to it. I'll take you on a tour and show our kids rooms when you calm down."

"Are you fucking crazy or stupid? My family will find me and kill you. You just signed your own death certificate."

"Yeah Paree, I'm crazy about you. I know you killed my wife and kids so that we could be together. That shit just showed me how much you care, so here we are together, and I hope you're ready to be a mother because I want my kids back."

"You got me fucked up. I wouldn't birth your ugly ass kids in this world if my life depended on it!"

"Funny you said that because your life does depend on it," I said, turning to walk out the room.

I stopped dead in my tracks when I heard a cellphone ring. Paree looked at me and started kicking her legs wildly as I remembered I had dropped her phone inside of her purse, I reached in and grabbed her phone as "twin" flashed across the screen. I slid the bar over and rejected the call sending it straight to voicemail before powering it off.

"You don't need this anymore. I'm the only person you will be in contact with from here on out."

FIFTY-ONE
LONDON

I pulled over to the shoulder right behind Paree's car and stepped out, but she was nowhere in sight. I had been calling her phone nonstop since she gave me her location, and I called AAA to meet me there. It wasn't like her not to answer her phone, especially when she's the one that needed help. I walked over to her car, looked inside, and noticed all of her belongings were gone. I knew she wouldn't leave this spot without calling to tell me, so I knew something wasn't right. I pulled my phone from my pocket, dialed her number again, and still didn't get an answer. After giving the AAA driver all of my information and a location to drop her car off, I turned to go back to my car but not before stepping down on something. I looked down and noticed a cell phone. I quickly bent over and picked it up. It wasn't an iPhone, so I know it didn't belong to Paree. I pressed the side button to power it on, but it was dead, stuffed it in my pocket, and dialed my mother's number. I knew she was about raise all kind of hell.

I SAT on the couch silently as my mother flipped the hell out and paced the floor. I didn't want to tell her that Paree was missing because I knew it would hurt her and she was going through enough, but I had to think about my sister. I just pray to God she's ok. I told her ass not to leave the crib, but she just had to be the rebel she's always been. If you tell Paree to go right, she would make a left. That's just her. I called Malik and asked him had he seen her. He said no, but he would be over asap to assist us in finding her. I told him that wasn't necessary, but he wouldn't take no for an answer.

I was kicking my own ass because I should've known she was lying when she said she was going to the gas station up the street for some blunts because we never ran out of blunts. YG stood near the window drinking a bottle of water before my mother stopped pacing and turned to him.

"Where is Bear?" My mother asked.

"I have the slightest idea. That nigga's been bugging ever since that shit happened to his people," YG responded.

I knew I should've been told my mother everything that has been going on right under her nose, but I knew she would tear my head off my shoulders if she found out Bear had raped Paree. I contemplated for about five minutes before I conjured up enough courage to tell them everything that has been going on.

"Ma, I need to tell you something," I said as she turned her attention away from YG to me.

"What London? Tell me this isn't one of those childish ass games you and your sister like to play. Paree bring yo ass out here!" she yelled.

I wish this were a prank that we were pulling like we often did as kids but the shit I'm about to say is definitely not a game.

"She's not here, ma. The same day that we had the barbeque and Rio got killed, Bear raped Paree."

"WHAT THE FUCK DO YOU MEAN?" she yelled while YG gave me a stale look.

I was shaking uncontrollably as I forced the next sentence out of my mouth as tears formed in my eyes.

"I didn't mean to put him on her, but when I found out she gave me that pill, I lost it. I swear I didn't mean to," I said as my mother snatched me up out of my seat by my collar while I wrapped my hands around her wrist.

"What the fuck is wrong with y'all? I don't understand. Kayo left his fucking mark on earth with the two of you. I really should beat the fuck out you, but I will probably end up killing you out of anger!" she spat as a mist of spit hit my face.

"Momma, please just listen to me! We killed his family to pay him back for raping her, so I think he has Paree. Ma, he's obsessed with her."

"Oh my God, this shit unbelievable. YG get on top of it. Find his whereabouts; I'm gone kill this nigga," she said now pacing again.

I sat there scared to make a move because I had never seen the look that covered my mother's face. She looked like Satan's spawn.

"London, was her keys in her car when you got there?" my mother asked I guess trying to put two and two together.

I shook my head no before remembering the cell phone I found and pulling it out of my pocket.

"I found this phone by her car, but it's dead," I said as my mother took it from my hand and looked directly at YG.

"That's why his shit going straight to voicemail," YG said as my mother cursed aloud and connected the phone to a charger.

"That's a dead man, I'm sick of muthafuckas trying me!" my mother yelled, causing me to jump.

The doorbell rang, and I jumped up to answer it because I knew it was Malik. I opened the door and turned to walk back in the living room, but not before telling Malik to close the door.

"My cousin with me, is that cool?" Malik asked as Sincere walked in behind him.

"Yeah, what's up Sin?" I said followed by a head nod.

"What up, you cool?" he asked as I shook my head yes.

The truth is my head is all fucked up. I don't know what I'm gone do if something happens to my sister. I'm praying for the best, but also preparing myself for the worse.

We walked back into the living room, and my mother looked up like she had just seen a ghost before softly saying, "Sincere."

FIFTY-TWO

KYANA

I looked up and thought I had seen a ghost. It looked like I was staring directly into Kayo's eyes. The only difference between Sincere and Kayo when he was younger were the tattoos that covered Sincere's body. For the first time in a long time, I was speechless. I stood there with an appalling expression spread across my face. He looked at me with curiosity as to say how do I know his name. I wanted to hug him, but my feet felt like they were cemented to the floor. I searched high and low for the relative that took him in after Neka and Kayo died, but every address I went to, the houses were vacant. I just wanted to know he was ok. I never stopped thinking about this kid.

"How do you know my name?" he finally asked.

"I knew your mother. She was a very close friend of mine." I replied as Sincere slightly lowered his head.

"Oh yeah?" he replied with little emotion.

"Yeah, it's a shame what happened to her and your father. I knew them both very well," I said, trying to see where his head was at.

"Wait what you mean? I think you have me confused with somebody else. My pops ain't dead. He's good."

"It's Paree!" London yelled as my heart fell into my ass from Sincere's last comment.

I could barely focus on what London was saying because Sincere had just fucked my whole understanding up. This shit can't be true. I watched this nigga die, and ten years later, he reappears? What kind of Tupac, Makaveli shit is this? I have to see it to believe it. As soon as I get my baby back, I'm jumping right on top of this shit. I know damn well Kayo hasn't been alive all of these years and never tried to seek revenge. There's no way in hell he's been walking the same streets as me, and we haven't crossed paths.

"Paree, what the fuck, where are you? Are you ok?"

"Ok, we'll be there shortly twin, I love you," London said, ending the call while trying to do something else on her phone.

"Where is she?" I asked with my hands on my hips.

"Hold on, ma. I'm tracking her phone...225 Burnside Circle. Bear has her. Come on y'all. We gotta go!"

FIFTY-THREE
PAREE

I laid there and thought anything I possibly could to take my mind off Bear as feasted on my pussy for the hundredth time. My pussy dry was as a desert, but he thought he was doing a damn good job as I fake moaned so that he wouldn't get angry again and hit me. My mind was all over the place as I thought of ways to kill him, but that shit was impossible with my hands being tied up. I don't know how long I've been here, but I know if I don't get away soon I'm going to crack the fuck up. I faked an organism as soon a light bulb popped on in my head.

"You like daddy tongue, baby?" Bear asked, struggling to stand his big ass up while wiping his mouth.

"Yes daddy, but I'm tired of being tied up. I want to see the rest of our house."

"Paree, you think I'm stupid, don't you?"

"No baby, come here," I seductively said while opening and closing my legs.

I don't know where I'm going with these charades, but I hope he falls for the shit. He stood there with his head tilted to the side as he lustfully watched me. I could see a bulge forming in his pants, which let me know I had him right where I needed him to be.

"Untie me baby so that I can take care of that the right way."

He smiled and walked over to the door locking it with the key from the inside before sliding the key into the small pocket on his jeans. He walked to the head of the bed and pulled his little dick from his boxers. He looked down at me with a deranged look in eyes while stroking himself. He never took his eyes off of me as he grabbed my hair and pulled my head near his dick. I closed my eyes and stuck my tongue out licking the tip while he slightly moaned. I made sure to tease him to the point where he wanted the full service. I flicked my tongue back and forth before wrapping my lips around the head and then stopping.

"Baby my neck hurt, I can't suck it right lying like this," I whined.

To my surprise, he didn't say a word. He just untied me. I grabbed my wrist and rubbed them before pulling him onto the bed. I wanted full control of his body. I planned on fucking him into a coma because that was clearly my only option. I stood straight up in the bed and pulled my shirt over my head becoming completely naked as his eyes lit up like a Christmas tree. I stood directly over his and message clit while he rubbed my legs.

"This is my show, so keep your hands to yourself. You had your turn," I said, sticking my index and middle finger inside of my pussy before sticking them in his mouth.

"Damn baby, you taste so good."

"Shhhh...let me take care of you."

I dropped down, sat my pussy directly on his face, and let him lick it a couple of times before standing back up. I dropped down and crawled to the other end of the bed giving a clear view of my ass while looking back at him. His dick was harder than Chinese math as it poked out of his boxers. I thanked God that he was a fat fly nigga that didn't have a body odor. He actually smelled like the Gucci cologne he always wore. That alone made this process a little easier. I closed my eyes and imagined he was Malik lying there. I fully removed his dick from his boxers, let spit drip from my mouth down the shaft of his dick, and massaged it with my hand. He was already squirming, and I hadn't even put my mouth on him. I watched as his toes curled. I did this for about two minutes before I turned my mouth into a Hoover vacuum. I did everything I thought Malik would like. It wasn't long before he had a fist full of my hair, causing me to stop and open my eyes.

"What the fuck did I tell you? Didn't I say that this was my show? I'm trying to figure out why you can't let me suck your dick how I want to."

"I'm sorry, baby. I won't do again. Please keep going," he begged like a big kid.

"You promise?"

"Yes, I promise."

I moved my hair to the side and picked up where I left off slurping and sucking him while he now moaned loudly. I felt like shit as tears rolled down my face. I didn't want him to bust just yet, so I stopped and asked God to protect me as I did the unthinkable and sat down on his dick raw. I bounced up and down on the tip as he gripped my hips, I didn't move his hands I just let him have his way as I moaned with him. I tried to focus and not call out Malik's name as I felt his body tensing up. I knew he was about to cum but damn sure not inside of me. I jumped up and used my hands to finish the job while telling him to put his kids on my face. No sooner than those words left, my mouth that shit was shooting out like a volcano had erupted.

I climbed to the head of the bed, laid my head on his chest while he mumbled a few words, and drifted off into a deep sleep. I didn't know if he was a light sleeper, so I slightly moved a few times to see if he would wake up, but he didn't, and that alone gave me the green light. I moved my body like a snake and slid to the floor. I crawled over to his jeans and removed the key. I still heard him snoring, so I kept moving swiftly, I stuck the key in the door and unlocked it just in time before he sat straight up in the bed and yelled.

"Bitch, I'm gone kill you!"

He was a few seconds too slow. I snatched the door open and quickly locked it from the outside. I turned around and froze in my tracks as I was met by the largest Pitbull I had ever seen in my life. It looked at me and sniffed me as stood there frozen solid while Bear yelled, "kill!" from the other side of the door.

The dog, to my surprise, turned and ran down the stairs wagging its tail. I guess he was tired of Bear's shit too. I entered the first room I saw which was a second bedroom. I looked around for my purse, and God must've heard my cries because it was sitting the corner on a chair. I ran top speed and grabbed it, dumping everything out on the bed, but my phone was not there.

"Fuck! Think bitch think," I said under my breath.

Something kept making me look at the dresser, so I jumped up and started pulling them open. This crazy ass nigga had a whole panty drawer set up for me with matching bras. I went through every drawer. I got all the way to the last drawer and boom my phone was laying right there. I grabbed it and powered it on while Bear was still yelling and beating on the other door. As soon as it came on messages from London, Malik, and my mother started coming through back to back. I went straight to London's name and called, she answered on the first ring.

"Paree what the fuck, where are you? Are you ok?" she asked quickly.

"London shut up and let me talk. I'm ok. Bear kidnapped me. I don't know where I am, but I'm turning on my GPS use the Find A Friend app and come get me. He's locked in the other room, so hurry up before he gets out."

"Ok. We'll be there shortly, twin. I love you."

"Love you too, now hurry up. My phone is about to die."

I had four percent on my phone when I dialed 911. The operator picked up asking a ton of questions that I didn't know the answer to. She asked me to name the landmarks around me, but there weren't any just trees. The phone died in the middle of the call I just prayed

London traced my location before it powered off. I sat there and listened for the front door while Bear apologized and cursed. He was really fucked up in the head.

After he yelled for about forty-five more minutes he became silent, I walked over to the door and put my ear against it. Then a loud knock came from the other side that scared the fuck out of me, causing me to jump back. I don't understand how the fuck he got out that room.

"Open this muthafuckin' door, Paree!" Bear yelled while the dog growled viciously.

"The police are on their way, Bear. It's over. You have a chance to get away just go!"

"I'm not leaving here without you. Paree, I love you, and I'm sorry. Please just open the door and talk to me. I won't hurt you."

"NO!"

"OPEN THIS FUCKING DOOR, BITCH!"

POW! was all I heard as I jumped from in front of the door. The dog was no longer barking, and I could hear Bear quickly moving from in front of the door. I wanted to look out, but fuck that. I was staying put until I knew I was safe.

"Don't run now muthafucka, where the fuck is my baby? Tear this bitch up and find my daughter!" I heard my mother yell from downstairs.

I quickly snatched the door open without thinking twice and was met by a fist. All I remember was Bear dragging me back into the room and locking us in. I slowly opened my eyes and looked up at Bear as he paced the floor and had a conversation with himself while holding his pistol. He quickly snatched me up off the floor and motioned for me to go to stand in the corner as he aimed the gun at the door. I covered my ears as shots rang out from every direction. When they were done shooting the entire door was gone, and niggas rushed in from the other side. Bear was hit a few times, but he wasn't dead.

My mother walked in and hit him the face with the butt of her gun repeatedly while London took off her hoodie and put it on me to cover my naked body. I was shocked but also glad to see Malik as he scooped me up off the floor bridal style.

"PAREE!" Bear yelled while blood flew from his mouth before my mother shot him between the eyes and walked out with us in tow.

FIFTY-FOUR
SINCERE

I have so many fucked up thoughts running through my head, so I knew I had to have a heart to heart with my pop. Why did they OG think he was dead? It's definitely some more to the bullshit ass story he was feeding me. First, he had me thinking this was some beef over the blocks out west, and then he turns around and tells me she killed my mother. I go to murk her and come to find out she's a friend of his. I knew he wouldn't tell me the whole truth so I'm taking matters into my own hands. I just have to see what's really to Kyana. I will never forget the look in her eyes when she looked up and saw me standing there. I knew exactly how to find out everything I needed to know.

Malik, the twins, and I sat in the parking lot of Dave and Buster's smoking a blunt before we went in. Malik told me he was meeting them there because Paree needed to take her mind off all the shit that happened to her with that crazy nigga. I immediately invited myself because this would be the perfect time to get into their heads so that they can tell me more about Kyana. I wanted to know exactly how she knew my parents before I proceeded to kill her like I was ordered to do in the first place. I knew the twins knew the game, and since

Kyana is their mother, they would only give limited information. I knew they weren't stupid, but I had my way with words.

We finally got out and walked inside, and to my surprise, it wasn't too crowded. I knew Malik was going to have Paree tied up, so I made sure I stayed on London's heels. Paree was a crazy ass chick anyway, and she would've asked my ass why I was being so nosey. I stood next to London while she played the Wheel of Fortune game and sparked up a conversation.

"Yo, you suck at this shit."

"Mannn, this damn thing has to be broke because I'm cold at this game."

"Why you break my boy heart like you did?" I asked, leaning against the game she was playing.

"Jason? Fuck that nigga. Shid, he broke my heart when I caught him in the car with Cami's dirty ass," she said, giving me her undivided attention like I needed at the moment.

"Yeah, that nigga's been tweaking lately. He don't even come out the crib."

"Good, he's a fucking menace to society," she said, causing me to chuckle.

"So y'all OG is the infamous Kyana? That explains why y'all pushing eighty thousand-dollar whips."

"Yeah, busted. We usually don't tell anyone who our mother is because you never know what a motherfucker has up their sleeve. I observe people closely, and I've been observing you, Sincere. So, what's up?"

"Ain't shit up, what you getting at?" I asked because she had caught me off guard.

"I see how you move. You're just like me you watch everything around you, so what are you trying to learn, or should I say "who" are you trying to learn?" she asked, looking me square in the eyes as if she was challenging me.

I was never the type of nigga to crack under pressure, but there was a look in her eyes that were similar to mine. I stared at her for the first time, and you would've thought I was looking directly at my father. I knew it had to be the weed fucking with my mind, so I broke the eye contact and looked away.

"Come on, Sincere. Don't bitch up on me. What's yo motive cause right now you acting real suspect."

"Yo, who is your father?"

"What?"

"I never hear y'all talk about your father."

"Aw nigga, if that's all you wanted to know, you could've been asked. Shid, you had me thinking foul thoughts about yo ass. Our father died years ago. I don't remember much about him, but he was a heavy. His name was Kayo. You a street nigga I'm pretty sure you've heard of him," she said, causing me to spit the Sprite out that I was drinking on the floor.

Everything she said after "Kayo" fell death on my ears. I knew it was bullshit behind this shit. I swear to God I hope she's lying to me right now. I asked my pop if I had siblings and that nigga looked me in my eyes and told me no on multiple occasions. He only wanted me to kill Kyana so that I wouldn't find out about this shit. She probably didn't even kill my momma. Furious wasn't the fucking word. I'm pretty sure I turned firetruck red in the face.

"Kayo huh, that's crazy because that's my pop's name, and he's alive and fucking well, sister."

"Fuck outta here, there's a million Kayo's in the world, and I'm positive mine is dead and gone."

"London, there's only one Kayo Castillo," I said, walking out leaving her standing there in awe.

FIFTY-FIVE
KAYO

I sat behind my desk in my office while Chanel looked up at me and moved her tongue around the tip of my dick. I rested my hand on the back of her head and slowly worked every inch of my dick into her mouth. I made her dye her hair blonde and get a weave like Kyana used to wear. Chanel was strictly into women when I first met her, but whatever Kayo wants Kayo gets. I'm the only man she's ever been with, so you know her love runs deep for a nigga. I met her a couple of years ago. I was driving and not paying attention when I slightly ran right into the back of her, and the rest is history, and now she's in love with a real nigga.

"Stand up," I ordered while she stood to her feet placing one foot up on the desk.

She stood there with freshly waxed pussy in my face, and I went in face first as she tried to keep her balance. I wrapped one arm around her leg to lock her in the position she was standing in. I took her pearl into my mouth and made love to it with my tongue while she grabbed my head and fed me. I knew once I locked those legs and started sucking on her clit that she was going to tap out. I felt her body tensing up and knew she was about to cum, so I immediately released my grip from her legs and roughly sat her on top of the desk. I teased her rubbing the tip of my dick across her clit as she pulled me closer, trying to get me to put it in. I looked down as her juices covered the tip of my dick as I push it in and out. I wanted her to beg for this dick.

"You want this dick, baby?"

"Yes, please put it in."

"My baby want this dick? I asked, giving her inch by inch."

"Yesssss baby, please."

That's all I needed to hear. I pulled her to the edge of the desk and gave her exactly what she asked me for. I had her stretched out feet to shoulders while I punished her pussy. I was hitting every spot with precision while she screamed my name. I wrapped one hand around her neck and applied minimum pressure. I looked down as she bit her bottom lip, making my dick even harder. I pulled out and slightly pressed down on her abdomen before going back in full throttle. I knew I had her soul when her warm juices squirted out that pussy. I made her cum at least three times before I finally released my kids all over her stomach.

"Why do always pull out? What I'm not good enough to have your child?" Chanel asked immediately pissing me off.

"I told you I don't want any more kids. If that's what you're looking for, find another nigga," I replied, walking over to the bathroom attached to my office.

"Pick your words wisely, for real."

"Take your own advice, Chanel," I said, walking up standing inches away from her face.

Chanel has always had tough streak inside of her, but I knew to calm her ass right down. She knows I don't tolerate any disrespect, which is why I always end up having to choke her little ass up. I wasn't worried about her fucking another nigga. The most she would do is fuck another bitch and bring her home so that I could have them both. Chanel's freaky ass was a different type of female than I was used to because Kyana would've never allowed no shit like that to take place.

I stood there looking Chanel directly in the eyes as she battled me with hers. I grabbed her collarbone and applied pressure instantly making her knees buckle.

"Please stop! You're hurting meeeee!" she yelled out.

"Learn how to control your tongue, and I'll control my hands," I replied as someone banged on the door like they had a fucking problem.

I pushed pass Chanel and power walked to the door before snatching it open.

"Why the fuck are you banging on my door like that, Sincere?" I yelled as he ignored me and forced his way in.

I knew for a fact this lil nigga had officially lost his mind. I stood there with my hand still on the doorknob while looking at Sincere pace the floor. I told Chanel to excuse herself, and she left without hesitation. She got lucky because Sincere saved her from an ass whooping.

"You know pop, I used to think you were like a fucking king or something, but overall a real man," Sincere said while pointing his finger at me as if he was lecturing me.

"Look, I don't know what the fuck is wrong with you, but you better realize who you're talking to right now. You better show some fucking respect, Sincere!" I said, walking over to my desk.

"I don't respect no nigga that lies about his kids, Kayo," he replied saying my name sarcastically.

"Sincere, what the fuck are you talking about?"

I could tell my son was upset, but I was clueless as to why. Maybe he's upset because he didn't get his mother's revenge. I had one of my killers to go ahead of Sincere and kill Kyana. I knew he couldn't do it, and I couldn't risk her getting inside of his head. I had everything mapped out in my head how I was going to bring my kids together. I wanted them to run this empire together, and I knew that would never happen with Kyana in the picture.

"So, you don't have a set of twins?"

"Yeah, I "had" a set of twins, but they passed at birth, how did you find out them?" I lied.

"What?" Sincere said astonished by the words that had just left my mouth.

"Yeah, I never told you about them because I knew your mom was enough. I didn't want to put anything else on your mind," I said, lowering my head.

"My bad, pop. I was in the barbershop, some old niggas start talking, and yo name came up. They said you married the prettiest bitch out the hood and had twins with her before you got killed."

All this shit that was supposed to remain a secret was resurfacing because motherfuckers don't know how to mind their own fucking business. Now I have figure out how to sugarcoat this shit to Sincere, so he that doesn't lose his head because I need him for this takeover. I need him to have a clear view of the future I have planned for us.

"Listen, have a seat. It's time I tell you what's up."

"Nah pop, just tell me what's up," Sincere replied, leaning against the wall with his arms folded across his chest.

"Ok, I had a set of twins with the woman I sent you to kill. Her name was Kyana, and she was my ex-wife. I had an affair on her with your mother who was her best friend. Kyana flipped off the deep end when she found out about the affair and learned that I also fathered you. They were both pregnant at the same time, but the twins didn't make it. Kyana caught up to your mother and killed her. She thought she had killed me also, but I faked my death to keep you safe. That's why I always told to never discuss me with anyone."

"This is some shit off of a movie, so it's your fault my mother is dead? You sure you faked your death to protect me, pop. It sounds like you were trying to hide from your past," he replied, stroking his chin.

"I don't run from shit Sincere, and had I not faked my death and moved you into this nice ass house and neighborhood, Kyana would've killed your black ass too. Instead of standing here sizing me up, yo ass should be thanking me."

The crazy part about this whole conversation is he is correct. I made sure I covered my ass for all of these years with top of the line security. I knew Rio was still out there, but I wasn't worried, I'll have him canceled by the weekend. I had plenty of opportunities to kill Kyana and come out of hiding, but that would've been stupid on my part. I was still making money off of Kyana as a "dead" man. I was her "connect" for all of these years, and she didn't even know it. I made sure I kept the prices low and the product A-1. She thought the "connect" resided in Cuba, but I've been right here in her city. Kyana did exactly what I needed her to do— build a fucking empire for me to take over. The bitch wasn't as smart as she thought she was.

"You right pop, I apologize. So now that Kyana is out the way, what's next?"

"You're next. I'm ready to bring you in as my right-hand man. Sincere being a boss is in your blood, so I already know this shit is going to come natural to you. Kyana was our biggest rival, but now that she's gone, the whole city is ours," I said, answering my cell phone and excusing myself.

FIFTY-SIX

KYANA

"A double shot of Hennessy, please. Ok, I'm back. Now listen to me, you don't have to stay there and take that shit. You still have your whole life ahead of you. I will never tell you anything wrong, and you know I don't sugarcoat shit. You need to get away from that nigga before it's too late," I held my phone up to my ear and shifted in my seat.

The bartender walked over and placed a napkin along with my shot in front of me. I ended my call and stirred the ice around in my glass.

"I'm sorry, I'm usually not the loud ghetto type, but I just hate to see a female get treated any type way by a nothing ass nigga," I said to the lady.

"Oh no, you weren't bothering me. Sometimes people need that honesty," she said knocking a shot back, I could tell she had been binge drinking.

"Yeah I know, I love my friend to death, but I can only give her advice. It's up to her to use it. I'm glad I don't have to deal with niggas. She's a prime example of why I play for the opposite team," I said, knocking my shot back and ordering another one.

I looked over at the woman who now looked like she was undressing me with her eyes and smiled before she introduced herself.

"That's very interesting, I'm Chanel by the way," she said, holding her freshly manicured hand out in my direction.

"Nice to meet you, I'm Kelly," I replied while holding on to her longer than I should have.

"A beautiful name for a beautiful woman."

And just like that, I entered Kayo's world, I planned on making her take me directly to Kayo's ass. After Sincere exposed that Kayo is still alive, I did what I should've done years ago, and that's researched Kayo's ass. Not only has this nigga been alive for the past decade, but he was right under my nose the entire time. I have been kicking my own ass ever since I found out. I slipped hard. I also found out Kayo had Sincere working as his hitman, which doesn't surprise me. The night Rio died that hit was for me, but I dodged that bullet just to be alive to put one in Kayo's head. Kayo has always been all for self, fuck the fact of putting his child's life in danger. I was working with limited time because I have to kill Kayo before my girls find out about him because for the first time, I don't have the answers to any of their questions.

"Has anyone ever told you look like..."

"Boo-Boo Kitty from *Empire*...yes, they have," I replied, smiling while completing my sentence.

"Yeah, but a prettier version..." she replied, stating facts.

"If I didn't know any better I would think you were flirting with me, Ms. Kelly."

"Maybe, Ms. Chanel," I replied, licking my lips.

I swear I have never been into women, but I might just let this bitch taste it before I kill her man. We sat there and talked about everything we would do to one another, and I must say, that nigga Kayo had a freak on his hands. I knew I had her ready when I leaned in closely and whispered in her ear.

"I'm going to leave you with my number, sexy. Call me when

you're ready for me," I said before sticking the napkin I wrote my number on down the front of her blouse.

I dropped a hundred-dollar bill on the bar to cover my tab and hers before walking out. If she's feeling me like I know she is, I'll be getting a call from her later on tonight. Now that that's out the way, I can go home and relax.

I pulled into my driveway and sat there taking it all in. I never in a million years thought I would grow up and became a queen pin. I was kind of banking on a hair stylist. I went through a lot to get to where I am in life, and I'll be damned if Kayo fucks up what I built. The vibrating of my phone caused me to quickly lift my head off the steering wheel and reach for my pistol. I hurried and answered before London thought something was wrong.

"What's up, babeeee?"

"Shut up, lil girl. Where's your sister?" I said finally stepping out the car.

I decided to come to the old house tonight because I didn't feel like taking the drive to the new house. As soon as I walked in, I could feel Rio's presence.

"In the house getting dressed we're going out. Ma, I need to ask you something."

"What's up, baby girl?" I said, turning on the lights.

"Did Kayo have any kids besides us because Sincere tripped me out the other night talking about Kayo is alive, and he's his father also?" she asked, causing me to stop dead in my tracks.

Fuck...Fuck...Fuck think, Kyana.

"Who knows how many kids Kayo's ass have running around Chicago. All I know about is mine and Kayo is dead, I don't know what Sincere is talking about," I replied, lying right through my teeth as London fell silent on the other end.

I walked upstairs to my guest bedroom and stripped out of my clothes. I didn't feel comfortable being in my bedroom. I went to the bathroom and ran me a hot bath in hopes of relaxing and releasing the million thoughts that crowded my brain. I knew I should've told the girls that Sincere is their brother, but I can't bring myself to tell them that. I just hope they don't call themselves liking on one another. I told them the truth about Kayo all the way up until now. I know Kayo will stop at nothing to kill me, but I'm a few steps ahead of him. I bet he thinks killing me will make it easier for him to come out of hiding and takeover, but that's bullshit. Shit will never be that sweet.

I stepped out of the tub and slipped on a full-length silk robe before sliding my leg holster up my leg securing my pistol. I had no security here with me, just me and my drink. I dimmed the lights in my living room and let The Isley Brother's "Choosy Lover" fill the emptiness in the room. I took a sip of the Hennessy in my glass and took a seat on my couch. I laid my head back and immediately felt a cool wind hit me. I didn't budge. I just sat there. I knew someone was there. Furthermore, I knew who when they slightly kicked one of the large vases that sat near my front door. They didn't say a word, they simply cocked their pistol and stood there.

"Your hands are shaking, Sincere. You're going to miss your target," I said.

"I never miss my target, Kyana."

"Put the gun down and have a seat. I've been expecting you."

"You can't play mind games with me. You weren't expecting shit."

"I told you once, and I won't say it again. Watch your mouth in my house. Kayo sent you here to try and kill me, not giving a fuck about you or your life. Some kind of parent he is," I said, sipping my drink never turning around.

I was the least bit worried about Sincere pulling the trigger. If he were here to kill me, I would've been dead a few minutes ago. I know he came here with questions that Kayo more than likely lied about. I still look at Sincere as that little boy I loved, and I will not lie to him about anything, even me killing his mother. I feel just as dirty as Kayo when I think about the kids and how fucked up this situation is. I knew it was only a matter of time before I have to explain this shit to all of them.

Sincere finally lowered his gun, walked around the couch, and sat across from me.

"What's the real reason you're here?" I asked as he leaned forward and rested his elbows on his knees.

"Kyana, what's the story behind you and my father?"

"He gave you a bullshit story, and you don't believe it. You were always a smart boy. Your father and I were married..." I said but stopped in mid-sentence when the front door swung open.

Paree and London walked in laughing.

"Damn ma, why it's so sexy in here," Paree said, walking into the living room and stopping abruptly.

"What are you all doing here?" I asked.

"I needed to grab something, but the real question is what's going on here?" London asked.

Well damn, I know I said I was going to have to explain the shit, but I wasn't ready yet.

"Have a seat next to your brother."

"Brother?" Paree asked, which let me know London hadn't told her anything.

"Yes brother, he's Kayo's son."

"So, it's true, huh?" London asked, walking over taking a seat next to Sincere while Paree stood in the same spot.

"Why am I the only one shocked right now? Y'all knew and didn't tell me?"

"You were going through enough, baby. please have a seat," I said as she slowly walked over to join her siblings.

I looked at the three of them together and felt myself getting emotional. I tried to get my thoughts and words together before speaking.

"Now Sincere, as I was saying. Your father and I were married. Your mother was my best friend, but they were having an affair behind my back for years, and she ended up getting pregnant right before I found out I was pregnant with them. I didn't find out until you all were around eight years old when I overheard them having a conversation about the affair on Christmas day. I tried to keep it together for the sake of you all, but every time I looked at you, I wanted them dead. I'm sorry Sincere, but yes, I killed your mother because she crossed me, I can understand if you hate me for that, but I loved you then, and I still love you now. I never wanted to separate you all, but I had no choice."

They all set there with different facial expressions. I knew I was dropping a lot on Sincere, but he needs to hear the truth, not that shit that Kayo was talking.

"So, you knew we had a whole brother and didn't tell us. This is some crazy shit. You said you would never lie to us," Paree said.

"Watch your mouth and yes I know it's crazy, but I didn't tell you all because I didn't know where to find Sincere, and I didn't want you all out there trying to find him. Yes, I kept you two away from Kayo for my own selfish reasons, and I am sorry, I was wrong, but Kayo means no one any good, not even you Sincere."

"So, is Kayo dead or alive?" Paree asked looking at Sincere.

"He's alive, but he thinks you all are dead. He said you all died at birth," Sincere replied, causing my blood to boil.

The nerve of that bitch ass nigga.

"Sincere that's bullshit. Kayo watched them grow up. He's a lair. You all were around one another every day until I divorced Kayo. You practically lived with us. I have always treated you like my own," I said as tears formed in my eyes.

"I think I remember, but why would he lie to me though? The man looked me in the face and lied," Sincere asked with pain in each word.

"That's Kayo's selfish ass."

"Wait a minute, ma. I thought Rio killed Kayo," London said.

"Yeah me too, but I guess it's impossible to kill Satan."

"I knew it was something about you when I first met you. You looked familiar to me," London said, looking at Sincere.

"How long have you all been around one another?" I asked curiously.

"For a couple of months now," Paree answered.

Kayo is one slick ass nigga who fakes their death for a decade and sends their child to do their dirty work. I could tell by the way this conversation is going my girls are going to try and reach out to their father, but that shit will only happen over my dead body. All three of them sat there wrapped up in their own thoughts, so I excused myself to take the call that was coming through my cell phone.

"Hello."

"Hi, beautiful."

"Heyyy, I wasn't expecting to hear from you this soon."

"Oh, I'm sorry were you busy?"

"Never too busy for you Ms. Chanel, what's up?"

"I was wondering if you wanted to come over."

"Sure, I have to get dressed. Text me the address."

"Ok will do, see you soon."

Dumb bitch.

FIFTY-SEVEN

PAREE

"Paree, momma gave us specific instructions not to reach out to this man. You are always doing the opposite of what someone tells you," London lectured as I followed behind Sincere's car from a distance.

After the sit down we all had, Sincere was furious with Kayo, but I on the other wanted to see what he looked like. I know I was anti-Kayo at first, but that was because I never thought I'd see the nigga. I want to see his face when he finally sees us, what will he say? Am I really like my father? I want to look the man that broke my mother's heart right in the face.

"Damn London, calm down. Mommy isn't going to find out. We're not getting out. I just want to see where they live."

"You are lying, Paree. I know you."

"I promise," I replied pulling over as Sincere turned into the driveway of a beautiful home.

I watched Sincere get out and walk up the porch that led up to the huge house. I thought our crib was big, but this is over the top. If we have eight bedrooms, they have to have at least ten. I'm not exaggerating. A huge dog ran toward Sincere, and he started wrestling with it. A few seconds later, a tall, handsome man appeared in the doorway. Both London and I tried to zoom in with our eyes but couldn't really see anything. I immediately unhooked my seatbelt as London shook her head.

"You promised, bitch."

"I lied. I wanna see his ass," I replied as London sat there.

I got out and walked alongside the gate, I could see Sincere and the man having words back and forth before Sincere hopped back in his car and zoomed out without noticing me. The man cursed loudly before walking back into the house. I looked back at London as her scary ass looked on from the car. I was about to take a few more steps when my heart fell in my ass. My feet were glued to the pavement when I saw my mother's Bentley pull into the driveway. What the fuck is really going on? I turned around and sprinted back to my car when I was in the clear.

"See bitch, I told you. I bet she saw yo ass," London said as I tried to catch my breath.

"What the fuck is she doing here? It's some bullshit going on and "WE" gone get to the bottom of it," I replied with my hand still covering my chest.

"No "WE" not doing shit, I don't care about none of this shit. I'm sick of it. Everybody's lying if you ask me."

"But, I thought you were team Kayo. "What if" remember that? Now you wanna bitch up because shit got real, literally," I said, drinking my bottle of water.

"I'm not bitching up. I'm just saying what's the point. Momma's not gone let us fuck with Kayo anyway. We know Sincere is our brother, so let's move on."

"We're eighteen, that's our decision, and I just wanna know what's going on. Are you in or out?"

"Bitch, do I really have a choice? You drove, come on man!" she said roughly unfastening her seatbelt.

I knocked the rest of my water back before hopping back out of the car, London wasn't trying to sneak or shit, she was just walking toward the door. I jogged up to her and pulled her back by her shirt.

"Bitch, wait! You just gone walk up to the door?"

"Yeah, what the fuck we sneaking for? I don't have time for the games, Paree."

"We don't know what we're walking into, you tripping. Let me get in the front before you get our asses killed."

I tiptoed up the stairs and leaned over the banister. I didn't see any movement inside, so I tried to open the front door, but it was locked. London nodded her head toward the side of the house as I ran back down the stairs. I was now following London to the side of the house where there was a set of sliding doors. She slid the door, and to our surprise, it was open. As soon as she opened the door, the big ass dog ran out doing full speed causing both of us to scream and run inside. Luckily, we ended up in what had to be Sincere's bedroom judging by the large sneaker selection that was nicely set in the far corner of the big ass bedroom. I could smell his cologne lingering in the air as we made our way over to the door that stood wide open.

I could hear a male's voice softly talking followed by a woman's voice as we got closer to the door. For the first time in a long time, I was nervous as hell. I was ready to run my ass back outside, but that quickly went out the window when I thought about "Cujo" running out. London put her finger over her lip, stuck her head out, and quickly pulled it back in while frantically pointing to the left. We both swiftly moved behind the door as the man that had to be Kayo walked past and followed the woman up the stairs. I could smell cigar smoke and cologne as he walked past. I stepped from behind the door and slightly peeked out. I motioned for London to follow me as I moved through the house like a ninja, our mother was nowhere in sight. I looked around the dim room, making my way to the same stairs Kayo walked up a few minutes ago. I put my foot on the first step and froze in my tracks when London screamed out in pain.

"Don't move little bitch!" was all I heard as I heard before a pistol was pressed to my temple.

FIFTY-EIGHT

KAYO

I know I hurt Chanel's feelings earlier because she stormed out with tears in her eyes. I think Kyana fucked it up for every other woman in the world when she walked out on me because I treated them like shit. I have never loved another woman like I loved Kyana. Even though we put each other through hell, if she were alive, I would still take her back. I know I must figure out a way to tell Sincere the truth about the twins without him looking at me differently. I almost had to put hands on him earlier because of his mouth. God and I never had a close relationship, but I often prayed to him to and asked him to place forgiveness in my kids' hearts. I know I have no other choice but to step up and be in my girls' lives, even though I faked my death, I never missed a beat when it came to them. I had every graduation, recital, and birthday party on video because I was present. I could tell them about any event that took place in their lives without missing a single detail. I love my kids with everything in me.

I stood at the bar in my office and poured myself a shot trying to clear my head. I swear my life is some shit out of a movie or them crazy ass books Kyana used to read to me. I heard the front door open and close followed by two women laughing and talking. My dick was almost standing up because I knew Chanel had brought another bitch home for us to play with. I didn't bother walking out there because I could hear Chanel's stiletto clicking across the floor as she got closer to the door. I knocked my cup and poured another as she lightly knocked on the door.

"Come in."

"Hey baby, what you up too?"

"Nothing much, what's up with you?" I asked.

"Ohhh nothing, I have someone I want you to meet upstairs."

"Who is she, and I hope she looks better than the last bitch you brought home? She smelled like cigarettes."

"Kelly's on a whole different level. She is by far the most gorgeous women I have ever laid eyes on. She's upstairs changing into something sexy for us. I'm positive you'll love her!" Chanel said, tracing my dick with her finger and walking out.

I watched her ass bounce out the door before killing the shot I was holding. I took a seat behind my desk and strolled through my old Facebook account. It was weird as hell seeing "rest in peace" posted all over the page, I bet I'll freak these muthafuckas out if I upload a status. I chucked to myself before Chanel peeked her head in and motioned for me to follow her. I stood up and walked out behind her as she held my hand. The house looked real sexy with the lights dim putting me straight in the mood. Once we made it upstairs, she stopped me before peeking inside of our bedroom and smiling. Chanel had me thirsty to see just how beautiful this woman is.

"You ready, baby?"

"I'm always ready," I said, popping her on her ass.

We walked in, and the room was semi-dark, but I could see a set of beautiful legs at the foot of the bed. The woman laid back on the bed with a black silk scarf covering half her face. I wanted to see if her face was as beautiful as her body as she laid there wearing a black one-piece silk lingerie that was sheer on the breasts area. She had her hands behind her head and under the pillow that she was lying on. I walked over and traced her body as Chanel massaged her breasts, she moaned softly.

As soon the moan escaped her mouth I froze, I know that voice. I know this body, and I know I had to kill one of my best workers for telling me the hit was a go. I slowly backtracked my steps while pulling my pistol from my waist. No sooner than I could get my hand on around the handle, Kyana was sitting up straight, with a pistol aimed at me.

"Kelly, what are you doing?!" Chanel yelled, looking back and forth from Kyana to me.

I wanted to pull the trigger, but I couldn't.

"Kyana...Kyana...Kyana, you're always coming up with a clever plan that never works."

"Kyana?!" Chanel said, climbing off the bed stepped off to the side.

"Yes, it's Kyana, not Kelly. I have nothing against you, Chanel. You have a choice to walk or die with yo nigga," Kyana said, but Chanel didn't budge.

I just stood there and stared. Kyana was still indeed the most beautiful woman in the world to me. Even with a gun pointed at me, my dick still got hard at the sight of my first love. Chanel knew all about Kyana and how much I loved and hated her ass.

"SHOOT THAT BITCH!"

"Bitch, he will shoot you before he shoots me. Shoot me, KAYO!" Kyana said, stating nothing but facts.

She knew she still had the juice, and she made that clear when she called my bluff. Chanel looked up at me as I watched Kyana cock her pistol. I cocked mine right after her, but a scream followed by a female's voice came from downstairs. Kyana's eye grew wide as she leaned forward as if she was trying to hear.

"That's my baby voice, shit!" Kyana yelled, jumping off the bed and pushing past me.

I ran out right behind her as Chanel followed me, Kyana stopped at the top of the stairs and aimed her pistol. I stepped on the side of her and became furious when I saw my security and the worker that I sent to "kill" Kyana with their guns up to my daughter's head.

"What the fuck are y'all doing?!" I yelled.

"We caught these bitches trying to creep upstairs. I will blow your fucking head off if move again!" the worker yelled.

Kyana lined her pistol up with his head perfectly, shot my security, and turned her pistol to the worker, but I shot him before she could. Chanel screamed and covered her ears. Kyana immediately ran down the stairs and checked on our babies. Every emotion hit me as I pulled my phone out and called the clean-up crew. Chanel threw her hands up in the air before speaking.

"What the fuck is going on, and who the fuck are they?!" Chanel yelled, pointing down toward the girls and Kyana.

"Mannn ma, who is this bitch and who is she talking to?"

"A fucking dummy that he better put in her place before I put my foot in her ass."

"I don't have to stick around for this dumb shit. Call me when you done playing house."

"Who the fuck are you talking like that?" I yelled, grabbing her throat and applying pressure.

"Let go of me," Chanel said as her face turned red.

I release her neck, and she fell to the floor. If looks could kill, I would be a dead man. She picked herself up off the floor as Kyana and the girls watched. She ran down the stairs and out the door. She slammed the door so hard that the windows shook. I didn't react I just simply walked down the stairs to check on my kid.

"Hold up ma, what are you doing up in this house dressed like a playboy bunny?" Paree asked. I knew it was her because of the beauty mark on her cheek.

"Don't question me, little girl. Why are y'all here?"

"Mrs. Smith came to kill me "again" I guess, and you two came to see me."

"So Kayo, you really faked your death and missed ten years of our lives?" London asked with her arms folded across her chest.

I could tell London had Kyana's sassy attitude while Paree was just like me nonchalant with no filter.

"I really had no choice because you two would've probably been orphans. Believe me, it was killing me to watch you all grow up from a distance, but Kyana did an excellent job. I never missed a beat. I was at every birthday party and graduation. I know you just had your first heartbreak, and you just fell in love for the first time. I know everything. When you all were getting those random gifts and large sums of money in the mail, that was me. I loved you two from the first day I laid eyes on you at the hospital. I fucked up, and as a man, and as your father I apologize."

"That's so sweet. Father of the fuckin' year award goes to you!" Sincere appeared out of nowhere slowly clapping his hands sarcastically.

"Sincere, let me explain this to you," I said totally caught off guard.

"Fuck you!"

FIFTY-NINE
SINCERE

I pulled back up to the house after blowing up on my pop. I don't give a fuck how he put it, the nigga looked me dead in the face and lied. All I asked him for was the truth, and he couldn't give me that, so fuck him. I'm about to grab my shit and keep it moving. I'm done playing with his ass. I pulled right behind a white Bentley. the license plate read *"Bosslady"* . I saw the same car at the twins' crib when Paree got kidnapped. I know damn well they're not around this bitch in cahoots.

I walked around the side of the house and walked in through my bedroom. I could hear voices as I got closer to the hallway outside of my bedroom. I stood in place for a minute and listened to my father pour his heart out to the twins about how sorry he is, but this nigga told me they died at birth. Pissed off would be an understatement right now.

"That was so sweet. Father of the fuckin' year award goes to you!"

"Fuck! Sincere, let me explain this to you."

"Fuck you!"

"What the fuck did you just say?!" my pop said, stepping around the twins and Kyana started walking toward me.

Kyana grabbed my pop's arm, but he kept coming toward me. I was ready for whatever though. He came and stood directly in front of me, but I didn't budge.

"Man, you heard what I said the first time, FUCK YOU! You ain't shit but a liar. You looked me in my face and told me they died at birth, but the whole time you knew they were alive. What "real" nigga hides from their children for ten years?"

Before I could finish speaking my mind, he leaned his head back and headbutted me in the forehead, causing my shit to leak. I wiped my head and reached for my pistol. Before I could grab it, he hit with a two-piece spicy instantly leaking my lip and slightly dazing me. I stumbled back into the wall and was finally able to pull my pistol from pants.

"Shoot me, muthafucka. I want you to, I'm right the fuck here!" he said, pounding on his chest hard as hell.

I aimed my gun at his chest with tears in my eyes and cocked it. Kyana ran over and stood between us.

"Kyana move. Let him show me how tough he is! Nigga couldn't even kill you, so I know he ain't gone shoot shit."

"Shut up, Kayo. He is a child, and he's hurt! Sincere baby, listen to me. You're angry right now. Calm down before you do something you regret."

"The only thing I regret is being brought into this world by a snake ass nigga who doesn't take care of kids. Kyana, you want to know a secret. Fuck it. I'm gone tell you anyway. Kayo has been your connect for years. The nigga has been talking to a couple of under-cover cops too so be careful. Tell her, Kayo," I said as Kyana turned her attention and her pistol to Kayo.

"You trying to kill me is one thing Kayo, but damn, when did we start playing with police?"

"Kyana, you know me better than anyone, and you know I hate them pig ass people. Now if you muthafuckas not gone pull them triggers, get them guns the fuck out of my face," he said without an ounce of fear."

I was praying Kyana just pulled the trigger because he was right. I didn't have it in me to shoot him, but I wouldn't mind watching someone else do it. I'm next in line to run this shit anyway, so they could kill each other for all I care.

"Yo Sincere, chill. Come on, bro. Come take a ride with me," Paree said, walking toward me.

"Yeah "sis" I'll take a ride with you. Anything to get out of the presence of yo daddy," I said, lowering my gun but never breaking eye contact with my pop.

"Come on, ma," London said as I followed Paree to the door.

"You all go ahead. I need to talk to Kayo."

"Are you serious? He wants you dead, ma, that's suicide," London said, making a valid point.

Kyana chuckled before speaking and lowering her gone.

"I'm good, baby. Kayo isn't a threat to me. Go ahead with your brother and sister. I love y'all."

SIXTY

KYANA

"Ten years, Kayo? Who does that and how the fuck are you still alive? I don't understand."

I know y'all probably thinking I'm a dumb bitch for even talking to Kayo after everything that he put me through, but I really need to know how he pulled this shit off. Kayo has always been a cleaver ass person and a thinker, but he always ended up making poor decisions. I never thought I'd have a chance to look into this nigga's eyes again. He stood there staring at me, and I had to look away because as much as I hated the man, I still had love for him.

"I had to do what I had to do. You weren't letting up. I had on a bulletproof vest. I told you I'm always one step ahead. I had many opportunities to kill you, but that would only make shit hot. I was cool working with you behind the scenes, you tore me down and built me right back up without even knowing, and that's how I know we belong together."

"Kayo, you and I both know that shit is a dead issue. You already crossed me once, so I would never double back on you. I really want to put a bullet in your head, but I'll spare you. Just continue to stay out my way," I said, tying my robe tightly around my waist.

"Fuck that, Kyana. Come home. I miss my family. I gave you ten years, and I need you back in my life."

"Kayo you had me, and you should've kept me. Let me ask you something."

"I'm listening," he replied, folding his arms across his chest while looking me in the eyes.

"What made you sleep with Neka out of all people?"

"I fucked up. I'm a man, and I can admit when I'm wrong. I was thinking with my dick. I regret everything about Neka except for Sincere. I can't change what I did. I only move forward."

Even after ten years talking about this shit still hurt my heart.

"I'm not even mad at you, Kayo. You what you did, and it's done. I prayed and forgave you a long time ago, and I asked God to have mercy on your soul."

"I appreciate that. So, does mean we're friends again?" he asked, licking his lips.

"Nope, CO-PARENTS! That's it! And speaking of parenting, you suck at it. You didn't have to hit Sincere like that. He was only speaking his mind."

"The shit was bound to happen, but did hear how that lil nigga was talking to me?"

"He's you all over. You remember how you were when you were his age, a straight hothead," I said as Kayo walked up behind and wrapped his arms around my waist. I quickly stepped back.

"Yeah, I know, but you know what?"

"What?" I asked turning around to face him as his cologne filled my nostrils.

"I'm glad this shit is out in the open. I want to be under one roof with all of my kids and you again," he said, placing a soft kiss on my lips.

"Kayo, don't kiss me, and this is as close as you will get to being under the same roof with me. My kids are old enough to understand what's going on, so playing house isn't necessary, besides you have

Chanel's dick dumb ass to keep you company," I said, walking into the living room like it was my house.

"Aww, is my baby jealous?" he sarcastically asked as he followed me.

"Of what? You know better, I am Kyana Jones. I don't have a jealous bone in my body. I'm that bitch."

Kayo came and stood right in front me with his dick protruding through his pants. I looked up at Kayo and locked eyes with him, and our past, present, and future flashed right before my eyes. I stood there as he walked over to the fireplace and pressed play on the Bluetooth speaker. Lauren Hill's "Ex-factor" came through the speakers, out of all songs this. She sang exactly what it felt like to love Kayo Castillo. This man has always been my weakness.

It could all be so simple
But you'd rather make it hard
Loving you is like a battle
And we both end up with scars
Tell me, who I have to be
To get some reciprocity
No one loves you more than me
And no one ever will

HE RAN his hands through my hair and massaged my scalp. I stood there lost in the moment. Once again, he was controlling my body. My mind told me to leave, but my heart said to stand still, and I followed my heart. I felt like we were teenagers again, and he was about to take my virginity for the second time.

I keep letting you back in
How can I explain myself?
As painful as this thing has been
I just can't be with no one else
See I know what we've got to do
You let go, and I'll let go too

'Cause no one's hurt me more than you
And no one ever will...

Before I knew it, he had pushed me back on the couch and buried his face in my pussy.

"Tell me this pussy is still mine, Kyana," he said while tongue kissing my clit.

I could feel myself on the verge of an organism as he picked up the pace. He managed to ease his hands under my legs, bouncing me up and down like I weighed nothing. I wrapped my arms around his neck and moaned loudly. I dug my nails into his back as he slurped, sucked, and licked every part of my pussy. I laid back and closed my eyes. We were so wrapped up in one another that we didn't hear the front open, but when it slammed, I popped my eyes open and pushed Kayo back. We were both unarmed as Chanel stood there with tears running down her face and a .50 caliber Desert Eagle aimed at us.

"Chanel, let me explain this to you. Put the gun down before you fuck around and shoot somebody." Kayo said calmly, slowly standing to his feet.

"Oh, I am gonna shoot...you and that bitch!"

SIXTY-ONE
PAREE

Every day I wake up to a new surprise. First I get kidnapped and raped, and then I find out my father is alive, and to put the fucking icing on the cake, Sincere is my brother. I'm glad he was the rude muthafucka he was when I first met because this would be even more awkward and nasty. I can't lie though. Sincere fits right in with us. Once we got in the car, we all rode in silence and put two blunts in rotation. I didn't want to upset the nigga more than what he was but fuck that. This nigga would fuck around and explode holding that shit in.

"You cool?" I asked Sincere before passing the blunt to London in the back seat.

"Nah, I'm not. I thought that man was the realest nigga in the world. My whole life I wanted to be just like him, but what kind of real nigga does the shit that he did?"

"I understand your point of view, but nigga don't stress yourself out over his lies and mistakes. He's the one who has to answer to God," London said, sounding like a damn preacher.

"Fuck that. You have every right to be mad. I hate a fuckin' liar.

I'm glad he stayed the fuck away from me with that fuck shit, straight up," I chimed in before releasing the smoke from my lungs.

"Right, I just need to clear my mind and figure out my next move because I'm not going to the crib. Drop me off at Malik's crib, sis," Sincere replied, causing me to smile on the inside because he called me "sis."

"Want me to take you take to Taylor's crib?" I asked, joking.

"Hell naw, that bitch got a hit out on me," he replied before flashing that million-dollar smile.

"Boy bye, Taylor ain't got no hitters, and she won't hurt a fly," London said, causing us to laugh.

The way the three of us vibe you could easily tell we had the same blood flowing through our veins, everything felt genuine. I'm happy shit hit the fan, I just wish it would've come out sooner because I love this feeling I have inside. I promise I'm not going to let nothing, and no one come between me and my siblings. Since we were in venting mode, I thought this would be the perfect time to tell them that I'm pregnant. I swear the shit hasn't fully registered in my head, I was just bumping pussies a month ago, and now I'm carrying a child.

I opted out on telling them because I didn't want to hurt London's feelings besides I haven't told Malik yet. We pulled into Malik's driveway, and I notice a candy apple red 745 BMW parked directly behind Malik's truck. I thought nothing of it because he told me some of the guys were coming over to chill. I noticed Sincere's demeanor change when he saw the car, which told me he regrets popping up unannounced.

"Aight umma holla at y'all. Thanks for the ride," Sincere said reaching for the door handle.

Before his foot could touch the pavement, Malik came walking out of the house behind a slim thick ass chick with at least four bundles of the finest weave in her head, curled by the gods. She was dressed in a pair all-white of ripped up jeans, and a white Versace fitted tee with the Medusa head in gold on the front. The gold

Giuseppe Zanotti stiletto pumps on her feet screamed bad bitch. It felt like all eyes were on me as Malik was cursing the girl and calling her out of her name. I had seen enough. I unbuckled my seatbelt in one swift move and was out the car.

"Yeah Malik, this what we doing now, huh?

"Baby hold up. This bitch is nothing!" Malik yelled, pointing at the girl.

"I'm gone show yo ass "nothing" Malik, you know better than to play with me. You better tell this bitch like all the other hoes...we got years in this shit, and I damn sure ain't going nowhere for a while now."

I didn't ask any questions. I just started swinging. She was quick on her feet, but not quick enough to dodge the punches I was throwing. London and Sincere stood to the side and watched me stomp, beat, and drag the girl all over the driveway. It wasn't until she screamed out "I'm pregnant" that I stopped swinging. She had blood coming from her nose and mouth as she picked herself up off the ground.

"Pregnant by who?" I asked, awaiting an answer as she looked from Malik to me.

"By me bae, I fucked up. That's why I was just arguing with the bitch. I told her she couldn't keep it. That shit is over, and I swear I don't want nobody but you."

"So, you wanna have our baby showers together or separately?" I asked as everyone stood there in shock.

"Wait you pregnant too? London asked.

"Not for long, I refuse to be one of those bitches. I ain't with none of that goofy shit, so I'm gone do us both a favor and get rid of it. You got me fucked up. Let's go, twin," I said, storming back to my car as Malik yelled out for me.

"PAREE! PAREEE, COME ON BABY! DON'T DO THIS!"

I made it to my car and sped off as soon as London's door closed. I was doing eighty down a one way I just wanted to get as far away from Malik as I could. My heart felt like it was going fall out of my chest. I waited until we got a few feet away from his house before I broke completely down, I just wanted my momma right now, and that's exactly where I was headed. The devil has it out for me, and my luck ain't worth shit. I just can't be happy, damn.

"Twin, it's ok baby. He clearly loves you. He dissed her to your face. At least he told you the truth. He could've denied it."

"Fuck him, man. That's why I never gave niggas the time of day. I feel so fucking stupid. I knew the shit was too good to be true," I said, hitting my steering wheel and pressing down on the gas.

"SHIT PAREE, STOPPPP!" London yelled.

It was too late. I was doing eighty down Kayo's block, and *BOOM* was all I heard before London and I went flying through the windshield.

SIXTY-TWO

CHANEL

I fought back and forth with myself on whether I should just leave town or go back and get the man that I love. I had given Kayo all of me for the longest, and he has a whole family. I changed my entire lifestyle for this man. I was in my last year of college and two classes away from graduating. I got so caught up in his web that I started missing class and eventually stopped going, dedicating myself to Kayo. My entire family cut me off because they didn't approve of the life I was living. Kayo made sure I wanted for nothing and treated me like a queen in the beginning, but he started changing a few months ago. He gave me a life that I wasn't accustomed to, and I'll be damned if I give it all up. I worked too hard.

I pulled back up to the house Kayo and I shared. I noticed Kyana's car still parked in front, I don't know what the fuck is going on between her and Kayo, but I'm about to get to the bottom of it. I grabbed the bottle of Hennessy that I was drinking and took it to the head before reaching down and grabbing the gun that I purchased a while back. I had all kinds of thoughts running through my mind. I have to go in here and get my man. I prep talked myself before stumbling out of the car. I swear liquor hits you ten times harder when you stand up, I'm glad I made it home without catching a DUI.

I walked up the stairs and twisted the knob praying it was open because I ran out earlier without my house keys. To my surprise, it was unlocked, and I wasted no time entering. The house was dim, and Lauren Hill played softly through the speakers in our living room. I could hear slight moaning as I got closer to the living room. I froze in my steps as I watched Kyana laid back on my couch gripping the back of Kayo's head as he feasted on her pussy like it was the last supper. They were so wrapped up in one another that they didn't notice my presence. I took my time loading my gun, and I even took another gulp from my drink before aiming my gun at Kyana. When I cocked my gun, she looked up at me and quickly pushed Kayo back.

"Chanel, let me explain this to you. Put the gun down before you fuck around and shoot somebody."

"Oh, I am gonna shoot...you and that bitch!"

"Chanel, baby, put the gun down. Come here."

"Don't walk up on me, Kayo! Tell me what the fuck is going on, and I wish you would lie!" I yelled as he stood still, I couldn't help but to look down at his semi-hard dick.

I looked around Kayo and noticed Kyana playing with her pretty pussy. I tried to block her out. I don't know if it's the liquor or what, but she is turning me on.

"You like that shit, don't you? Come here, baby. Come taste it," Kayo said, extending his hand.

"I don't wanna taste that shit. She blew that."

"Bitch, fuck you!" Kyana said as if I didn't have a gun aimed at her.

"You should choose your words wisely when you have a gun pointed at you! You want to be me so bad, but Kayo belongs to me," I slurred.

"First and foremost, I don't want this nigga. I just got caught up in the moment sweetheart. You can have the man. But keep this in mind I have been his bitch since I was sixteen, and I'm thirty-five now, so you do the math."

I stood there and listened to her tell me that the man that I've given my all to belongs to her, and it was cutting me deep. I didn't believe her. He told me he was only with her for a short period of time, so I needed to hear it from Kayo. I wanted him to tell her to stop making shit up.

"Stop making shit up, bitch. He told me he was only with you for about six months. You are a non-factor, I'm wifey!"

"You're proud of that?"

"Ok that's enough," Kayo said as we kept going back and forth.

"Yup bitch, you see this mansion you chilling in, I'm the head bitch in charge."

"Hoe please, this is nothing! But I'm gone let you be great," she said, sitting up on the couch.

I tried to hold my grounds, but this bitch was hitting me below the belt, I had no win against her. I feel so stupid. I grabbed my bottle and turned it up as tears flowed freely from my eyes.

"Kayo, tell her she's a lie. Tell her how you said we were going to get married next year, tell her how you said you would always love me. TELL HER!" I yelled while holding the gun with shaking hands.

When he stood there speechless, he confirmed that everything she was saying was the truth, and everything he told me was a lie. I turned my gun from her to him. There was no possible way I was going to be the only person hurt in this room.

"Chanel, wait!" he yelled as I left off one shot hitting him in the thigh as Kyana dived for her pistol that wasn't too far away. She tried but she was too slow, I let another shot off this time hitting Kyana in her back, Kayo yelled out as he watched her gasp for air. She was still trying to crawl to her gun.

"You see, this could've all been avoided had you told her the fucking truth. You should've told her you love me. You proved you don't, so fuck you!"

"Put the gun down! I love you, Chanel!" he yelled as I tried my best to aim at his head.

"Too late..." I said, sending a bullet straight through his skull.

Kyana was a tough cookie. She was still fighting, I watched her lay face down as her back heavily caved in and out and blood surrounded her. I walked over and placed my gun to the back of her head.

"You see Kyana these are the consequences when you let a nigga play with your heart!" I whispered before pulling the trigger.

I almost threw up as I watched her head open, and her brains splatter.

Oh my god, what the fuck did do? I have to go! I grabbed the bottle I was drinking from and ran out of the front door, I was seeing double as the liquor had its way with me. I was in no shape to drive, but I couldn't risk getting caught. I jumped in my car and sped off. I was driving down the block as fast as I could to get away. My vision was extremely blurred from the tears, my body was shaking, and everything was moving fast so fast that I didn't see the car that was coming toward me head on. I slammed on my brakes, but it was too late. All I remember was seeing two people ejected from the other car before my head hit the steering wheel and everything faded to black...

SIXTY-THREE
SINCERE

"Yo," I answered to the unknown number that flashed across my screen.

Malik and I sat on his porch talking about all the shit that's going on in our fucked up lives. Here he is in love with my little sister, but he probably lost her because he slipped up and popped his ex-bitch off. My relationship with my pop is dead, and I don't think we gone be fixing that shit anytime soon. I don't have shit to say the man. I just want to forget about all the shit. I do plan on getting to know the twins better. I see me all in them, especially that crazy ass Paree. I can even get used to having Kyana around, but I know her, and my pop will never be cool like that. I swear I'm too young to be stressed the fuck out like this.

"Hello, Sincere!" my neighbor, Mrs. Reid screamed through the phone.

Mrs. Reid is an older lady, and she would always bring cakes and shit over to me and my pop.

"Mrs. Reid, what's wrong?" I asked sitting up.

"There's been an accident at your house."

"What kind of accident?" I asked now standing to my feet as a nervous feeling filled my body.

"Remain calm and get here as soon as you can," she replied as I ended the call and told Malik, "let's go!"

We hopped in his truck and headed straight to my crib. I had all kind of shit clouding my brain. I know this nigga didn't kill Kyana and get caught. Shit, maybe she offed his ass, and Chanel found him, I don't know. I couldn't even sit still in my seat. The five-minute ride to my crib was turning into an hour because the traffic was bumper to bumper. There had to be an accident or something because this shit rarely happens. I could see the police lights along with the para-medics and fire truck lights. All of the cars in front of us were slowing down being nosey, which is why there's probably so much traffic.

"Dammmmmmnnn Lord, look how the fuck them cars are smashed up. Aw my god nigga, the bodies still there," Malik said, sitting up looking at the accident.

I could see two bodies on top of a car, but as we got closer, my heart fell in my ass. I unlocked the door and jumped out as Malik tried to figure out what I was doing. I recognized Chanel's BMW, and as walked closer I could see the license plate on the other car, it read "*twin2*".

I dropped my head as Malik came running toward me, I stopped him and pushed him back the other way, but he snatched away. He walked a little closer and noticed the twins' lifeless bodies lying on top of Chanel's car. I ran over and grabbed him when he yelled out "FUCK!"

I dropped a few tears as the police asked if I could identify the bodies. I said yes, and they let me cross the tape, Malik stood back with his hands folded on top of his head. I gave them the twins' name, but I didn't tell them I was their brother, I said I knew them from the area. I also identified Chanel as a friend of the family. They had her laid down on the ground covered with a white sheet. They asked me a few questions about their parents, and I said I would try to contact their mother.

"Man, cover them the fuck up. They got all these nosey ass people looking and shit!" Malik snapped at the police as they told him to calm down.

I had to get Malik away because I knew his temper and the last thing I needed was one of them cracker muthafuckas "accidently" shooting him.

Malik and I got back inside the car and rode in silence. I could see the hurt all on my cousin's face. I knew he loved Paree, and he's probably blaming himself, not to mention she was carrying his baby. I don't know how I'm supposed to tell Kyana her kids are dead, but I have too. I know she's caught plenty bodies in her days and maybe this is her Karma, I just hope my pops Karma don't hit me like that. I have seen a lot of dead bodies but seeing them lying there fucked with my mental.

"You cool bro?" I asked finally breaking the silence in the car.

"Nah, I'm not. That's my baby laying on that car, man. I shouldn't have let her leave," he said, breaking down.

"I already know you loved her. I was ready to get closer to them, but God had different plans. I just don't know how to tell they OG. She's gone be sick. I hate this shit happened."

We pulled up to my house and looked at one another there were no police, just my neighbor sitting on the porch. She jumped up when I hopped out the car.

"Mrs. Reid, I thought you said something happened," I said with a confused look on my face.

"I was bringing a pie over and heard some arguing, so I decided to come back another time, but before I could make it down the stairs, I heard gunshots. That's when I ran and called you and the police. Those pigs still haven't made it," she said as Malik ran up the stairs with me in tow.

Malik turned the corner before me. He tried to block me the same way I did him at the crime scene, but I had already caught a glimpse of my pop and Kyana's bodies. They were both unrecognizable because of the shots they took to the head.

"What the fuck is going on? Mannnn, damn!" I yelled.

I swear my whole life had just crumbled within an hour, and I don't know how I should feel right now. Malik immediately got on the phone with our people to have the bodies removed and transfer to the funeral home we do business with. I guess my fucked up family will finally be together. I swear if I could, I would've done shit differently. I know shit wasn't supposed to end like this...

NO WEAPON FORMED against me shall prosper, it won't work
No weapon formed against me shall prosper, it won't work
Say No weapon formed against me shall prosper, it won't work
Say No weapon formed against me shall prosper, it won't work
God will do what He said He would do
He will stand by His word
And He will come through
God will do what He said He would do
He will stand by His word
And He will come through
No weapon formed against me shall prosper, it won't work
No weapon formed against me shall prosper, it won't work

I SAT in the front row with Malik and Brandy on each side of me, who would've thought the redhead bitch from the hotel party would be my lady. She has been A-1 since day one though. I had a pair of dark Ray-Ban frames covering my eyes as people walked up and viewed the four pictures of Kyana, Kayo, and the twins that I had sitting on top of their caskets. I could see the shocked and confused expressions that covered most of the guest faces when they saw a casket for my pops. Due to the injuries, none of the four could have an open casket. They were very well known, so there were all nationalities and people from all calibers of the drug game there to pay their respects. My grandmother Amelia Castillo and Uncle Santana sat directly behind me surrounded by an excessive amount of security. She occasionally leaned forward and rubbed my back. Sympathy was the last thing I needed right now. I needed to figure out my move. Kyana's right-hand man YG had one request, and that was to be able to stand by her one last time, so that's exactly what he did. He stood next to Kyana's casket the entire funeral. I decided to have all of them cremated because I didn't want to just put them in the ground and leave them. Kyana's family knew exactly who I was and was very cooperative and helpful throughout this entire process.

After the services, I walked outside and stood near my car. I said my goodbyes to my grandmother. She tried to convince to move to PR with her, but Chicago is my home. I leaned against my car and flamed up a blunt as a fat white man, and a sexy ass white lady came walking my way. She was dressed in a fitted black dress with a pair of red bottom stilettos on her feet. Her hair was pulled up into a neat ponytail, and a pair of glasses sat on her face giving off a sophisticated look. I didn't put my blunt out as they approached me and stood in front of me holding manila folders.

"Hello, Sincere."

"How can I help you?"

"Actually, you can't, but I need to go over the last Will of my client with you, and this gentleman will be doing the same for his client. I know you might not be up to handling business at a time like this, but this will only take a second."

"Your clients?"

"I represented Kyana and this gentleman represented Kayo. This won't take long, Kyana put your name alongside your sisters when you were younger to have access to all of her possessions if anything were to happen to her, and your father did the same. So, with that being said, every home, car, and bank account that belonged to the two of them, now belongs to you. I just need you to look over everything and sign a few documents."

"Huh?"

"Yeah, I know it's crazy regular kid one day and multi-millionaire the next, I'm sorry for your loss, and I will be more than happy to work with you moving forward."

"Yeah, I look forward to working with you too," I said, shaking her hand.

I was tired as hell, so I told Malik I was about to head to the crib. I just wanted to relax and get my thoughts together. I thought about what area I wanted to move in because I planned on selling the house. It has too many memories. I pulled into the driveway and saw my pop's car sitting there, and that's when it hit me, I don't have nobody left. I sat there and broke down for the first time since all this happened. I let the tears fall from my eyes before banging my hands on the steering wheel. I had a pint of Rémy on my backseat, so I grabbed it and took a drink. I wiped my face and finally got out. I walked past and rubbed my pop's car. I took a seat on the porch and rested my head in my hands. "Damn pop, I'm sorry, I didn't mean none of that shit I said." I looked up when I heard someone walking toward me. I looked up and instantly regretted not having my gun on me.

"How does it feel, Sincere? How does it feel to have your blood snatched away from you?"

"You should know, is that why you came here, to see if my pain is equivalent to yours? What do you want, Taylor? I don't have time for your shit today."

"Nah, I came here so you can look me in the eyes when I kill you, the same way my brother looked you in yours when you killed him. Fuck you, tell my brother and best friends I love them."

Before I could react, I was staring down the barrel of a .9mm handgun...Damn, I guess Karma really doesn't have a deadline...*POW!*

CPSIA information can be obtained
at www.ICGtesting.com
Printed in the USA
LVHW041503120619
621002LV00002B/309/P